"LET'S PRETEND I'M YOUR SISTER."

The twinkle in Carrie's eyes matched the mischief in her voice.

"Or even better," Mac said, digging into his pocket, "let's pretend you're my fiancée." Mac took her left hand and slipped a ring onto her finger. "Newly engaged women are supposed to smile, aren't they? Or maybe they're supposed to be kissed first, and then they smile."

He said it lightly, and the kiss was light, too. But something happened. Slowly, Mac bent his head until his lips touched hers and they were kissing again, not at all lightly. When the kiss ended, she opened her eyes and saw that he was badly shaken, too.

"You really throw yourself into your work, don't you?" she managed to say.

"Only when it's for a good cause," he teased, but the look in his eyes was no laughing matter.

ABOUT THE AUTHOR

The first story Robyn Anzelon remembers was the
tale of how she came to be in her family. *Searching*
was inspired by the fact that she, herself, was
adopted. Though she has written other books, this
one is closest to her heart. Also close to her heart
are her husband and daughter with whom she lives
in California. Robyn says, "It's because of them I
believe so much in love and romance, and why I
know I will always write."

Books by Robyn Anzelon

Robyn Anzelon
SEARCHING

Harlequin Books

TORONTO • NEW YORK • LONDON
AMSTERDAM • PARIS • SYDNEY • HAMBURG
STOCKHOLM • ATHENS • TOKYO • MILAN

Published February 1986

First printing December 1985

ISBN 0-373-70198-5

Printed in Canada

For my sister, with love
may your odyssey, wherever it leads,
bring you happiness....

CHAPTER ONE

HE STOOD MOTIONLESS in front of the window, blocking the morning's sunshine like an angry storm cloud.

"I'm going to do this story," he said. "If not for you, Libby, then for someone else."

He used her name, but Libby Sandowski had the distinct impression that Mac Kincaid's ultimatum was as much for himself as for her, a feeling strengthened by the fact that he didn't turn from the window to face her. San Francisco was looking her crisp, clear best this morning, but Libby very much doubted Mac was admiring the view. She'd known him long enough to easily read his body language, and his hands were giving him away. Jammed deep into the back pockets of his jeans, so deep that the denim was pulled taut across that sexy male tush of his, Mac's hands clearly said he wasn't thinking of sunlight glinting on the Golden Gate.

"I didn't say I wouldn't use the story," she said, absently raising a hand to tuck a renegade strand of steel-wool-gray hair back into the Katharine Hepburn-esque topknot pinned at the crown of her head. "I merely suggested that you might be too close to this one. Too emotionally involved."

He turned then, swinging around sharply. "Hell, yes, I'm involved!" he snapped. "But that doesn't mean I can't handle it. Have I ever blown a story?"

"No, you haven't." Libby didn't hesitate. She'd already been city editor at the *Times* when Mac had dropped out of college to join the paper as a very junior staff reporter. Over the next twelve years, she'd risen to managing editor while he had become an award-winning, top-notch investigative reporter. She knew Mac Kincaid—very well.

He was good, very good, at his job. He took too many risks, of course. He was too damned independent, too much of a loner. And he became too personally involved in every story. On two occasions—that she knew about—he'd forgotten the pen was supposed to be mightier than the sword, or the fist, and tried to right an obvious injustice on the spot. But no matter how deeply a story touched him, Mac had never once let personal feelings cloud his judgment or destroy his fairness.

Which didn't change her opinion of this particular story one iota.

"You haven't blown a story yet, Mac," she said. "But it happens to the best of us. Believe me, I know."

Mac looked at Libby, into the steel-blue eyes that could be hard as flint, but were soft now, soft and shadowed—and believed her. The back of his neck prickled, the way it always did when his reporter's curiosity was aroused, and several very probing questions formed in his mind. But suddenly, Libby looked away and swiveled her chair around to face the desk.

"This story won't help your mother, Mac," she said quietly. "Or Beth."

There was a long—a very long—silence during which the only sound was the click...swish...click of the pendulum of the antique school clock on the wall counting out the passing seconds.

"That's a pretty cheap shot, Libby, even for you," Mac said at last.

"Maybe," she admitted without a trace of apology. "But it's also relevant, isn't it?"

The clock clicked out several more seconds while Mac crossed from the window to the far side of the desk. He threw himself down into the softly cushioned tub chair the staff had unaffectionately dubbed the "hot seat" and, leaning forward, fished a paper clip from the silvery snarl filling a Japanese teacup on the desk. Staring at Libby, he fingered the clip, pulling and twisting the wire into different shapes.

"Not really all that relevant," he finally answered her. "I realize that in my mother's case the damage has already been done. But my doing this story might keep the same thing from happening to someone else."

"It might. It also might cause more problems for your family."

"Why should it? I don't have to use my mother's experience."

"No, it will be your experience you'll be using, Mac, whether you mean to or not. And it's going to be hard on you...and consequently on your family." Libby waited a moment, but he didn't respond. "Have you told them what you're planning?" she asked.

The paper clip Mac was torturing snapped in two. "I don't need my family's okay for my stories, thank God!" he said, flinging the broken clip into the metal wastebasket beside the desk. "It's bad enough that I have to put up with you treating me like a kid fresh from journalism school who doesn't know a byline from his own a—"

Mac broke off abruptly as if realizing only that moment what he was saying. Slumping back in the chair, he rubbed at his eyes with both fists.

Like an exhausted little boy, Libby thought, watching him. She'd seen that touchingly childlike gesture before—after he'd returned from Ireland with his story on what the never-ending civil strife was doing to the children of that country; after he'd interviewed the thirteen families who had each lost a child to a murderer who'd been convicted, declared insane, and released five years later to kill eleven more times before he was caught; when he'd finished his undercover research into the abuses of the elderly, abandoned and virtually forgotten in supposed convalescent hospitals that were little more than living graves. Those times, and others, she'd seen him rub his eyes as if he were trying to rub away the things he'd seen. Each time she'd known nothing he could do would ever really erase any of it, but writing the articles, using his words to push for change, could at least make the pain easier to bear.

But this time she was afraid there would be no release in the writing. None at all.

"I'm sorry, Libby," Mac apologized, lowering his fists and snatching up another paper clip in one fluid motion. "You struck a nerve, I guess. I haven't told the family, but I will, of course. I'm just waiting for the . . . right time. Because I am going to do this story. You might be right about the risks, but that's a chance I'm willing to take. The story's a good one. It needs doing. It's the kind of thing I'm good at. And besides—'' he paused, taking a deep breath ''—I have to do it.''

''Dammit, I knew that was coming,'' Libby groaned, shaking her head. ''And what about the stories you're already working on—the one on medical malpractice suits and the other on that Federal Drug Administration thing?''

''The malpractice story is almost wrapped up, I just need a few more confirmations before we run with it,'' Mac said confidently. ''And the rumors about some shady doings in the F.D.A. are still just that, but I'm working on some sources. Libby, I'll handle it all, believe me.''

''All right, Mac, you win. Go ahead. Do it. Just don't say I didn't warn you....''

Mac smiled, as much for her style as for her acquiescence. ''I won't, Libby. Thanks.''

This time Libby's groan was a silent one brought on by Mac's smile. Oh, to be thirty years younger! That smile of his made her want to leap across the desk right into his lap—a not very practical wish for a fifty-six-year-old, three times divorced workaholic with an ulcer and a faceful of worry lines. Nevertheless...

Mac Kincaid had that indefinable something that could melt a female heart at forty paces, and frequently did. It wasn't just good looks—though he had those, too. His hair was a deep lustrous brown, and somehow always looked about due for a cut. His eyes were brown, too, but a warmer brown spiked with gold, and they and the brows above them slanted down just slightly at the outer corners, giving him a perpetually wistful look that was incredibly sensual. His mouth, with the roguish small scar just to the left of it, was nice—until he smiled. Then it was dynamite.

The only trouble was, he didn't smile often enough, at least not lately. And the article he was proposing to do wasn't going to help. Unless . . .

Suddenly Libby had an idea, a perfectly marvelous idea. Mac wouldn't see it that way, of course, so getting him to agree was going to require a brisk finesse. But she hadn't got to be managing editor of a metropolitan daily without learning something about finessing.

She smiled. "So, now that you've sweet-talked your way around my better judgment, what's your plan?"

"Well, I've done some preliminary research and interviewed a number of people already, and there's a conference on the subject down in Southern California this weekend I was thinking of going to," Mac answered, sending another silvery victim pinging into the wastebasket. "What happened to my mother isn't unique; everyone admits it's occurring more and more—but no one's talking about how. Obviously, the only way I'm going to get the information I need is to go underground, pose as one of them, go through the regular routine and see where it leads."

Libby had expected as much; Mac had done undercover research before, as the scar beside his mouth testified.

"This isn't going to be an easy pose for you to pull off," she said. "Wouldn't it be simpler if you could work with someone who has the right background, who can present legitimate papers, history, etc.?"

"It might—but I doubt I can find anyone with the right background who would also be impartial enough to handle it."

Libby's smile broadened as she reached for her Ro-ladex address file. Giving it a spin with one hand, she reached for a pad and pencil with another. "I think I can help you there, Mac Kincaid," she said.

CHAPTER TWO

BENEATH A WATER-COLOR-WASHED cerulean sky, San Francisco Bay was the deep sparkling blue of melted sapphires. The heat of the spring sunshine mixed pleasantly with the crisp chill of a salt-sweetened breeze. The elegant skyline of the city, the intricate artistry of its bay-spanning bridges, the lush greens of the Marin headlands, Angel Island and the distant Mt. Tamalpais, provided a diversified feast for the eyes. It was a gorgeous morning, the kind that made people—even long-time residents who should have known better— hum sentimental tunes about leaving their hearts in the City by the Bay.

But Mac Kincaid wasn't humming as he stood at the rail of the ferryboat blustering its way north across the water toward Sausalito. His mood had much more in common with the boat's grumbling, sputtering engines.

Libby had conned him, royally, he thought, pressing a thumbnail into the soft rim of the Styrofoam coffee cup he held. He should have seen it coming, but he'd been so relieved she'd agreed to his story idea that he hadn't even noticed the trap until it had snapped shut— leaving him stuck with "Dear Carrie."

Dear Carrie! Dear God! What was Libby thinking of? When she had copied some information from her address file and smilingly handed the slip of paper to him, saying here was someone who would be perfect to help him with his investigation, he'd expected to see the name of one of the other *Times* reporters. But though the name belonged to a writer for the newspaper, Carrie Prescott wasn't a reporter. Not by a long shot.

She did a column for the *Times*, a sort of "Dear Abby" for teenagers. "Carrie's Mailbox" responded to letters concerning typical adolescent problems—a majority of which, not surprisingly, related to sex.

Mac had never met Carrie Prescott, though he had read the column—under protest the first time, when Tessa, the youngest of his six sisters, had thrust a copy under his nose. "Carrie understands," she'd told him, stabbing a finger at the letter concerning the problems of the youngest in a large, very loving, very protective family. He'd had to admit, if somewhat grudgingly, that Carrie's reply to "Always the Baby" had been reasonable, sympathetic and right on target. And he'd found himself looking for the column on his own at times after that and enjoying the deft blend of nonjudgmental honesty and gentle humor.

He knew, as well, that Carrie Prescott had come to the column by way of three very well-received young adult novels, one of which had received a prestigious Newbery Medal.

Still, a couple of books and an advice column for hormone-beseiged children didn't make the woman a serious journalist, and Mac foresaw all sorts of difficulties in trying to work with an amateur. And this case was just too damned important, for him to let anything, or anyone, get in the way.

Which was exactly what he had told Libby the minute he'd read the name she'd written. But the old harridan hadn't taken no for an answer, as usual. "She can give you the perspective you'll need to do the story right," she'd insisted, and when Libby Sandowski insisted, it was like being caught in an avalanche—if you didn't get out of the way in time, you got snowed under.

So Mac had reluctantly agreed—to talk to Miss Prescott, no more. And had secretly decided he would talk to "Dear Carrie," all right. He would talk, and present Libby's suggestion in such a way that Carrie Prescott would most certainly refuse. Then, having lived up to the letter, if not the intent, of Libby's law, he'd be able to get on with his work in peace.

But first he had to waste the morning on a ridiculous charade, he thought as the ferry bumped against the Sausalito dock. Not that Sausalito was a bad place to waste a morning. He'd always liked the small town tucked snugly against the tree-cloaked hills overlooking Richardson Bay. Its history ran the gamut: a refuge for wealthy San Franciscans when Victorian mansions and horse-drawn carriages ranged over the hillsides; a shipping center with a reputation for sinful bordellos and gambling dens after the railroad reached it in 1875; a retreat for artists, writers and intellectuals, its reputation only slightly less scandalous, in the 1950s. And just enough of its various pasts remained to add charm to its present.

Mac tossed the Styrofoam cup, its rim now crimped like a finished piecrust, into the trash container beside the door as he left the ferry. Sausalito's main street edged the waterfront and yacht-filled harbor, making it a pleasant walk as he headed north toward the houseboat community at the far end of town.

Docks led out to groupings of the houseboats the way streets led to regular houses in more conventional developments. Each dock had an artistically unique gate and was lettered—Dock A, B and so on—but Mac found it much easier to locate the one leading to Carrie Prescott's houseboat using Libby's description of the gate rather than the unobtrusive identifying letters. Mermaid Gate, Libby had called it, and sure enough it was, he discovered. Carved mermaids swam, lounged on rocks and combed their streaming hair in voluptuous abandon all across the sweeping wooden arch that supported the gate—a carved wooden panel set into wrought iron. A single mermaid graced the panel, in intriguing detail.

The artist had undoubtedly been male, Mac judged, grinning in spite of his disgruntled mood. The mermaid's long flowing tresses were arranged to accentuate, not disguise, her well-developed womanly charms, while her fishy tail was flipping saucily upward. Her smile was no less enchanting, tilting the corners of her mouth in a manner somehow both shy and seductive at the same time. Her raised hand cupped the gate's latch, and Mac almost felt he was taking liberties as he lifted the latch she offered and pulled open the gate.

Like the gates, the houseboats were architecturally and artistically varied, from nautical to whimsical, from elegant to ramshackle. Carrie Prescott's, on the left at the end of the short dock, seemed to be something right out of Hansel and Gretel. Rounded ''gingerbread'' shingles layered the walls and mansard roof, the tall brown pepper-pot chimney was surely chocolate, and a ''peppermint stick'' white railing edged the sun deck. Lacy white curtains fluttered at one open window and bright spring flowers overflowed several wooden tubs set around the deck.

But Mac barely noticed the flowers. He was staring at the young woman also on the deck, the woman who had to be Carrie Prescott. She was standing in front of an easel, all her attention focused on the canvas there, and Mac moved a few cautious steps closer, not wanting to believe what he was seeing. It wasn't that she didn't look a day over sixteen that made him swear softly under his breath. It wasn't her hip-length fair hair, hanging loose and flowing or her long prairie-style dress, her bare feet or the childish way she was nibbling the end of a wooden-handled paintbrush as she contemplated the canvas. What made him feel like turning around and marching right back to Libby's office was the fact that as the breeze rose off the water and smoothed the cotton dress against her body, it was decidedly obvious that Miss Prescott was six or seven months pregnant.

Damn it all! Mac swore softly. He was going to murder Libby Sandowski! What was she trying to do to him? He was certain she'd said *Miss* Prescott. So how was he supposed to bring up the subject of adoption to this young woman who obviously hadn't been taking her own column's frequently repeated advice about contraception and responsibility in sexual relations? Damn Libby!

Mac, used to taking any kind of risk to get a story, wasn't up to this one. He had just decided to turn tail and run when the girl looked up.

"Hi," she said, flipping a ribbon of hair back over one shoulder. "I'm Robin. You must be looking for Carrie."

Strangely, it was a statement, not a question, and the girl's eyes, the unusual blue of shadows on snow, were far too intense for Mac's comfort. But at the moment all he could feel was overwhelming relief that this fey-eyed child—this *pregnant*, fey-eyed child—wasn't the contact Libby had saddled him with.

"I'm Mac Kincaid," he introduced himself. "Libby Sandowski at the *Times* suggested I talk to Miss Prescott about a story I'm working on."

"Carrie's in the sun room—first door on the right." She waved her paintbrush toward the open door of the houseboat, but her winter-blue gaze didn't leave his face. "Don't bother knocking, just go on in. Carrie doesn't hear phones, door bells or anything when she's working."

"I wouldn't want to interrupt," Mac said quickly, wondering if one aborted attempt to meet Carrie Prescott would satisfy Libby. "I could come back later."

"Oh, I don't think she'll mind—in this case," she said enigmatically. "She's probably ready for a break by now, anyway."

Carrie was indeed ready for a break. Lying in the huge macraméd hammock strung across one corner of the houseboat's sun room, she was working. She'd been working for the past hour and twenty minutes. The only trouble was, she hadn't got past the first "Carrie's Mailbox" letter she was supposed to be answering. Frowning, she picked up the sheet of powder-pink paper once again.

The letter began in a childish scrawl of perfumed purple ink. Dear Carrie, I'm thirteen years old and I haven't been really really in love *yet*! All my friends have, at least twice! What should I do? When will I meet Mr. Right? And how will I know when a guy is really *right*? Help, Carrie!.... Spinster.

Touchingly amusing as the letter was, it wasn't at all unique. Carrie had answered questions like these many times before. But this time the answers weren't coming easily—she'd written only one bit of wisdom on this page of her spiral notebook, and "Damned if I know" wasn't the answer "Spinster" needed.

Disgusted, Carrie tore the page from the notebook, crumpled it and tossed it across the room. But before the paper hit the grass-green carpet, a small black paw darted out from behind a leg of the desk and batted it in a different direction like a baseball player connecting with a pitched ball. The crumpled paper sailed into a far corner, joining five or six earlier sacrifices—other useless answers to "Spinster."

"For a half-blind, arthritic old bag of bones, you sure have good aim, Pandora," Carrie said, smiling at the cat who padded slowly out from her hiding place to stand below the hammock and give one scratchily pitiful yowl. Knowing the old feline could never make it up into the hammock, Carrie reached down and scooped her up, almost flipping herself out of the hammock in the process. With an asthmatic sigh, Pandora settled down on Carrie's stomach.

Pandora was named for Carrie's second book, *Pandora's Promise*, with good reason. Carrie had arranged to meet the local veterinarian at his office one morning before opening, to ask him some questions about collies for the book she was working on at the time. She'd come home with Pandora.

The cat had been left on the vet's doorstep in a cardboard box with a makeshift lid taped over the top. It happened often, the vet had told her. Kittens, puppies, and even old ones, like this one, who weren't sick or injured, just elderly. Homes could sometimes be found for young ones. But the old ones...

Carrie had looked at the black cat, a scrawny creature just sitting in the box, even though the lid was off, as if resigned to her fate. Carrie hadn't meant to, but she'd reached out and stroked the hunched furry body. And the cat had started purring.

Now Carrie stared into wide, sea-green cat eyes. "Why am I having such a time answering this not very unusual letter, Pandy?" she asked. "Is it because half my mind is worrying about the fact that I still haven't come up with an idea for the next book?"

The slitted eyes blinked noncommittally.

"Maybe it's because it's spring and too nice a day to be inside working?" Carrie offered.

Pandora's nose twitched ever so slightly.

"I suppose you think it's because this coming Saturday I'll be exactly double Spinster's thirteen years, and I could by rights be asking the very same questions," Carrie said, scratching the cat's graying chin. "I suppose that's what you think, isn't it?"

Pandora meowed her off-key meow that sounded in this case remarkably affirmative.

"Rotten, Pandy, rotten," Carrie murmured, moving her fingers down to the cat's neck. "You could have politely disagreed."

But Carrie didn't disagree with her own assessment. She hadn't been in love yet, not the "really really" kind Spinster was talking about. And like Spinster, all her friends claimed to have been—at least twice, Carrie thought wryly, remembering the numerous divorces and remarriages among the people she knew. But for Carrie, there had only been instances of strong liking, attraction and—as in the case of her disastrous two-year relationship with Doug Bannerman—mad infatuation.

So the letter had touched a nerve that for some reason was unusually raw—undoubtedly because of her fast-approaching birthday. Birthdays were special to Carrie, but she hadn't made plans for this one; on the contrary, she'd rejected invitations from friends and her parents. It was almost as if she'd been waiting for something else, something unexpected, something...

Restlessly, she wriggled deeper into the hammock, ignoring Pandora's meowed complaint at the disturbance. All the psychoanalyzing wasn't getting Spinster's letter answered. Picking up the sheet of pink paper again, Carrie reread the questions and decided she might as well start with Mr. Right. Surely she could give Spinster a few hints on how to tell "Right" from "Wrong." Surely she'd learned something about that over the years.

Letting her mind wander, she thought of the man—a stranger—she'd glimpsed in a restaurant one recent night. Darkly, sexily handsome, he'd been kissing the wrist of his dinner partner with a fervent intimacy that had sent a hot shivery sensation through Carrie. And even though she'd been with friends, suddenly she'd felt very alone.

She thought of the first boy she'd ever "loved"—a skinny freckle-faced redhead who'd saved her from being a wallflower at her first school dance. He'd walked her home from school every day for a month after that, and even kissed her once—an awkward, off-center and perfectly wonderful, young girl's first kiss.

She thought of the young man she'd dated in college—before Doug—who had wanted so much to marry her. He'd been sweet, generous, sensitive, a wonderful man she'd liked, admired, even loved—though not in the way he'd wanted her to. He was a doctor now and happily married with two children, and he and Carrie were still what they had always been—friends.

And then there had been Doug. Brilliant, impulsive, temperamental Doug, who could sulk for two days over some imagined slight and then come home one afternoon with hothouse orchids, vintage champagne, sweet apologies and sweeter kisses. Who'd been jealous, selfish, cruel; and romantic, intoxicating, captivating.

Once, at the age of twelve, she had spent a weekend cutting up magazine pictures and pasting together eyes, noses, hair, chins, mouths and bodies, trying to make a composite of her ideal mate. Now, closing her eyes, she tried to put together all the images—a sensuous stranger, a first love, a friend and Doug—in much the same way she'd tried to assemble Mr. Right from cutouts and paste. She'd been attracted to those four individuals, in totally different ways and for different reasons. If somehow the things she had found attractive about each of them could be merged, perhaps her Mr. Right would appear.

Tall and dark with freckles, she wondered, smiling. Healing the sick by day and nibbling her wrist in restaurants by night? A tempestuously passionate man like Doug, but one who could still care more for someone else than himself? What would make her ideal man, the one she could fall truly in love with?

"Carrie Prescott?"

Carrie heard her name, but the voice speaking it was so perfect—deep, resonant, with a slight huskiness, like the voice of a man who's just made long, satisfying love to the woman whose name he was now turning into an endearment—that it seemed more of an extension of her meandering thoughts than part of reality. Yes, that voice would do quite well for Mr. Right, she thought, her smile broadening, the image of her ideal suddenly not seeming so formless. Warm brown eyes that could fill with fiery longing would match that voice. And a generous mouth, one soft from the kisses of lovemaking, that would curve easily into a full, sensitive smile. And strong hands to hold a woman softly or caress her heatedly, passionately. And a lean, hard body....

The voice fueled the daydream, but the touch on her shoulder was too concrete to do the same.

"Miss Prescott..." came the voice again and the warmth of a hand on her shoulder.

Carrie's eyes flew open to a figure bending toward her. Startled, she bolted upright...and the hammock responded like a rubber band stretched and suddenly released. In one quick, unstoppable motion, it flipped over, dumping Carrie, her papers and Pandora unceremoniously onto the floor at the feet of the man who'd touched her.

Despite age and arthritis, Pandora screeched and barely touched down before she streaked out of the room in a blur of indignant black. Carrie wasn't quite so resilient. The fall knocked the wind out of her and all she could do was sit there, head bowed, her ears ringing, while a giant fist closed around her lungs, squeezing tighter and tighter.

Suddenly there was a hand pressed against the middle of her back, rubbing warm soothing circles there, and a voice—that voice—was coaxing her to "Relax, Carrie, just relax. You'll be all right in a moment."

And she was. As if the hand and voice were magic, the crushing fist relaxed, and Carrie sucked in what seemed like a roomful of sweet, fresh oxygen.

Inhaling deeply, she slowly raised her head to look into the face of the man who was crouched beside her, still rubbing her back—and lost her breath all over again.

God, it was *the* face! she thought. The one she'd just been imagining. The mouth was right—full lipped, with the promise of a smile quite evident. And the eyes were deep and brown and lit with such concern that you could almost warm yourself in them, like reaching cold hands out to the blaze of a campfire. She hadn't imagined the small scar just to the left of his mouth, but it added the perfect hint of mystery.

"You're him!" she exclaimed, the words slipping breathlessly out on the wave of her amazement.

Mac stared at Carrie Prescott, stared deep into her wide green eyes that were filled with the kind of wonder usually reserved for Christmas morning. "I certainly hope so," he said.

CHAPTER THREE

TO LIFE'S LITTLE MOMENTS of panic or extreme embarrassment, Carrie always reacted in the same way. She started talking, about anything, babbling on just to kill time until she regained composure and control.

Being dumped like a rag doll on the floor of the sun room, surrounded by the oversize confetti of her papers and staring at a man who'd materialized from a daydream, qualified this as one of those moments.

"Isn't this where the violins should come in?" she muttered.

"Violins?" The man so close beside her quirked one dark brow.

She nodded. "You know...scene one, take one: the mysterious and attractive stranger appears out of nowhere; cue the clutzy heroine who falls at his feet; they stare deep into each other's eyes and murmur words with overtones of Kismet...and then the violin music starts...."

He laughed, and his laughter was liquid sunshine, filling the room. "I can't wait to find out what happens in scene two," he said.

The laughter was warm, but it was the fire in his velvety brown eyes that brought a sunburn's heat to Carrie's cheeks. Slowly, caressingly, his gaze was moving from her face downward—across the front of her old college sweatshirt, lingering briefly at the white

U.C.L.A. imprinted there, gliding over her ragged-edged white denim shorts, slipping down the bareness of her legs, down. . . .

Her skin tingled deliciously—too deliciously—wherever his eyes touched, and Carrie was just ready to yell, "Cut!" when he suddenly rocked back on his heels, grinning broadly, and the script changed.

"Good grief!" he cried, "do those things bite?"

Even without looking down, Carrie knew exactly what "things" he meant. Her slippers. Her monstrously huge, hideously fuzzy, hot-pink slippers. Her wonderful, faithful, only-things-ever-to-keep-her-chronically-ice-cold-feet-warm-while-she-worked slippers. This man, who was at least halfway responsible for the bruise she could already feel blossoming into purple glory on one hipbone and whose too-bold eyes had taken liberties no doctor would dare, was now insulting her marvelous slippers—and she still didn't even know who he was! A small smile tickled the corners of her mouth.

"They only bite strangers," she replied pointedly, and vigorously wiggled her toes. The mounds of pink fluff bounced up and down like two vicious, voracious creatures.

He laughed again, at the same time flinging his hands upward, palms facing her. "I'll talk, I'll talk!" he intoned. "I'm Mac Kincaid, I work at the *Times*, Libby Sandowski suggested I talk to you about a story I'm working on, and I apologize profusely for startling you right out of your hammock. Is that sufficient to make you call off your fuzzy watchdogs?"

It was—more than sufficient. Carrie had recognized the name even before Mac Kincaid had completed his introduction. You didn't work for the *Times* for long without hearing about him, about the numerous journalistic awards he'd earned for himself and the paper, and most especially about his near-legendary exploits while pursuing stories. And he was good—even before she'd started working for Libby, Carrie had read everything he wrote, and loved it all. He focused on the problems of ordinary people, not on the headline-grabbing scandals of the rich and famous. He was hard-hitting, ramming home the truth even when it wasn't palatable. But he was always fair and unbiased, and very often his reports resulted in changes for the better. Rumor had it that he'd had more than one offer of an anchor spot on a television news program, and looking at him, Carrie was sure it was true. That face would have millions of women panting for the six o'clock news.

And she was sprawled in front of him wearing a droopy old sweatshirt, raggedy white shorts and slippers that looked like hand-me-downs from the Easter Bunny! All at once Carrie felt an overwhelming and traitorous urge to kick her beloved slippers underneath the nearest piece of furniture.

She did the next best thing. Drawing her feet inward, she stood quickly, even before Mac Kincaid could push himself upright and offer her a hand. Holding herself as straight and tall as her five foot two and a half inch— she always insisted on the half inch—frame would allow, Carrie smiled. Regally, she hoped.

"That introduction is enough to earn you a reprieve, anyway, Mr. Kincaid," she said. "If you don't mind leaving the scene of the crime, we could adjourn to the kitchen and a glass of something... Iced tea, perhaps?"

Mac wasn't thirsty and he loathed tea in any form. But he liked Carrie Prescott's smile—half embarrassment, half challenge. It was an intriguing combination and somehow strangely familiar.

His neck prickling, he said, "Iced tea sounds fine. And it's Mac, please."

In the next few minutes Mac Kincaid found a number of other things to like about Carrie Prescott. He liked the faint scent of her, part soapy-clean, part spring flowers, that he smelled as she moved past him to lead the way to the sunshiny kitchen. He liked the full curves her breasts pushed into the shapeless sweatshirt she wore and was fascinated by the tantalizingly soft shell pink of her heels, which popped out of her funny slippers as she stretched on tiptoe to take two glasses from a cupboard. He liked her hair. Cut in a softly layered China-doll style, it was the rich color of cinnamon shot with sunlight, and brushed softly against her cheek and the back of her neck as she bent to pluck a lemon from the dwarf citrus tree growing in a sunny corner. But most especially he liked her smile and the rosy blush that accompanied it, as she looked up from slipping lemon slices over the rims of the glasses and caught him watching her.

"What story?" Carrie asked as she carried the tea things to an oak table in the windowed breakfast nook at the far end of the room. With a thrust of her chin she gestured Mac into one of the two chairs there.

He sat, his thoughts still on her smile, on where he could have seen one like it before. It wasn't until one of her dark brows arched questioningly into her cinnamon-colored bangs, that he even realized she'd asked a question.

"Uhmm...sorry," he apologized hastily. "I was thinking about, uhm...what was it you said?"

"I said, what story is it that Libby thinks I could help you with?" she repeated, setting a glass on a paper napkin in front of him.

For a moment, he couldn't remember. Then, with a jolt of astonishment that he could have forgotten even for an instant, he did. He remembered the story and the reasons behind it and why he was talking to "Dear Carrie."

He reached out, slowly drawing the glass and napkin closer like a poker player shielding his cards. "It's on adoption search," he stated.

"Adoption search?" she echoed curiously, but she was wondering more about the sudden subtle change in Mac Kincaid's expression than about his story topic. One minute he'd been half smiling and watching her with an intensity that was as flattering as it was disturbing. The next, although the half smile was still in place, it looked almost frozen there, and a small muscle beside his mouth was twitching tensely.

"That's current jargonese for the search by adopted people for their biological history and birth parents," he explained, "or by a birth parent who's given up a child and wants to later find that child...."

"I know the term," she interrupted. "I just don't know why Libby would think I could help you with that subject."

"You are adopted, aren't you?"

Carrie nodded, taking a sip of tea. "Yes, but Libby knows I've never been interested in searching for my biological background. We discussed the subject once after the paper covered one of those airport reunions where the woman who gave up her child twenty-five years ago meets that child—now an adult—for the first time. I told her exactly how I felt—that I couldn't begin to comprehend what motivated someone to search and that I thought a lot of people probably got hurt in the process. So why would she think I could help you?''

"For precisely that reason—you aren't interested in searching, but you do have the right background." Mac was making accordion pleats in a corner of his paper napkin. "You see, I want to investigate all aspects of adoption search—what motivates people to do it, why others are opposed to it, and what can happen when the search ends, successfully or not. But I want to concentrate on the ways the searchers get their information when records and files regarding adoptions are supposedly sealed. I think it's sometimes done illegally, and I know some very nice people are getting hurt in the process. But the only way to get that part of the story is to go undercover, to tap into the adoption search groups, pretend to be a searcher and see what happens. That's where you come in."

"How?"

"By working with me," Mac said.

"Working . . . with you?" Carrie lifted her glass and took another sip of the cold liquid, but it didn't quench the inexplicable sudden dryness in her mouth. Putting the glass down, she folded her hands on the table.

He nodded slowly. "Yes. I'd like you to pretend to search for your biological background. Numerous adoption search groups have sprung up over the past few years, and there are frequent conferences and meetings on searching and adoptees' rights. Using your background, we can join a group or two, attend some meetings, and see where it leads—hopefully, to the information I need."

Carrie turned to stare out the window at the wind-ruffled water of the bay. "That doesn't sound quite...honest."

"Neither is what some of these people are doing!"

Mac knew the minute the words left his mouth that they were coming out too sharply, too adamantly, so he wasn't surprised when Carrie turned back to look at him, her brows lost in her bangs again.

"What I mean," he said evenly, "is that when you're investigating something like this where illegalities may be involved, total honesty doesn't work."

"I understand that," she said. Carrie had no doubt that going undercover was often the best, sometimes the only, way of finding the truth. An insider would obviously have access to information, secrets even, that would be kept from a reporter. She remembered reading about other investigations of Mac's, where he'd gone undercover to gather information and documentation, and how she'd applauded the results. But when she thought of doing it herself, of purposely deceiving people, it seemed so...different.

"I just don't think I could pretend...lie...very convincingly," she said.

Mac didn't think she could either, not with her eyes. He'd seen scoreboards that gave away less. Storm clouds of doubt were darkening the clear green of those expressive eyes to jade now, and she blinked slowly, her sable lashes dipping as if tallying each thought—for and against his proposal—before going on to another. He could see the vote was going against him, and with a start he realized he didn't want it to. Not at all.

Half an hour before, he'd arrived at Dear Carrie's, intending to swiftly maneuver her into a quick refusal to Libby's ridiculous "suggestion" so that he could get on with his work in peace. But now, when he had her refusal almost in hand, he didn't want it. Somehow, sometime, that intention had gone right out the window. He didn't know exactly why or when; he was only certain it had.

"You don't have to lie," he argued. "You are adopted and you can go through the motions of searching. I'll do the rest."

"But I—"

"I know it's a lot to ask of you—that you have your own work and all. But Libby's willing to pay for your time on this, and she even suggested you might gather some useful material for a book, since lots of teenagers are curious about adoption and searching."

"A book..." Carrie repeated thoughtfully. A book about adoption search. It was an interesting idea, one she'd considered before, but had always rejected because of her own lack of understanding of all sides of the issue. She'd received more than one letter from troubled adopted teens whose typical adolescent identity crises seemed to be intensified by the unknowns in their lives. She'd sympathized with, but never really understood, their often desperate desire to know the facts of their pasts. If she went along with Mac's investigation, mightn't she gain the perspective she needed to do a book—a very good book?

But still there was the deception involved....

"I don't know," she said uncertainly. "What would I have to do? When would we start?"

"Are you free this weekend?"

"This weekend?" *As in her birthday?*

He nodded. "There's a conference down in Anaheim—at the Disneyland Hotel, of all places. It's put on by one of the leading adoptees' rights groups and should provide a basic overview of their ideas, methods and opinions. We could go—if you're free."

"Well, I . . ."

"I could pick you up Friday evening, we'd fly down, attend the conference Saturday and be back Sunday. I can't promise it will be fun, but it should be . . . interesting."

"This weekend is rather . . ."

With one hand, Mac pushed his cold glass to one side, the tea still untasted. He leaned forward. "I've already read everything I could on the topic. I've interviewed people involved in search groups as well as those who are opposed to searching, including several who've been 'found' with unpleasant results. But I still need more. And you—and a little harmless pretense—can help me get it." He reached out and both his hands closed around hers. "Please, Carrie, I need you."

His touch was hot and cold. One of his hands still carried the chill of the glass he'd moved, the other was fiery warm, yet each seemed to be burning Carrie's skin in a disturbingly intense way. He needed her.

"Okay, Mac," she told him. "I'll do it."

CARRIE SAID GOODBYE to Mac Kincaid at the door of the houseboat and quickly retreated back to the delft-and-white kitchen. But not quickly enough; Robin was right behind her.

"Well?" the girl demanded, blue eyes gleaming.

Carrie took the two glasses from the table and carried them to the sink. "Well what?"

"Well, when are you seeing him again?"

"What makes you think—"

"Car-rie! It's not nice to tease a pregnant lady!" Robin protested.

Carrie laughed. "Friday night."

"I knew it!" the girl exclaimed. "He's perfect. The two of you will be super together."

"Robin, there's no 'two of us.' He just wants some help on a story he's doing." She returned to the table and reached for the napkins they'd used. But she paused, holding the one Mac had folded and refolded as he'd talked. Thoughtfully, she studied the dog-eared paper. "I'm not sure I should have agreed, either."

"Why not?"

"Well, the story's on adoption search..." Carrie hesitated, glancing at her young, unmarried and very pregnant houseguest, wondering how Robin would feel about this particular subject. She knew so little about Robin, really, and almost nothing of her plans and feelings about her pregnancy. She'd tried to talk to the girl, had offered a shoulder to cry on and to help in any way she could several times in the month Robin had been staying with her. Robin's response had always been an understanding nod, a serene smile and a polite "Thank you for the offer," nothing more. So Carrie had no idea whether talk of adoption would bother Robin or not. In a way, she almost hoped it would—just to get the girl talking about her difficult situation.

But Robin's expression held only curiosity and a dash of impatience, as she waited for Carrie to continue. Carrie sighed and dragged her thoughts back to her own predicament.

"I'm adopted and he wants to use my background; wants me to pretend to be searching for my biological parents," she explained. "And... I don't know... the idea worries me."

"Why?"

"I'm not sure really." She fingered the pleated napkin. "For one thing, he seems...tense, or something, when he talks about it, almost as if there's something he's not saying. And there's the pretense. And to go poking around in my past...I don't know...."

Robin cocked her head. "Are you afraid of what you might find out, Carrie?"

"Of course not," Carrie declared quickly. "I've never cared about the circumstances of my adoption. I know all I want to know about that, and I have parents I love and who love me. Which is why it seems silly to get involved in a search, even if it is solely to help Mac Kincaid...and now I'm committed to spending the weekend with a man I hardly know...."

"The weekend!"

"We'll be working. There's a conference in Southern California...."

"No wonder you're worried!" Robin cut in, grinning. "A whole weekend with that gorgeous hunk...sigh!"

Carrie made a face at the girl, but didn't reply. Actually, until this very moment, she'd been too busy worrying about Mac Kincaid's story to think about anything else—like spending the weekend with the man.

Crumpling the two napkins into paper balls, she lobbed them neatly into the nearby wastebasket. But even that activity didn't mask the shiver that shot through her. A weekend...Friday, Saturday, Sunday...with Mac Kincaid.

She thought of the touch of his hand hot against her back, of his hands covering hers, of that strange moment when she'd first looked into his eyes and said, "You're him!" And suddenly she was wondering if all along she'd been worrying about the wrong thing.

THINKING OF THE COMING WEEKEND, Mac walked back through Sausalito toward the ferry. He'd been dreading the conference, even while knowing he had to attend. You never knew where an important lead might turn up, but a whole day of listening to the same poor-me stories, the same excuses, the same party line diatribes, had been almost more than he'd thought he could stand. But now that Carrie would be there with him, the prospect didn't seem so bad. At least there'd be someone on his side this time. No, the thought of the coming weekend didn't seem bad at all. Nor did the thought of working with Carrie Prescott.

He'd never admit it to Libby, but the old witch had been right—Carrie was going to be a great help to him in his investigation. Her background would provide the perfect cover and she was obviously sympathetic to his point of view. With her help, he should be able to move faster and get the whole thing over with sooner. It was going to work out perfectly.

His thoughts busy, Mac barely noticed the indulgent smiles of an elderly couple he passed. The smart-alec smirk of a jean-clad kid, who probably should have been in school at this hour, he ignored. But the grin that a silver-haired, three-piece-suited bank-president type belatedly turned into a cough behind a discreetly raised hand, did register. Suddenly Mac realized the smiles, the smirk and the grin had all been directed at him.

Because he was whistling. He was strolling along, smiling to himself, thinking of Carrie Prescott and the weekend and whistling. Whistling, of all things, that damnable song. "I left my heart . . ."

What the hell! he thought, cutting off the whistle and the smile, and increasing his pace to a brisk walk as he boarded the ferry for the return trip to San Francisco.

What in blazes was the matter with him? He hadn't felt this ridiculous since junior high school, when Patsy Louise Carson had let all her girlfriends read the note he'd written her declaring his undying love. No wonder people had been staring and grinning.

Scowling, he thudded up the narrow stairway to the open-air top deck of the boat. But as the ferry pulled away from the dock and chugged out into the bay, Mac was facing back toward Sausalito. Mellow morning sunshine and a backdrop of blue sky had turned the small town into a picture postcard. The breeze and the spray kicked up by the ferry's passage were briskly cool against his face. Far down along the curve of shoreline was the cluster of houseboats. He couldn't distinguish Carrie's gingerbread-styled boat among the others, but he knew it was there. He could picture it vividly in his mind. Just as he could picture her.

What the hell! he thought again. But this time he was smiling . . . and whistling.

CHAPTER FOUR

THE FOLLOWING DAY, Carrie and Robin returned from an emergency clothes shopping trip to find Eddie Van Ormer waiting on the front deck of their houseboat, a cardboard box at his feet.

Eddie lived two doors away, in a boxy redwood-shingled houseboat smelling alternately of wet clay, wood shavings or exotic spices, depending on which of his diverse talents he was exercising at the moment. Sixty-four years had etched a network of lines into Eddie's craggy face, but most of them were laugh lines that only made him look younger. And his squarish hands, that could mold a blob of clay into a woman's face, carve a piece of driftwood into a leaping porpoise, and stir-fry octopus into a delicious delicacy, would never be old.

On the day Carrie had moved into her houseboat, Eddie had arrived at the door, calling himself the officially unofficial welcoming committee, and offering chicken Kiev, pilaf and a bottle of California chardonnay. He was a recent widower, and Carrie was fresh from New York and Doug Bannerman. Two of the walking wounded, Eddie said. It might have been that commonality of bruised hearts, or something else, but a wonderful friendship had blossomed between them and grown deeper ever since. So Eddie dropped in frequently and was seldom empty-handed.

Carrie wasn't surprised, therefore, when he tapped the box and said, "Got somethin' for you, Carrie, my darlin'."

"A new carving?" she guessed, brushing a curly wood shaving from the collar of his plaid flannel shirt as she kissed his leathery cheek. Eddie wagged his head.

"No, this present's not from me," he told her, lifting the box and following her and Robin into the living room. He set it on the redwood-burl table in front of the small fireplace. "It was delivered this afternoon by a rather intense and dashing young man, who looked extremely disappointed to find you not at home. He paced out on your deck for ten minutes, until I took pity and offered to guard his treasure until your return. He wrote you a note, too. Let's see, where did I put it?" Eddie started patting his pockets.

"I'll bet it's from Mac!" Robin exclaimed.

It was indeed from Mac, Carrie saw when Eddie dredged the note from deep inside one jeans pocket, but the message held more impatience than disappointment. The words boldly scrawled across the piece of paper torn from a small reporter's notebook were punctuated with brusque dashes and abrupt exclamation points, and his name slashed across the bottom of the page. Carrie— Thought you might want a preview of the conference—shows what we're up against! Don't let it scare you off, though—we'll survive. See you Friday! Mac

"Kind of a swashbuckling flourish to that signature, isn't there?" Eddie said, reading over Carrie's shoulder. "He's a new boyfriend?"

She tossed the note onto the table and reached for the box. "Not old, or new, or a pirate. Mac Kincaid is a reporter, and we're doing some work together, that's all.

This 'present' is undoubtedly just something to do with that.'' She unfolded the interlocked sections of the lid.

The box held several books, a couple of magazines, a file folder of clippings from the *Times* library and several pages of typed notes, and a brochure for the conference. One book, *Lost and Found* by Betty J. Lifton, was a collection of stories about adoptees and their searches, another was titled *Adoption Search*, and seemed to be a ''how to'' guide. Carrie picked up the conference brochure, glanced at the title, *Opening Doors*, and dropped it back into the box.

''Just work,'' she said, picking up the box and heading for her bedroom.

''Funny,'' Eddie said.

Carrie stopped and looked back over her shoulder. ''What's funny?''

''Oh...'' he said shrugging, ''this Mac...he just didn't pace like a man delivering work. Funny.''

''Funny,'' Robin echoed, then pressed her fist against her mouth, not quite holding in her laughter.

''Not funny at all,'' Carrie declared, continuing toward her room. But she was smiling as she set Mac Kincaid's box gently on the end of her bed.

ROLLING FROM HER STOMACH onto one side, Carrie snuggled deeper into the bed covers. A moment later she flipped to the other side. Then onto her back.

Silvery moonlight drifted through the skylight over her bed, and Carrie threw an arm up over her eyes. But printed words replaced the slash of light, parading disturbingly across the screen of her closed eyelids.

Sitting up, she switched on the small lamp on the nightstand and reached for the book she'd been reading half an hour before. She rested it against her upraised knees and its pages fluttered open to the chapter she'd last read.

Earlier, she'd glanced through the material in the box Mac had left for her, the majority of which was monotonously similar to things about adoption and searching she'd read in the past. Only Mac's typed notes and this book, the how-to-search book, had caught her special interest.

Mac's notes described interviews he'd had with three women, two birth mothers and one adoptee, who had been found. In all three cases, indications were that the searchers—two relinquished children and one birth mother, correspondingly—had completed their searches through illegal means. For the three women who were found this way, the results had not been pleasant.

Two of the stories were typed out in question-and-answer form, as if they were transcripts of a taped interview. Both these women felt their lives had been interrupted at a particularly bad time, the birth mother just after her husband's death, the adoptee after the difficult birth of her child. The third woman's story was different. According to Mac's description, the searching adoptee had contacted one of the woman's *other* children before the woman herself, causing an estrangement between that daughter and her mother—and then discovered her information was wrong and she was not the woman's child after all.

All three stories were touching, presenting a side of searching seldom in the media. One other thing about the notes was touching, as well. Mac Kincaid was a lousy typist and his typewriter keys needed cleaning desperately. The "e," "o" and "a" were indistinguishable blotchy black egg shapes, and strikeovers were common—especially in words with "th" in them.

In Mac's hands—or his typewriter roll, to be precise—
"there" was one big smudge.

The "how to" book was interesting in a different
way. It opened with the typical arguments for the rights
of adoptees and birth parents to know the truth—arguments Carrie had skimmed, having heard them and
been unconvinced, before. But then it moved on to just
how one should go about searching and what one might
expect to find.

Carrie had found herself reading every single word.
And thinking about what she'd read long after she'd
turned off the light.

Now, she tossed aside the book and kicked off her
covers. Slipping out of bed, she put on her robe and
jammed her feet into her pink slippers. Tiptoeing, she
headed for the sun room, and the shoe box in the bottom drawer of her desk.

It was a Buster Brown shoe box, though most of the
smiling Buster Brown and his dog Tige printed on the
lid had long ago been worn away, and its corners were
held together with tape. For years it had been her treasure chest, repository of her most important posses-
sions. At various stages it had held collections of trading
cards, seashells and pop beads; napkins, programs and
ticket stubs; dried corsages, snapshots and love letters.
But when she'd moved to San Francisco from New York
a year and a half ago, the box had been relegated to
safe-deposit box status.

Setting it in front of her on the desk top, Carrie
opened the box. And smiled.

She knew it couldn't be so, but for a moment she
smelled brand new black patent leather, and she was
seven again, wearing lovely new pumps with heels that
clicked smartly against the front walk of the house as

she skipped outside to meet her father, just home from work. "Look, Daddy," she cried, and he swung her up in strong arms and called her his "wonderful grown-up lady."

But it wasn't that year she wanted to remember now. Reaching into the box, Carrie removed the deed to the houseboat, her car's pink slip, a spare set of keys, a glowing review of her first book and her diploma from U.C.L.A. There were other bits and pieces, too, that she set aside, coming at last to the small folded square of paper she was looking for.

She'd looked at her birth certificate before. As a child she'd studied it with the same self-centered and natural curiosity that had made her go through her baby pictures time and again. But she'd cared only about the personal facts, her birthday, her birth weight and so on. Once she'd outgrown that stage, it had become just another piece of paper, necessary on occasion, such as when she'd applied for a passport for a post-college trip to Scotland, or when she'd needed the exact time of her birth for a friend who wanted to plot her astrological chart.

Now, though, as she unfolded it, she felt more like that long ago curious child. One corner of the paper was bent, and she smoothed it flat. She ran a fingertip over the rough impression left by the state seal and she read the words filling each space thoroughly, as she'd never really read them before.

Certificate of Live Birth, a district number, a certificate number. Her name: Carrie Ann Prescott. Female, a single birth. The date, the hour. The place.

In the spaces for place of birth, the city, county and state were listed. But the space for the hospital was blank. As was the space farther down, where the attending physician's signature should have testified to the truth of the above statements. Those two spaces were blank, just as the book had said they might be.

Carrie knew she shouldn't feel so surprised . . . so uncomfortable. Somewhere along the line she'd learned that when an adoption was final, the child's birth certificate was amended to show the names of her adoptive parents, and the first certificate showing the birth parents' names was sealed permanently away. So she'd always been aware that the certified copy she was now holding was actually of her amended birth certificate, not the true original.

She understood the reasons behind the amending of the birth certificate. Secrecy. Protecting the privacy of those involved. But until now, she'd never noticed how far that secrecy extended—even to leaving out information and signatures that might be identifying.

Just as the book had said. It had also claimed that occasionally, information was even falsified so as to further preserve secrecy. Instances of birth places, doctors' names, even birth dates, being altered were known.

Carrie looked once more at the paper, at her birth date—her birthday—and at the blank spaces, then put the certificate and the other things back into the box and shoved the lid on top. She flipped the switch on the Tiffany-styled desk lamp, plunging the room into darkness.

But instead of returning to her room, Carrie leaned back in the chair and drew her slippered feet up to tuck them beneath her robe. She'd never really noticed the blank spaces on her birth certificate before, or if she had, hadn't cared. And she didn't care now, not really. It didn't matter what hospital she'd been born in—

maybe she'd even been born the old-fashioned, new fangled way, at home. She didn't need to know the name of the doctor who'd delivered her. If she suddenly discovered her birthday was actually a few days earlier or later than she'd always thought, would it change anything? Of course not.

But she was still sitting there, in the chair, in the dark, when Pandora padded curiously in. She meowed twice, as if asking why Carrie wasn't returning to bed, then meowed again, plaintively. Carrie reached down and lifted the cat up onto her lap. Pandora paced a slow, small circle before plopping down and nudging her head under Carrie's hand. Purring, the cat fell quickly and placidly asleep.

Carrie didn't.

CHAPTER FIVE

LATE FRIDAY AFTERNOON, Carrie was in her room, re-assuring herself one more time that the contents of her packed suitcase bore no resemblance to sweatshirts and pink slippers, when Mac Kincaid arrived.

Though she'd never heard Mac's knock before, she knew instantly that the three short confident raps were his. Eddie would probably say the knock had a swash-buckling flourish, like Mac's signature, Carrie thought with a small smile.

She was grateful that Robin was there to answer that flourishing knock, though. It didn't stop her stomach from turning a somersault as Robin called out, "It's Mac, Carrie." But it did delay, however briefly, the moment when she would have to face him.

She was nervous. She'd spent the past several days being nervous. Nervous about the investigative work she and Mac would be doing, nervous about spending the weekend with a virtual stranger, nervous about the rocket ship ride her stomach seemed to take every time she put on her pink slippers or drank iced tea or sat in the hammock.

But nervous or not, she couldn't keep Mac waiting forever. Gently nudging a curious Pandora out of the way, Carrie closed the lid of her suitcase. She started to lock it when the sound of Mac's laughter sent its siren song through the closed bedroom door, and she paused, head cocked to catch every warm nuance, every bright tone.

She liked Mac Kincaid's laughter. She'd liked it the other day when he'd laughed at her joke about the violins and at her threatening slippers. It was easy and warm, spontaneous and affectionate, like a kiss between old friends. Her mother had once told her, listen to the way a person laughs, and at what, and if it makes you think of good things, that's all you need to know. Mac's laughter made Carrie think of the first daffodils and robins of spring, crackling fires and hot buttered rums on a rainy night, golden-oldie love songs and spending a romantic weekend with a man you—

Carrie snapped the suitcase locks closed with unnecessary vigor and swung the case off the bed.

Mac was sitting on the couch, twisting keys around a gold key ring and telling Robin the location of a discount art store in the city when Carrie entered the room. He finished the directions without a break or even a noticeable pause, but from the moment he saw Carrie, his mouth was on auto pilot. His eyes locked with hers and he could have been reciting the Gettysburg Address for all he knew, or cared.

In the past two days he'd halfway managed to convince himself that he'd imagined the impact of their first meeting, that Carrie Prescott was just another attractive woman, and nothing more. But now, one glimpse of her walking through the doorway, gracefully dodging the scrawny black cat twining around her ankles, and he knew he hadn't imagined a thing. A peach-pink dress looking temptingly soft clung to every curve of her body, the weight of the suitcase she was carrying made one shoulder dip almost provocatively, and that bewitchingly familiar smile was on her face. There was something about her that affected him in a way no other woman ever had. Already, a whistled tune was playing in his head.

"Hi," he said, standing and moving toward her, extending a hand. "Here, let me take your suitcase."

"Thanks," she replied softly, and then didn't know what else to say. Mac looked even more...right than he had the other day. He wore a chest-hugging navy sweater vest over a sky-blue shirt, and worsted wool slacks of charcoal gray that molded lean hips and muscular legs. His thick brown hair showed the traces of a recent combing, but already a wayward lock was drifting across his forehead, and Carrie's fingers itched to touch it, to brush it back and then wait for it to fall forward again. She was staring, she knew, but he was gazing at her just as intently, and when his fingertips brushed against her hand as he took her bag from her, it felt as if two live wires had just touched together.

"I hate to intrude," Robin said, smiling impishly, "but don't you two have somewhere to go?"

A grin lifted the corners of Mac's mouth, but his eyes didn't leave Carrie. "Can't we give the kid a quarter and send her to the movies?"

"It costs five dollars to get into a show nowadays," Carrie answered, wishing she didn't sound so breathless.

"I guess it'd be cheaper for us to leave, then," he said with a shrug. "Shall we?"

Carrie nodded, but turned to Robin, who was still smiling knowingly. She was wearing the long maternity T-shirt Carrie had given her, over faded jeans with mismatched patches on the knees. The T-shirt was crimson with a big shocking pink heart centered at stomach level, and the jeans, Carrie knew, would be unzipped most of the way. Pink ribbons tied Robin's long hair into two ponytails, her feet were bare, as usual, and she looked about twelve years old.

It was strange, Carrie thought, how Robin could, at times, seem far older than she was, while at others, like now, she looked too much a child to be pregnant with one.

Carrie crossed the room to where Robin was half sitting, half leaning on the wide arm of the upholstered chair.

"Are you sure you'll be all right?" she asked. "Eddie's going to be home all weekend, so if you need anything..."

Robin's ponytails swung back and forth. "I won't. But I may claim starvation so he'll fix me some of his pizza."

"You have the number of the hotel, don't you?"

"That and Eddie's number and Libby's number, the emergency numbers to match every catastrophe known to woman, the veterinarian's number—Carrie, I probably even have your social security number! I'll be fine. Now go and have good time." And Robin winked.

The wink ended Carrie's mother-henning faster than any assurances could have. Giving the girl a hug, Carrie turned back to Mac.

"I guess I'm ready," she said, not at all sure she was.

She was even less sure when she and Mac headed down the dock. It was a beautiful spring afternoon, one of those rare ones where the golden light of the lowering sun was unimpeded by San Fransciso fog, and the breeze off the water felt almost warm. The soft tapping of their footsteps added a pleasant counterpoint to the medley of late afternoon sounds—water lapping gently against the boats, the plaintive cry of a lone sea gull, the sizzle of someone's early dinner frying...and, unfortunately, the squeak, squ-eak of Mrs. Brindle's rocking chair.

Mrs. Brindle was one thing Carrie hadn't thought to worry about concerning her trip with Mac. And now it was too late to avoid her.

Eugenie Brindle was eighty-seven years old, ninety-seven percent deaf, and one hundred percent snoopy. She spent much of her time ensconced in her rocker on her houseboat's front porch like a sea urchin on a rock, waiting for tidbits of gossip to float by. These she seized with gleeful enthusiasm and delivered outrageous commentary at the top of her lungs. Carrie, seeing the woman's faded blue eyes widen as they neared, knew exactly who was about to become the subject of Eugenie's next broadcast.

"Carrie Ann Prescott! Going out, are you? With this spiffy young man? Lucky you! Is that your suitcase he's carrying? Must be more than a one-nighter, hmmm? Where are you taking her, young man?"

Carrie tried to cut in, tried to stem the tide, but Eugenie's forte was non-stop interrogation. It didn't bother her a bit that she seldom gave her victims time to reply to her questions; she was perfectly capable of supplying most of her own answers. She blathered on, and Carrie wanted to sink into the ground.

"And how did you ever get our sweet Carrie to agree to this, I wonder? She doesn't go in for fooling around as a rule, you know. Very old-fashioned, is Carrie. She had such a broken heart when she first came to live here, you know. When was that, Carrie? A year ago, or two? I forget...must be all mended now, though, if she's gallivanting about with the likes of you...."

"Mrs. Brindle, we have a plane to catch," Carrie took advantage of one of the woman's rare pauses, tossed in her excuse and fled. Behind her she heard Mac saying a polite goodbye. But Eugenie, as usual, wasn't listening.

"I'll bet you're pleased as punch that she's going off with you, aren't you, young man? But take good care of her, hear? I like Carrie. Don't you dare break her heart."

Mac caught up with Carrie at the Mermaid Gate, where she couldn't seem to work the simple latch. He flipped it easily and pulled open the gate, chuckling. She strode briskly through the opening, but then whirled and faced him.

"Mac Kincaid, stop laughing!" she ordered, wondering why she'd ever thought his laughter was nice. "I'm embarrassed as hell, and you're just making it worse."

Instantly Mac sobered. "Hey, I wasn't laughing at you, just at that woman's delightful chutzpah." He moved closer to her, close enough to reach out and brush a strand of cinnamon-colored hair from the high curve of her cheek. But instead of taking his hand away when the small task was finished, he let it drift downward, until it came to rest against the top of her shoulder. His fingertips lightly grazed her neck.

"And what's to be embarrassed about, anyway?" he added gently. "Mrs. Brindle thinks you're sweet, I'm spiffy, and we're going off together for the weekend. I'd say she's right on target, wouldn't you?"

He waited for the beginnings of Carrie's smile, then added, "And I know for sure she was right about one thing."

His fingers were moving slightly, caressing her neck like butterfly wings, and Carrie's pulse started beating double time.

"What?" was all she could manage.

"I am 'pleased as punch' that you're coming with me," he said simply.

Happiness was a sudden heat, filling her, warming her, melting away her embarrassment and the last vestiges of her nervousness at the same time. Carrie looked deep into Mac's warm brown eyes, and silently blessed Eugenie Brindle's gossipy old heart.

"I am, too," she told him. And meant it.

Mac smiled. "Good, then can we get a move on? This thing—" he paused and hefted Carrie's suitcase up and down "—weighs a ton."

Carrie laughed, and Mac gestured to the left and put a hand lightly on her elbow as they started walking. "I should warn you about one thing," he said.

"Warn me?"

"About my car. You see, I live in Stinson Beach. But I had to be in the city late last night for an interview, so I stayed with one of my sisters, Beth and her husband, who have a condo on Russian Hill. In exchange for such occasional rooming privileges, I let Beth volunteer me for carpool duty for the kids from the preschool where she teaches. Today we went to the zoo."

Two images flashed through Carrie's mind—a disturbing one concerning the kind of interview that might take place late at night, the other a delightful picture of Mac Kincaid herding a flock of preschool children around the zoo. Neither explained a thing. Her brows rose quizzically.

"We stayed a bit longer than planned and the brats were tired, going on cranky," Mac went on, "so I

bought them some donuts and popcorn to keep them quiet on the ride home. By the time we got back it was late and there wasn't time to do anything about this...."
He stopped beside a car—a brand new BMW with pristine midnight-blue paint, a stylish sunroof and a temporary paper license taped in the front window.

Carrie looked at the sleek new car, still not certain what Mac was getting at. Then he opened the passenger door.

The two plush seats were the only relatively clean spots in the car, undoubtedly because of a recent hasty brushing. But it was going to take a lot more than a little brushing to get rid of the popcorn littering the floor mats, the donut crumbs and powdered sugar decorating the dashboard, and the network of small handprints crisscrossing the window glass.

"I should have left the little beasts at the zoo," he muttered, totally without conviction.

Carrie waited until Mac had closed her door and gone around to the back to stow her suitcase in the trunk before she let the smile come. She looked at the disaster inside the car, marveling. She knew no other man who would let his new and costly automobile be used as a snack room by a mob of preschoolers. Or sound as utterly unconvincing as Mac did when he grumped about the results.

The Friday afternoon traffic added an extra twenty minutes to the length of the ride to the airport, and still it seemed too short to Carrie. The sun was a huge golden ball floating low in the champagne sky as they crossed the Golden Gate Bridge, and the cool air rushing in through the car's open sunroof was tangy with the special scent that was part sea, part pine and part pure vintage San Francisco. Then they were heading south through the storybook city, which was being transformed by the magic of the setting sun. Windowed skyscrapers became castles of gold, aged Victorians regained their former glory, and the crush of cars on the freeway... well, that remained a noisy, smelly traffic jam. But Carrie didn't mind, because she and Mac were talking.

Mac related tales of his other "preschool herding expeditions." Carrie condensed some of the funniest of "Dear Carrie's" letters. They traded stories of their experiences with their mutual editor, Libby Sandowski. And they laughed together, in all the right places.

There were serious moments, too. Carrie learned that Mac had stumbled into journalism after finding his temperament unsuited to the medical career he'd first chosen.

"One of the recommended premed classes was 'Death and Dying,'" he told Carrie. "It was a good class. Maybe too good, because by the end of it I knew I could never handle not being able to save every patient. But giving up the lofty ideal of becoming a doctor was hard, and I finally tried to exorcise my feelings by writing about them. A friend who worked on the college newspaper read the piece, published it, and I was hooked." He paused and his eyes twinkled. "Too bad, in a way. I know I would have had a great bedside manner."

Mac discovered that Carrie had always wanted to write, though she'd never envisioned doing a column.

"But the kids who read my books kept sending letters, all asking similar questions," she explained. "And when *Yesterday's Promise* was serialized in the *Times*, the paper got letters, too. Libby contacted me, suggesting I try answering them in a regular column. I enjoy it, only now it may be syndicated, which will mean more letters and so on. And then there are the ones who call or show up on my doorstep, wanting personal advice.''

"Didn't anyone tell you that's what unlisted addresses and phone numbers are designed to prevent?''

"I know. I keep meaning to arrange it, but then I think of someone out there, needing help and not having anywhere else to go...like Robin.''

"Robin? You mean she showed up on your doorstep? In her...condition? I assumed she was a relative or something.''

"No, we only met about a month ago,'' Carrie said, thinking back. "She didn't come for advice, though. She had a copy of my second book, *Angie's Decision*, and wanted my autograph. *Angie's Decision* is about an unwed pregnant teenager and what she decides to do about her baby, so it wasn't hard to guess Robin's situation was probably similar. Only, Angie had family to turn to, and Robin didn't—her parents, a stepfather and alcoholic mother, threw her out when they learned she was pregnant.''

"They what?'' Mac's fingers drummed against the steering wheel.

"It happens more often than people think. But Robin was prepared—she had money saved and came to San Francisco to stay at a home for unwed mothers. Only she wasn't comfortable there and we got along so well, I asked her to stay with me. She has a part-time job now and has offered to get a place of her own, but I like having her.''

"She doesn't look old enough to be out on her own.''

"She's eighteen, and sometimes seems like eighteen going on fifty. But others...''

Mac nodded, understanding. "What's she planning to do when the baby's born?"

"I don't know," Carrie admitted. "I'm not sure she knows. I've tried to talk to her about it because it docsn't seem that she's made any plans at all, but she just smiles contentedly and...well, Robin's a little...oh, I don't know how to put it...."

"Fey?"

"Yes! That's perfect. Fey, otherworldly. She paints beautifully, and Eddie, our neighbor, tried to get her interested in showing in the gallery that handles his work. But she hasn't taken him up on his offer, and she hasn't asked for any advice about the baby, either."

"Maybe, she's already decided to do whatever Angie did in your book," Mac suggested.

Carrie gnawed her lip. "Maybe."

"And what was that?"

"She gave her baby up for adoption," Carrie said.

There was a long silence after that, and when they started talking again, they kept the subjects light, as if by mutual agreement.

"You should meet my sister, Tessa," Mac was saying as they reached the airport and headed into the multileveled parking garage. "She's a big fan of your and has been known to lie in wait for the paperboy on Sundays just to get the section with your column before Laraine, Andi, Deborah or Kelly have a chance."

"Tessa, Laraine, Andi or...?" Carrie had lost track.

"My sisters...Laraine, Andi, Deborah, Kelly and Tessa. Plus Beth, the married one who lives on Russian Hill and only has to fight her husband, and occasionally me, for the news."

"But that's six!"

"Right." Mac sounded proud, as if having six sisters was his own personal accomplishment. Then he added, as if reading Carrie's mind, "Believe me, surviving as the only brother, and the eldest, among that gaggle is something to be proud of."

Mac parked the car and they left its cozy warmth for the tomblike chill of the garage. He removed their suitcases from the trunk, then opened the back door to get his jacket. It had slipped off the seat and into a heap on the floor, and it wasn't the only thing that had.

"A friend of yours?" Carrie asked as Mac straightened, his jacket in one hand, a worn, furry brown teddy bear in the other.

"Not really," he replied, scowling into the fuzzy brown face. "This is Benjamin, Donnie Katzenberg's bear, which Donnie swore he would not forget if I would please, please, please let him take it along to the zoo. Benjamin Bear, without whom Donnie Katzenberg has not slept since the day of his birth."

"Without whom Donnie Katzenberg is probably not going to sleep all weekend, much to the despair of his mother and father?" Carrie guessed.

"Right," Mac agreed. Shoving back a cuff, he checked his watch, but he already knew there wasn't time to even consider going back to drop off the stuffed animal. Not if he and Carrie were going to make their plane. It was just a toy, of course, and Donnie Katzenberg would survive the weekend without it. Even if he was only four and a half years old, wore thick-lensed glasses that left deep grooves on the bridge of his nose and sucked his thumb when he was upset. Even if he really loved his blasted bear.

Tucking the bear under one arm, Mac slammed and locked the car door.

"Let's leave it at the ticket counter," he said, picking up the suitcases and starting toward the terminal. "I'll call Beth and she can let Donnie's parents know it's here; knowing Donnie and his bear, I'd bet they'll be out to pick it up tonight."

But Benjamin Bear didn't make it to the ticket counter. They were heading that way when Mac came to a sudden stop in the middle of the terminal.

Caught unaware, Carrie didn't put her brakes on in time and her knee bumped the corner of one of the suitcases he carried. She gave a small yelp of pain and Mac spun a full one hundred eighty degrees around to face her. But not with an apology.

"Carrie," he said hoarsely. "Don't say anything about the conference. Okay?"

"What?" Rubbing her knee, Carrie wondered what she'd just missed. She didn't have the faintest idea what Mac was talking about.

"I'll explain later. But please, just don't mention the conference," he said again, just as a small missile crashed into the back of his legs. With a last imploring look at Carrie, he dropped the suitcases and turned, scooping up a carrot-topped little boy. "Donnie! And what can I do for you, as if I didn't know?"

"Benjamin!" the child squealed. He had a fistful of watercolor pens in one waving hand, but snatched the bear from under Mac's arm with the other.

"You could say hello first, Donnie," a softer voice admonished, and a young woman appeared beside Mac, smiling.

She was pretty, even with a smudge of purple watercolor across one cheek. There was a tomboyishness about the short cut of her curly golden-brown hair, her tall, slim figure clad in jeans and a plaid shirt, and her undisguisedly freckled nose. But she wore a delicate gold chain on one wrist, her lips were touched with blushing pink lip gloss and her long-lashed hazel eyes, which were regarding Carrie even as she spoke to the child, were filled with appraisal that was definitely feminine.

"Beth, what are you doing here?" Mac demanded ungraciously, at the same time leaning over to brush a quick kiss against her cheek.

"Rescuing Benjamin Bear, of course," she replied. "Donnie missed him about five minutes after you left."

"Why you instead of Donnie's parents? I thought you and Stewart were going to a dinner tonight?"

"We are, but I'll be back in time—I hope. Donnie's folks were busy, and we had to catch you before you left."

"You're too soft when it comes to these kids." Mac touched his thumb to his tongue, then to his sister's cheek, rubbing away the purple smudge. "And their parents know it and take advantage of you, too, you know."

"And just who was it who let Donnie take Benjamin in the car in the first place?" Beth asked. "Against my advice, I might add. I warned you he always leaves it behind somewhere, but you let him con you, anyway. When it comes to the kids, you're the marshmallow, Mac Kincaid!"

"Marshmallow!"

If it hadn't been for Mac's outraged expression, Carrie might not have laughed, no matter how close Beth's comment came to her earlier assessment of his feelings for the children. As it was, she couldn't stop herself.

"See, Carrie agrees with me," Beth added undiplomatically, turning to her at the same time. "I assume you're Carrie, even though my grumpy brother has been too busy berating me to introduce us."

Mac rolled his eyes, but made the introductions. But the two women barely had a chance to exchange polite formalities before Mac was thrusting Donnie into his sister's arms and lifting the suitcases.

"Well, Donnie has his bear, we have a plane to catch, and you'd better get home to Stewart and your party."

Beth nodded. "Yes, why don't you go check the bags in. I'll wait here with Carrie."

Mac looked at Carrie, and then at his sister, then at Carrie again, and she could almost hear him repeating his earlier pleas about not mentioning the conference.

He needn't have bothered; there wasn't a chance for Carrie to mention anything. Mac was barely out of earshot when Beth grinned at her—a grin very like her brother's.

"Donnie's parents weren't busy," she confided. "I offered to bring Donnie because I wanted to meet you."

Carrie's eyes widened in surprise. "You did? Why?"

"Because ever since..." For a moment, a shadow seemed to dim the brightness of Beth's smile. But then she swallowed, and it was back again, in full force. "Well, for the past couple months, anyway, Mac hasn't been his usual cheerful self. But last night when he came over, he was whistling and smiling. And this afternoon, he asked me three different times if what he was wearing looked all right. And I wanted to see why."

Carrie could feel a blush beginning. The appraising glint was in Beth's eyes again, and this time Carrie understood it. Mac's sister was sizing up Carrie as a girlfriend for her brother—a girlfriend he was taking on a weekend trip. It didn't make sense—she should have known the trip was business. Except that Mac had asked Carrie not to mention the conference. Why? Because his sister didn't know about it? But why would he be keeping that a secret? And what could Carrie say to Beth?

"I...I doubt Mac's mood had anything to do with me," she said.

Beth shifted a bear-hugging Donnie from one hip to the other. "I don't."

"But we're just working together...."

"I know, Mac told me." Beth smiled, a smile as good as a proclamation announcing she didn't believe a word of it.

But why didn't she, Carrie wondered, a funny sort of prickling starting in her stomach. Did Mac usually claim he was going away on business when he took a woman off on a weekend trip? And did he do that often?

"Hey, don't look so horrified! This isn't an official Kincaid family inspection...." The shadow returned to her eyes, but was quickly dispelled. "That comes later," she threatened. "But I was born with a terminal case of nosiness and I love my big brother to bits and...and Mac would kill me—or worse—if he knew I was trying to pump you. He can think up the most awful kinds of revenge. When I was seven, he painted red spots all over my doll and told me she had jungle fever and would have to be burned in the fireplace so she wouldn't infect the rest of us. I was in the sixth grade when he told drippy Marvin Witherspoon that I was in love with him and wanted him to kiss me in the lunch room, and Marvin did—yuk!"

Carrie laughed, liking Mac's sister.

"In the tenth grade," she went on, "my gym shorts ripped during the boys versus girls softball game—Mac had snipped just enough threads to time it perfectly. And in the twelfth grade—''

"You deserved it all," Mac cut in, returning. "You were the pestiest little brat, always following me around and snooping into my business." He darted a glance at Carrie, then looked back at his sister. "And something tells me things haven't changed all that much."

"And you, Mac Kincaid, were always the most secretive brother in the world," Beth shot back, her glance darting to Carric, too, before returning to Mac. "I doubt you've changed, either."

"Beth . . ." Mac began ominously. But she'd turned to look at the clock on the terminal wall.

"Love to stay and listen to your lecture, big brother, but Stewart's going to have a fit if I'm late." She stood on tiptoe to kiss Mac. "Say goodbye, Donnie, and hold on to that bear. We've got to run." And she did, literally.

CHAPTER SIX

THERE WAS A PING and the No Smoking light blinked off. A second ping darkened the Seat Belt light. A moment later, the flight attendant started her safety monologue, which seemed to consist of one interminably long word. "TheBoeing727ispressurizedforyourcomfortshouldtherebealossofcabinpressure...."

"I'm sorry, Carrie," Mac said, flipping the silver lid of the armrest ashtray open and closed and open again. He'd waited to apologize and explain until they were on the plane; wanting the relative privacy of their seats; wanting, admittedly, more time to think of just how, and how much, to explain. But somehow, instead of working up a good explanation, he'd spent the intervening minutes worrying that Carrie might decide not to get on the plane with him at all.

And now they were sitting together in the forced intimacy of adjoining airline seats, on their way to the conference he had asked her not to mention to his sister. And it was time for him to tell her why.

"I didn't mean to put you in such an awkward position," he began. "I never guessed Beth would show up."

"Your sister doesn't think we're going to be working this weekend," Carrie said, studying the orange and pink upholstery of the seat in front of her. It was patterned in zigzagging lightning bolts, a design as chaotic as her feelings. She wanted to be angry, and wasn't, quite. She wanted to understand, and didn't, at all. Most of all, she wanted to not care why Mac Kincaid had lied to his sister, or about how often he took business trips that weren't business. But she did care, too much.

"I told her we were," Mac said.

"She didn't believe you."

"I know."

"Why didn't she?"

The ashtray cover clicked down, up, down, up. "Probably because I don't usually work with anyone on my stories, and I didn't want to mention the topic in this case just yet, so I hedged a bit, and Beth just assumed . . . and I couldn't convince her otherwise without telling her about the conference so—"

"So you conveniently let her assumption stand," Carrie finished for him. "But why? Why not just tell her the truth?"

"Because adoption is a sore subject for Beth."

Carrie twisted in her seat to look at Mac, her green eyes shadowed, like flawed emeralds. "It is?"

He nodded, stiffly. "Beth and Stewart want children, but after two years of trying and tests and even an operation, the doctors finally admitted Beth isn't going to be able to have a baby of her own. So she and Stewart were considering adoption, but—" he paused, just slightly "—but she heard some things about adoptees searching for their 'real' parents and such, and it put her off the whole idea. Stewart still wanted to, though, and he and Beth argued about it. And my mother was . . . involved in the disagreements, too, and she and Beth aren't even speaking now. So. . . ."

"Oh, Mac, how sad for your family," she murmured, her eyes turning liquid. "Was Beth's problem what originally interested you in adoption search?"

The ashtray lid snapped closed. "I guess you could say that," he said flatly. "And obviously I'll have to tell her, and the rest of the family, about the article before it's published. But stories don't always work out, and I didn't want to upset them needlessly. Of course, if I'd known you would be meeting Beth, I would have told her before, but at the time it seemed easier to let her think—"

"I know what she thought!" Carrie cut in, but she was smiling.

Mac caught the smile and cocked one eyebrow rakishly. "She liked you, anyway," he said. "Even if she does suspect you're a loose-moraled vixen out to snare her sweet and innocent brother."

"Sweet and innocent!"

"Sweet?"

Carrie laughed, and shifted in her seat, relaxing. She still didn't quite approve of his deceit, but she could understand it now. Poor Beth. And the whole family. She'd seen the closeness between Mac and his sister, heard it extend to his family when he spoke of his six sisters. It wasn't difficult to believe he would want to protect them from unnecessary hurt.

She believed Mac's explanation, but she also believed it wasn't the whole story. She'd watched him toying with the armrest ashtray, heard the slight pauses as he spoke, and thought of a little boy trying to explain his black eye while hiding his bruised knuckles. She was more certain than ever that he was holding something back, and she couldn't help wondering what, and why.

THEY FLEW THROUGH a sky darkening from orange to coral to purple and landed on the carpet of stars that was the greater Los Angeles basin at night. A rental car and a bizarre maze of interconnecting freeways carried them from the airport to the city of Anaheim, where the incongruous floodlit shape of Disneyland's Matterhorn appeared amidst a conglomeration of office and industrial buildings, hotels and restaurants. A few minutes later, Mac was guiding the car into a parking space in front of the famed amusement park's adjacent hotel.

Mac switched off the engine, but didn't immediately move to get out of the car. Instead, he turned to Carrie.

"There is something I should mention before we go in," he said. "I won't be using my own name, either here or at the conference. Not many people remember newspaper bylines, but I don't want to chance it. Being tagged as an investigative reporter might put our —" he paused, putting a hand over his heart and rolling his eyes upward "—sincerity in question."

"I imagine so," Carrie agreed, wrinkling her nose at his display. "What name will you be using?"

Mac leaned forward and crossed his arms over the rim of the steering wheel. Resting his chin on one wrist, he looked at Carrie. "You are about to learn one of my deepest darkest secrets, lady, and if you ever breathe a word of this to a living soul, I'll—"

"I wouldn't dare!" she declared. "I heard about your typical kinds of revenge from Beth, remember?"

"Just so we're clear," he said, nodding with mock soberness. "My full name is . . . Ashley MacAllister Kincaid."

Carrie stared in disbelief. "Ashley? As in *Gone with the Wind*?"

"Exactly," he confirmed dourly. "My mother was as infatuated as Scarlett when it came to the honorable Ashley Wilkes, an infatuation she unfortunately did not outgrow before my birth. So . . . Ashley."

Ashley. Carrie looked at Mac and couldn't stretch her imagination far enough to see him as an Ashley. Rhett Butler, yes, she thought. There was plenty of Rhett's bold unconventionality and intriguing sensuality in Mac. His darkly compelling eyes, the small scar beside his mouth, even the way he was leaning against the wheel—arms crossed oh so casually. Rhett—but not Ashley.

"My only consolation," he said, "was that Mac-Allister, her maiden and my middle name, lent itself so well to a substitute. I haven't used Ashley since I was old enough to enforce my wishes with a tantrum, and later a punch in an occasional nose . . . except when absolutely necessary, like now. Ashley MacAllister makes a convenient cover—one I certainly can't forget."

"I guess not." Carrie ran her tongue over the giggle tickling the roof of her mouth. "And shall I call you Ashley, or Ash, or . . . ?"

"Mac will be just fine," he cut in. "And you can use your own name—your being recognized would be a plus, actually. You can always say you're hoping to write a book glorifying your grand search—they'll love that."

"Rats! Here I was expecting false identity papers, a secret code word and a trench coat, and I don't even get a cover."

"Oh, but I do have a cover for you," Mac said, leaning back in his seat, far enough back so that he could dig deep into his pants pocket. "You're the future Mrs. Ashley MacAllister."

"What?" Carrie was trying not to notice how the charcoal-gray wool of his slacks was responding to his wriggling. She was very grateful when Mac seemed to find what he was searching for and pulled his hand from his pocket. He relaxed in his seat, and the charcoal-gray wool relaxed, too.

"We're engaged," he said. "Impending marriage and pregnancy are supposedly two of the most likely motivations for adoptees to begin a search. And since making you look pregnant seemed a bit difficult..." His eyes dropped to the flatness of her stomach.

Carrie folded her hands strategically. "Maybe you should have borrowed my background and Robin's shape," she suggested dryly.

"I'm satisfied with what I've got." Mac took her left hand and slipped a ring onto her finger.

It was ice against her skin, and refused to slide over her knuckle. Mac's eyes flicked up, crashing into hers, as he pushed a little harder. The ring slipped over her knuckle and into place, and it no longer felt cold.

Natural reflexes took over and Carrie stretched her hand out toward the light from a parking lot lamp shining in the front window. Wiggling her fingers, she shifted the ring this way and that, letting the stone fracture the pale light into rainbows.

It was a beautiful ring, its solitaire raised high on delicate golden prongs and burning with a deep inner fire. And it fit her finger perfectly.

"Mac, it's absolutely gorgeous," she breathed, fluttering her fingers again.

"Family heirloom," he said casually.

Carrie's hand froze in midair. "You mean it's real?"

"Sure. No fake diamonds for the Kincaids. That ring's passed through three generations of Kincaid brides. Mine will be the fourth."

"But I can't wear an heirloom," she protested, trying to pull the ring from her finger. "You don't play charades in the family jewels." She got it as far as the ridge of her knuckle, where it stuck again.

"It's my ring, and I can play whatever I want with it," he said, taking her hand. "You're not going to abscond with the Kincaid treasure, are you?"

"Of course not, but . . ."

"Then relax." He nudged the ring back into place, but didn't release her hand. And Carrie realized she didn't want him to. His hand was warm, the ring on her finger felt heavy, but somehow right, and little frissons of anticipation were zipping up and down her spine. She wanted...she wasn't sure what she wanted...or maybe she was, and that was precisely what was bothering her. It was too soon, the feeling was too strong. Unknowingly, she caught her bottom lip between her teeth.

Mac's other hand came up and he brushed a knuckle against the edge of the trapped lip. "Hey, don't blow your cover," he teased. "Newly engaged women are supposed to smile, aren't they? Or maybe they're supposed to be kissed first, and then they smile. I think that's it."

He said it lightly, and the kiss was light, too, a harmless, friendly kiss to top off the charade. At least that's what he told himself it was going to be.

But something happened. Mac's lips brushed against Carrie's lightly and he drew back, not intending anything more. But her mouth was soft and warm and sweet, the even sweeter scent of her was flowing intoxicatingly around him, and her hand trembled ever so slightly in his.

The tiny tremor hit him like a full-fledged earthquake. The small movement was unaffected, vulnerable, and unbelievably sexy. He looked down at her hand, soft and slim, nestled in his bigger, rougher one, and the contrast struck him as a miracle, like a perfect work of art, or a sunrise. Slowly, Mac bent his head until his lips touched hers, and they were kissing again, not at all lightly.

Someone had put the little rental car on a roller coaster track, Carrie decided as Mac's mouth moved against hers. Put it on track and then thrown it into high gear. A tingling fire was pouring through her, flaming brandy with all its heady golden warmth was flooding her veins. Mac's lips opened over hers, her own parted eagerly in response. The kiss deepened, their tongues meeting in silken thrusts. His arms went around her, his hands, strong and hot, pressed against her back, urging her closer to him, molding the soft angora of her dress against her skin.

The roller coaster swept onward, faster. A sweet aching was growing within Carrie, fed by the feel and taste of Mac's mouth, the sure, heated touch of his hands. And it wasn't just her lips and back he was touching, she felt Mac in every fiber of her body, in every singing nerve, with every crescendoing beat of her heart.

She leaned into his embrace, her arms twining around his neck, her fingertips tracing the taut muscles there before sliding into the silkiness of his hair. His mouth left hers to blaze a trail of velvety kisses down the side of her neck, and when his tongue dipped into the hollow of her throat, tasting the pulse beating there, Carrie heard the small involuntary sound she made, a soft purring, a plea . . . a surrender.

Reluctantly, she drew back, out of the hypnotic warmth of his arms, and opened her eyes. She smiled, shakily.

"You really throw yourself into a cover, don't you, Mr. MacAllister?"

Mac took a deep breath, and then a second one. His body was still pulsing with very ungentlemanly messages. And adolescent metaphors about racing engines thrown into reverse and stripped gears were zipping around in his brain. But Carrie's eyes were wide, and the plea in them was not the same plea that had been in her small moan of a moment before.

Mac breathed deeply again. "You should have seen me as a wino in the 'tenderloin,'" he said, and smiled back.

MR. MACALLISTER AND HIS FIANCÉE were given adjoining rooms overlooking the floodlit artificial lakes and greenery strung with tiny white lights at the center of the hotel complex. On the way up to their rooms, they shared an elevator with a family with five children, who were returning from a full day at the Magic Kingdom, if the Mickey Mouse ears on each head and tired smiles on each face were anything to judge by. The youngest girl, draped exhaustedly over Dad's shoulder, was still whining her displeasure at the prospect of bed instead of "one more ride." Mac made funny faces at her until her pout turned to giggles.

At the door to Carrie's room, Mac suggested they get unpacked and settled in and then go out for a late dinner. She agreed quickly, welcoming the chance to be alone for a few minutes, to get herself back in order.

But once alone, all she could think about was what had happened in the car, which didn't do a thing for restoring order. She tried to concentrate on shaking the wrinkles out of the clothes she removed from her suitcase, but she kept getting sidetracked by the sparkle of the ring on her finger. She tried to decide whether or not to change for dinner, but her thoughts kept drifting to Mac's kiss, and her reaction.

She knew the kiss had been just a bit of teasing, part of the charade, not serious. Her mind had known that, even at the time. But her body hadn't—hadn't known, or hadn't cared. Mac's kiss, his touch, had been like an instant wildfire, setting her aflame. Just thinking about it now started the fluttering sensation all over again deep inside her.

And she shouldn't be feeling that way about a man she barely knew. Mac Kincaid intrigued her, there was no denying it. But who wouldn't be intrigued by a man who appeared in the middle of a daydream about Mr. Right, and fit in so very perfectly? And true, he was, as Robin would put it, easy on the eyes, Carrie thought with a smile. His firm-lipped mouth, the slight downward slant of his brows over his dark gold-flecked eyes, the strongly muscled contours of his body, his hands that were so seldom still—he was definitely easy on her eyes. She liked his smile and especially his laugh; she liked the sensitivity he'd shown toward a little boy, his family, even a stranger in an elevator. She liked being in his arms.

But it was too much liking, too soon. So she was going to have to be very, very careful. Things had happened too fast with Doug Bannerman, too, and look what that had gotten her—months of heartache. Being attracted to Mac Kincaid was one thing; letting that attraction lure her down a garden path was another.

Of course, she told herself, heading into the small white-tiled bathroom, she was undoubtedly making a big affair out of a small kiss—and a playful one at that. For Mac, the kiss had been part of the game they would be playing for the next few weeks, or however long it took for him to do his investigation, nothing more. She was sure he wasn't mooning about in his room, thinking about the moments he'd held her in his arms. Certainly he wasn't still feeling hot and bothered.

But as she leaned over the marble-topped sink, cupping her hands beneath the water fizzing from the faucet, she heard the shower come on in the adjoining bathroom. And as she looked into the oval mirror above the sink, a broad smile spread across her face. In the next room, Mac Kincaid was showering, and she couldn't help wondering, was his shower warm, or cold? Maybe even as cold as the water she was about to splash over her still much-too-pink cheeks?

THEY ATE in a small Italian restaurant called Amore. A garland of tiny lights wound among wine bottles hanging from a latticework ceiling, a candle dripped a wax rainbow over a squat green bottle on their table and soft Italian love songs played in the background. It was no surprise that the majority of widely separated tables seated only two.

Soft lights, love songs, superb food, mellow wine, and Mac Kincaid.... It would have been a devastating combination, Carrie decided not long after they arrived, except that the conference was going to start at nine o'clock the next morning. And that thought was as good as any cold shower for dispelling a romantic atmosphere.

At the hotel, Carrie had finished unpacking and freshening up before Mac and had spent the intervening minutes looking over the conference brochure. The front of the brochure featured the conference name, Opening Doors, and an appropriately symbolic logo— a partly open door through which floated a flurry of tiny red hearts. But inside was a listing of the various workshop sessions. She had glanced down the list, at titles like "Who Am I?", "The Big Lie," "Steps in a Successful Search," "Finding," and "Tomorrow's Adoptions," and her stomach had flip-flopped uncomfortably. She'd thought of the next day, of attending the sessions Mac had starred in red ink, of pretending, and felt even worse.

And now, queasy knots of apprehension were keeping her from doing justice to the piquant antipasto, the richly seasoned rigatoni and buttery garlic toast on the table.

"What do you want me to do tomorrow?" she asked Mac, lifting her wineglass. On her finger, his ring made shooting stars out of candlelight.

He picked up his glass and clinked it gently against hers. "Oh, stare at me adoringly, blush a lot, maybe put your head on my shoulder when we're sitting together... all the typical fiancée things."

"Mac, really," she protested, putting down her wine without tasting it. "I'm... nervous."

"Don't be. There's nothing to it," he assured her. "We'll attend several of the sessions and workshops, but mostly we'll just talk to people. Our story is we're just starting your search, which covers our ignorance and also steers the conversation directly to searching.

We keep our ears open for any hint of ways to get into the supposedly sealed adoption files, grit our teeth, and echo the platitudes everyone else will be mouthing when necessary. The latter should be the only really difficult part."

Mac's velvety voice could have a very biting edge to it, Carrie realized. "You don't sound like you're expecting to have much fun," she observed.

"No, I don't suppose I do." Mac broke a teardrop of wax off the bottle holding the candle and rubbed it between two fingers thoughtfully. But when he spoke again, it wasn't to explain. "There is one thing you could do for me now, Carrie, if you wouldn't mind . . . tell me about your adoption so I don't contradict my fiancée's story tomorrow."

"I don't mind at all," she said, "but there isn't too much to tell, really. It was a private adoption. My mother couldn't carry a baby to term. She'd had several miscarriages and had been warned not to try again. So she and my father decided to adopt."

"Did you always know you were adopted?"

"Absolutely. In fact, my earliest memory is of the story my mother used to tell about my adoption. It was right in there with Winnie the Pooh and Cinderella, and she made it as wonderful as any fairy tale—only I liked it better because I was the star. She would hold me in her lap and tell me how much she and my father had wanted a baby, how they heard about me and that I was a colicky thing, always crying. But when they came to see me, and my mother picked me up the first time, I became fascinated with her bright-red nail polish and stopped crying, and that settled it. She and my father were sure about adopting me from that moment."

"So being adopted didn't bother you?"

"Never. It seemed as natural as anybody else's birth to me, and maybe even a bit better, because I always knew how very much my parents wanted me."

"What about the circumstances of your being relinquished. Did you ever wonder about that?"

"Well," she began slowly, "once when I was about thirteen and very preoccupied with things sexual, I did ask my mother why I'd been given up. The story was typical enough. A young, unmarried girl in 'trouble' did the best thing for everyone and gave up her baby, and my parents were forever grateful that she had." Carrie took a sip of wine. "Maybe it was the way my mother told me, straightforwardly with understanding, or whatever, but it satisfied my mild curiosity. I did wonder occasionally what the mystery woman had been like and what she might have felt at having to give up her baby. And I did have a funny dream...."

"A dream?" Mac picked another drop of wax off the bottle, his eyes on Carrie. But she didn't notice; she was staring into the candle flame, remembering.

"I'd almost forgotten..." she said. "But I had this recurring dream off and on for a couple of years, starting when I was about twelve, and I always assumed it had something to do with my adoption, though I couldn't say just what. I would dream of a big house with pale cream walls and a huge curved staircase leading from a tiled entryway up to a bedroom. And I was in that bedroom—crying and crying because I was alone. So very alone."

A shiver shook Carrie's shoulders and Mac reached out and took her hand. It was cold, and he laced his fingers with hers, holding tightly. Carrie blinked, as if breaking the candle's trance, and shrugged. "Weird, huh?" she said with forced lightness, and lifted her wineglass again.

"I don't think so," Mac said. "When I was eleven, I used to dream about a tribe of beautiful Amazon women who were waiting deep in the jungle for the one man who would be perfect enough to satisfy their Amazonian needs. Of course, at eleven, I wasn't quite sure what needs those were, but I was pretty confident I could satisfy them—at least in my dream. And night after night I led expeditions into the untamed wilderness, searching for the tribe at great risk, without concern for my own safety, surviving numerous perils. And finally I would discover their secret city of gold and they would surround me, a whole tribe of Wonder Women, and then...then I'd wake up." He heaved a huge sigh. "Now that's weird."

Carrie nearly choked on her wine. "Mac..." she wheezed. They grinned at each other.

"Did you ever mention your dream to your parents?" Mac asked when she was breathing steadily again.

She shook her head. "No...I'm not sure why. I guess I just didn't want to bother them with it." She paused. "And, as I said, I never felt a compelling need to know if it meant anything, or any other details about my adoption. They just never seemed to matter."

Mac smiled broadly, the tiny scar beside his mouth deepening to a dimple, as his thumb stroked the fleshy mound at the base of Carrie's palm. "It's really too bad," he murmured.

"What's too bad?" she asked as tiny sparks skittered up her arm.

"Too bad that you'll undoubtedly be the only adoptee at the conference tomorrow who feels that way, and because of our cover, you won't be able to say it," he answered. "That's not going to be easy."

CHAPTER SEVEN

MAC WAS RIGHT. For Carrie, nothing about the conference the next day was easy. From the opening welcome speech, through the various workshops, to the film at the end showing adoptee–birth parent reunions—all gloriously happy, of course—it was variously disturbing and exhilarating, but never easy.

A few months before, Carrie had attended the American Booksellers Association convention in San Francisco, and come home lugging a huge bag stuffed with promotional giveaways and free samples. At the Opening Doors conference she collected things, too. But these were intangible things like bits of conversation, impressions, expressions on faces, stories told; things she carried only in her mind, much heavier things.

Her collection started with a snatch of conversation overheard as she and Mac stood in line to pick up their registration packets before the opening session. Behind them, a wiry little man sporting a bristly mustache was speaking in a voice three times his size to an elderly woman, clearly not minding who else heard him.

"I can find anyone, you better believe it," he boasted. "Whether they want to be found or not. And it doesn't take me months or years, either. Weeks, days sometimes, is all I need, you better believe it. I've been a private investigator for fifteen years; I have connections."

"But it must be awfully expensive," the woman said, her voice quivery. "I'm on social security, you see..."

He didn't wait for the rest. "Hey, of course it costs. I'm a businessman, not a charity organization. But you say you've been searching for five years and so far, zilch. I say I can find the kid you gave up in a week. But naturally it's gonna cost...."

You better believe it, Carrie thought grimly.

Next into her bag of "goodies" went an impression, one that surprised her. The opening session speeches contained all the familiar platitudes of adoptee–birth parent rights advocacy: searching was right and absolutely necessary; all adoption records should be open to the adoptee and birth parents without restriction; ending secrecy could only have positive results regardless of the situation. There were melodramatic stories of crucial information withheld or outright lies told by cruel social workers and selfish adoptive parents; of adoptees whose severe psychological problems evaporated when their searches were completed; of birth mothers who once every year sat weeping over a cupcake with a candle stuck in it, mourning the birthday of the child they'd lost. Emotional tugs on the heartstrings were a lot more frequent than facts.

But running beneath the clichés and the syrupy stories was a thread of caring that Carrie sensed was genuine. True concern and a real desire to help flowed from the speakers to everyone in the room, to new searchers and old hands, and it both impressed Carrie and made her feel terribly guilty for her deception.

Guilt didn't make keeping up her end of the pretense any easier. And neither did Mac.

Not that he didn't play his part well ... he did. From the moment he picked her up for an early breakfast that morning, he was always beside her, the perfect future husband. He was attentive, he glibly introduced her as his fiancée who wanted to know the facts of her past before their marriage, he fielded questions. He was utterly convincing. Which was precisely what bothered Carrie.

Mac too smoothly slipped into the lie that was Ashley MacAllister lovingly supporting his fiancée in her quest for the truth. There was far too much realism for comfort in his pose as the enraptured lover, especially when it came to tender glances, draping an arm caressingly across her shoulder, sensuously stroking her palm with his thumb as he held her hand. He was too damned convincing, Carrie decided, discovering long before the first coffee break that enduring Mac's cover was going to be the hardest part of keeping to her own.

The first workshop was interesting, yet disturbing. "Who Am I?" presented some of the facts missing from the opening session and Carrie listened, a frown puckering her brow, to the discussion of how adoption affects the adoptee. Adolescent adoptees suffered above average incidences of delinquency, drug and alcohol abuse, unmarried pregnancy and alienation from family. And the problems seemed to often carry over into adulthood, with higher than normal rates of psychological and emotional problems requiring therapy showing up in older adoptees. Insecurity, lack of identity and emotional instability were common.

But why? Carrie left the workshop, her mind awhirl. Why should being adopted have an adverse affect on so many? Several possible theories had been presented: different family dynamics in an adoptive family; accentuated feelings of being different; the negative impact of having an unknown heredity and biological connection; and more. Yet no one theory applied in every case; no direct cause–effect relationships could be proven.

A lot of the theories, Carrie thought, seemed to boil down to the adoptee feeling rejected, a feeling that colored everything else in life, an insecurity never overcome. Yet she had grown up with the exact opposite feeling—of being loved and wanted as much as, or even more than, other children. Why? What had made things different for her? Was it her parents, her environment, her heredity... what? Why had she been so fortunate? And what would help the others?

She wanted to tell Mac what she was feeling, to ask him those same questions and see if he had any answers. But there wasn't time; the next workshop followed almost immediately.

"Deciding to Search" was supposed to deal with the impact of that decision on the adoptee, a spouse or children, the adoptive family and those who were found. And it did, but to Carrie's mind, in a very frustrating way.

There was an inherent bias underlying the discussion, she realized immediately. Searching was right. Absolutely. Without qualification or exception. And that bias colored everything that followed. Yes, it was admitted, there might be repercussions of a search. Adoptive parents or siblings might feel rejected and hurt. A spouse or children of a searcher might feel neglected or that they were taking a second place to what often became an expensive, all-consuming, draining concern of the searcher. The person being searched for and his or her family might feel invaded, distressed, shocked.

But though all these possibilities were mentioned, the mention always carried an addendum that to Carrie seemed as if nothing more than a shifting of responsibility from the searcher to the others affected. The adoptive family should not feel hurt, should, in fact, be willing to help the adoptee. The same was true of the spouse or children of the adoptee. And the ones being searched for, it was stated, usually got over their initial surprise and any negative feelings quickly. If they didn't, then *they* had a problem they would have to deal with.

Carrie sat in the small conference room beside Mac, and more than once wanted to argue, to point out the imbalances of that attitude, to scream even. But her cover wouldn't permit such heresies. She could only, as Mac had said the night before, grit her teeth and wait for the session to end.

She did, wondering at the same time how Mac was taking it. He didn't seem to be gritting his teeth, she thought, sneaking glances at him as the speakers droned on. He was lounging back in his chair, long legs stretched out in front of him and casually crossed at the ankles. His squarish jaw wasn't tensed, the only thing marring the unwrinkled plane of his forehead was a wayward lock of chocolaty brown hair. His eyes were on the speakers, he was listening intently, and even nodding occasionally, as if concurring with some point. It was odd that instead of taking notes, as he had in the first session, he was holding the leaded end of his pencil pinched between the thumb and forefinger of one hand and tapping the opposite palm with the eraser. But she doubted it meant anything. In every other way he looked just the way Ashley MacAllister should look, interested and in agreement.

Which was why it came as such a surprise when three-quarters of the way through the workshop, Mac snapped his pencil clean in half.

But at the coffee break, it was Carrie who couldn't hide her feelings about the story they heard.

As Mac had said, most of those at the conference were eager to talk about their personal situations. Janice Sedgewick, a large, middle-aged woman with small, opaque brown eyes, long, deliberately red hair and a grating voice, was doing just that when Carrie and Mac joined several other people sitting in the lobby outside the conference rooms.

"So, after several months, a...friend was able to get my mother's name for me," Janice said with a tiny sniff, her method, Carrie soon realized, of punctuating a sentence. "It took another six weeks to locate her—and then she refused to meet with me. She didn't want to give me my birth father's name, either, but I wouldn't take no for an answer." Sniff.

Carrie's brows inched upward.

"He was easier to find," Janice continued, "even though he had moved to another state. I wasn't going to chance another refusal by calling ahead, so I just flew out there. But when I arrived at his home, this old woman answered the door and told me I couldn't see her husband, he was too sick. I explained that he was my father and I had a right to see him. But she just got all huffy and said he was suffering from Alzheimer's disease, and since he couldn't remember her, his wife of forty-two years, he wasn't likely to recall a woman he'd had an affair with thirty-seven years before—and certainly wouldn't care about meeting the child of that affair." Sniff, sniff.

"You mean your birth father was married at the time he and your birth mother had their affair?" Carrie asked, stunned by the dreadfulness of the situation. "And his wife didn't know until you showed up at her door?"

Janice nodded.

"Oh, how awful." Carrie was thinking of a sick old man, without a memory, the poor wife he no longer recognized, and Janice, blundering into the touchy situation with such cruel results. "You must have felt horrible."

"I certainly did," Janice replied. "All that and she wouldn't even let me see him—can you imagine? But I haven't given up—I'll wear her down." Sniff, sniff.

The coffee she was drinking turned to acid in Carrie's stomach.

Even then, she might have handled it, if Janice hadn't in turn asked about Carrie's reason for attending the conference. As usual, Mac jumped in with their cover story.

"Good for you, Carrie," Janice said earnestly. "Searching is hard and very frustrating at times, but it's also very exciting, a very special adventure. And finding your real parents is worth whatever it takes, isn't it?" Sniff.

Adventure. Worth whatever it takes. *Real* parents. The words churned along with the acidic coffee in Carrie's stomach, frothing into a nauseating mixture that threatened to gag her, and she knew she couldn't stay there, not a minute more. Shakily, she put her coffee cup down on the nearby table and stood.

"I'm not looking for real parents," she told the woman. "I've had real parents for twenty-six years." And she turned and walked away.

She was sitting on an artificial rock beside an artificial waterfall on the hotel complex's large central courtyard when Mac caught up with her. The night before, fairy lights had glimmered in the trees and shrubs and sparkled in the water of the lakes. In daylight, the court looked more stagy, more like the extension of Disneyland it was. Yet the sound of the waterfall was soothing, the breeze rustling through the palm trees was cooling, and Carrie smiled at him as he sat down beside her. Mac took an instant liking to the place.

"Blew my cover, general," she said, sketching a salute. "Will it be the stockade or the firing squad?"

He chuckled. "We're not too hard on conscripted troops. Besides, there was no real damage done. The formidable Ms Sedgewick merely counseled me to be understanding of your outburst, explaining that many adoptees go through periods of denial during their search." His voice slid up an octave and into his nose. "It's just fear, dear. Some adoptees even go through most of their lives claiming they aren't the least bit interested in searching, you know. Of course, we're aware that they're just denying the truth, that they've been brainwashed into believing only bad adopted children hurt their adoptive parents by searching. They simply can't bring themselves to admit their need, the need all adoptees have. At least your fiancée isn't that bad off." And Mac sniffed.

The imitation was funny and perfectly on target, but Carrie didn't feel like laughing.

"You mean that...that woman actually said any adoptee who claims to be uninterested in searching is really deceiving himself?" she asked, disbelief clouding her eyes. "She really thinks there isn't a single adoptee who's truly happy and content not to know every last gory detail?''

"That's what she said," Mac confirmed.

"But that's bizarre. It's illogical, and unfair and…"

"Brilliant," he put in. "Take the offensive, label the other side as self-deluded, and you've hamstrung them before they've said a word. You can sympathetically pat them on the head when they try to disagree with you, but you certainly won't listen to what they have to say because you know they're just lying to themselves. Voilà! End of argument. And you're free to go on justifying whatever it is you want to do—in Janice's case, barging in on a sick old man and his wife."

Carrie looked up at him. "But Mac, it's so wrong. Doesn't it make you furious?"

Her green eyes glittered as brightly as the teardrops of water splashing from the waterfall into the pool beside her. Mac put his arm around her shoulders, pulling her against his side. Her head dropped naturally against his chest and a strand of her sweet-smelling hair tickled his chin. The warmth of her body huddled in the shelter of his was comforting, and he let his eyes drift closed. It felt so good to relax, to be able to quit pretending for just a moment. His fingers tightened on the softness of her upper arm.

"Yes, Carrie, it does make me furious," he murmured. "It really does."

BUT NOT ALL THEIR ENCOUNTERS were infuriating. They met many "varieties" of searchers, young and old, strident and hesitant, and heard many different stories, some funny, some sad, all touching. And as the day wore on, the people and the stories gathered in Carrie's mind like a party of bothersome poltergeists, stirring up questions, challenging long-held beliefs, making her wonder if she'd ever be able to sort it all out.

The last workshop of the afternoon was on sources and aids for searchers, and Carrie knew she should be paying strict attention. But her mind kept wandering. Mac was busily jotting down notes about government records, both open and closed, church records, hospital files, genealogical sources and so on. Carrie had her notebook open in front of her, too, but she was doodling, not taking notes. At first the doodles were just pointless shapes, squares, circles, stars, daisies. But one circle turned into a head, a girl's head, and her hair was made of question marks. And when Carrie'd filled in the girl's features, her mouth was a definite frown.

She was staring down at her childish drawing, musing over its meaning, when a hand holding a red felt-tipped pen covered it. When the hand moved away, the frown had been replaced with a pair of gigantic red lips lifted in a wide and happy smile.

Carrie turned a giggle into a cough and looked curiously at the man sitting on one side of her, red pen in hand. She guessed he was in his early thirties, though his professorish full beard and mustache made it difficult to judge. His hair, curling to the collar of his rugby shirt, was the same pale chestnut color as the neatly-trimmed beard. His eyes were a light brown, too, but they twinkled brightly as he reached out toward her notebook again.

"I'm Peter Millheiser," he wrote, "and it can't be as bad as all that." A large arrow indicated her formerly frowning doodle.

"Oh yes it can," Carrie wrote in return.

"You mean the conference?"

"Yes," she scribbled back. "It's overwhelming. So many unhappy people. It doesn't make adoption look very good."

"Don't let it get to you. There are plenty of happy adoptions. Mine was. And I work with a group that's making them even better."

Carrie was about to write "What group?" when the session ended with the audience breaking into applause for the speakers. Startled, she looked up. On the other side of her, Mac was clapping. But he was staring at her notebook.

The applause ended and they all stood. Peter Millheiser turned to Carrie.

"I'm glad that's over," he said, smiling at her. "Now we can talk out loud."

"Yes, I was afraid you'd get writer's cramp," Mac put in.

He was the taller by several inches, and Carrie had the impression he was making as much of his height as he possibly could as he stood beside Peter Millheiser. The comment wouldn't have sounded particularly friendly even if Mac hadn't deliberately folded his arms across his chest as he stood facing Peter Millheiser. Still, the other man's smile faltered only a fraction as he looked from Carrie to Mac and back again.

"Peter Millheiser, Mac...um, Ashley MacAllister," she introduced them, stumbling over the lie. And then she realized she hadn't introduced herself. "I'm Carrie Prescott."

"My fiancée," Mac added, as quick as ever at establishing their cover. Perhaps even quicker.

"Congratulations," Peter said smoothly.

"You mentioned a group you work with...?" Carrie shifted the conversation.

He nodded. "It's called Triangle, and is primarily an educational organization dealing with adoption."

Beside her Mac tensed. They weren't quite touching, but Carrie could still feel the rigidity go through his body.

"I think I've heard of Triangle," he said slowly. "You're based in the San Francisco area, aren't you?"

Peter looked pleased at Mac's recognition. "Right. In Berkeley, actually, where I live. We're headquartered in the spare room of my house for the time being."

"Triangle's something of a clearing-house for information on adoption studies and trends, isn't it? And you present workshops of your own?"

"You have heard of us, Mr. MacAllister," Peter said, nodding again while at the same time giving the remark a slightly questioning twist.

"It's Mac, please, and Carrie and I have a place in Sausalito," was his reply, the latter an embellishment of their cover Carrie could happily have done without. She hadn't counted on being "promoted" from fiancée to live-in lover.

"She's adopted and wants to search for her birth mother," Mac went on, blithely ignoring the frown she shot him. "She'd like to find some information on her background before we're married, and I want to help her, of course. But we're not sure about the best way to begin, or how it's going to affect us and those we love. We were hoping this conference would answer a lot of the questions, but I'm afraid it's only added more. It seems there are a lot of difficult issues involved in searching that I haven't considered before."

Carrie's frown changed to a look of surprise. Mac had just echoed her feelings and growing confusion.

Did he really feel that way, she wondered, or was the claim only part of his cover story?

"It was that way for me, too, when I began," Peter was saying.

"You've searched?" Carrie forced her attention from Mac to Peter.

"And found." He smiled, and gestured at the notebook she held. "I love my parents very much; they and my two adopted sisters are my family. But I also wanted to know my biological roots, my beginnings. So I searched. And I also became interested in the whole experience of adoption. But like you, I felt overwhelmed at first." He paused and glanced at Mac before continuing. "Since you're from the Bay area, maybe you'd like to attend some Triangle meetings. We go into the whole adoption experience, and in a positive way, I think. We have adoptees, birth parents and adoptive parents at our meetings, so it can get pretty wild at times, but it also keeps our perspective clear. We have a special search support group, too, that you might like to join."

"Sounds great," Mac agreed immediately, though there was a touch of asperity in his voice that didn't quite jell with his words.

Peter handed Carrie his card after jotting some dates and times on the back. She glanced at the notes, then at the front of the card with the name of the group and an address printed on it.

"Why Triangle? Does it stand for something special?"

"For the three components of every adoption," he answered her. "The child, the birth-family members, and the adoptive family—the adoption triangle. Too often in the past, only the needs of one or two sides of the triangle were considered when decisions about placement, secrecy, availability of information and so on were made. Which in turn led to many of the problems affecting adoptees and their families today. Triangle tries to deal with the problems and the needs of all three sides. I hope we'll see you at a meeting.''

"I hope so, too," she made the obvious reply, and then was surprised to realize she actually meant it. A day ago she wouldn't have been interested at all in any group dealing with adoption, she knew. But that was before the conference had planted so many questions in her mind, questions that were mushrooming and demanding answers. Triangle might have some of those answers.

But a moment later, Triangle lost a lot of its appeal as a familiar voice called Peter's name.

"Peter, dear, there you are! We're going to be late for the closing session!''

They all turned to see Janice Sedgewick advancing on them, red hair fanned out behind her like a squirrel's bushy tail. When Peter would have made the introductions, she cut him off.

"Oh, we met earlier. Carrie was a little upset then." Her small eyes shifted to Carrie. "But you look like you've recovered now, dear."

"Carrie and Mac are from Sausalito and may be coming to some Triangle meetings," Peter told the woman. "And they might be interested in the search support group, too."

"How nice." She sniffed.

"Janice runs the search group," Peter said.

"How nice," Carrie echoed dryly, wondering if she could unobtrusively drop the card Peter had given her into a trash can somewhere. But as if he'd guessed her intention, Mac took the card from her, tucking it into a pocket.

"We just can't wait to get started," he said, and smiled dazzlingly at Janice Sedgewick.

She sniffed.

CHAPTER EIGHT

THE CONFERENCE WAS OVER, and Carrie had never been so glad to see the end of anything before in her life. She knew the feeling wouldn't last. The questions were still there inside her head and would push forward again, demanding answers. But for the moment, all she wanted was to put it all out of her mind, to eliminate the words adoption and search from her vocabulary, to exorcise the poltergeists, if for only a little while.

Unfortunately, Mac didn't seem to feel the same way.

At his instigation, he and Carrie had left the final session the moment the applause started tapering off. He'd been silent as they'd taken the hotel elevator up to their floor. As Carrie had dredged her room key from the depths of her shoulder bag and unlocked her door, he hadn't said a word. When she'd opened the door, he'd followed her inside without waiting for an invitation.

But the moment she closed the door behind them, the words started spilling out, a torrent unleashed as he ripped the conference badge from the pocket of his wheat-colored corduroy sport coat.

"Thank God that's over," he said, shedding Ashley along with the badge. He scowled at the pink square he held. It carried the same hearts and open door logo as the conference brochure. "I should have known how bad it was going to be this morning, the minute I saw this ridiculous thing. Can they really expect people to believe that no matter what doors are forced open, only sweetness and light are going to pour out?"

"I think a lot of them do, sincerely," Carrie said, removing her badge more gently.

Mac crumpled his and dropped it into the straw wastebasket beside the dresser. "If they do, it's because they've deluded themselves into believing it. That's what groups are for, after all—community brainwashing, justification by consensus. Get a group together in support of some cause and they'll convince themselves in no time that their rights, their feelings are all that matter in the world, and the rights of the other guy be damned."

Carrie plopped down onto the end of the bed and nudged the shoe off one of her feet with the toe of the other. She supposed Mac was right, at least in many cases. Certainly she'd heard that attitude expressed by some of the people she'd talked with today—Janice Sedgewick for a prime example. But not everyone had been so strident and uncaring, though they'd all been equally desperate to find the truth of their pasts. They needed to know—that was the one thing she had learned conclusively. She still didn't understand why they felt that need, but she believed they truly did, and such an urgent need couldn't simply be dismissed. But neither could the right to privacy of others. So where did one person's rights end and another's begin?

Carrie didn't know. And, she thought, kicking off her second shoe and wiggling her toes, at this very minute she didn't care. She wasn't going to think about it just now. She couldn't.

But Mac hadn't noticed her silence. He was pacing in front of the room's single window like a caged lion, talking a mile a minute.

The chance meeting with Peter Millheiser was a stroke of good fortune, he was saying, shrugging out of his sport coat and tossing it over the back of a chair without breaking stride. Triangle was on his list of Bay area groups to be investigated, and Peter's invitation would accelerate the group's acceptance of them. So next on their agenda should be to start Carrie's search following suggested procedure. They'd skimmed by this weekend by claiming beginner's status, but from now on they would have to work at looking genuine if they were going to get anywhere.

As soon as they were back home, he went on, tugging loose the knot in his tie, they would have to gather all her adoption papers and start a search notebook— steps number one and number two in the recommended procedure. And step number three would be getting whatever information was available from her family.

Mac stopped in midpace, one hand on the collar button of his shirt. "Will you be able to do that, Carrie?" he asked her. "Ask your parents about your adoption, I mean? What would you give them as a reason for wanting to know?"

"The truth, of course," Carrie responded automatically. But actually, she hadn't thought before of her parents being involved. Now, sinking back on her elbows, she asked herself what her mother and father would think, how they would react to her pretended search. And what if the search were real?

She had a good and very loving relationship with her parents. Her father was a typical absentminded physics professor at Stanford University who'd never seen a reason why his daughter couldn't do anything in the world she wanted to. Her mother was a proud house-wife and mother.

She and her parents had gone through the usual trials and conflicts. Her adolescence had been a series of emotional tornadoes whirling through their lives. During her college years, when she'd been so sure she had all the answers, they'd disagreed on politics, religion and the future of the world. Their most serious rift, though, had been a result of her decision to accompany Doug Bannerman to New York, a decision they had vigorously opposed, an opposition Carrie had bitterly resented. But that rift had healed—even before she found out how right they were—without leaving any permanent scars, chiefly because love was a great medicine and they had plenty of it to go around. No matter how strongly they disagreed, no matter how loud the arguments, Carrie had always been confident of their love.

She knew now that love would govern their reaction to her investigation of her adoption, too, whether pretended or real. If she needed to do it, she was sure they would support her. But would they also be hurt?

Earlier that afternoon, in the workshop about the effects of searching on others, the possibility of adoptive parents feeling hurt had been briskly dismissed. Adoptive parents shouldn't feel hurt, adoptees weren't searching for replacement parents, the search would probably help the whole family's relationship, the reasoning had gone.

Easy statements to make—especially for adoptees and birth parents. But Carrie couldn't help feeling they wouldn't be so easily put into practice by even the most well-meaning and loving adoptive parents. If a child were to go to a parent and say he or she wanted to find another mother or father, wouldn't it be natural for the parent to feel rejected as if he or she had somehow failed that child? Logic might tell the parent the curiosity was natural, that the need to know was part of the adoption experience. But emotionally...emotionally it would still hurt.

If she were really searching, telling her parents would be hard. But since she wasn't....

"I'll just tell them the truth," Carrie repeated. "There won't be a problem, I'm sure."

"Great," Mac said, resuming his pacing. "I have a feeling that Triangle may be the key. We'll have to wait and see how far we have to pursue your search to make it look genuine...."

Mac went on talking, but Carrie wasn't listening. She was watching him. He'd unbuttoned the collar of his shirt and finished unknotting his tie, exposing a small triangle of tanned skin at his neck. When his pacing led him away from her, Carrie saw that the back of his cotton shirt was wrinkled from the day's wear. His russet brown slacks were creased, too, at the backs of the knees, and in front, low across his hips.

It was unfair, she thought, that a woman just looked careworn after a long, trying day like this one. But a man...Mac...looked great. There was something, well, downright sexy about his slightly rumpled look, the discarded formality of his sport coat and the barely undone shirt and the loose tie. Carrie remembered her grandmother, a spry, fun-loving and down-to-earth lady, telling her that imagination and mystery were the greatest aphrodisiacs in the world. Showing a little was a lot more seductive than showing it all, she'd claimed while deriding current fashion. Looking at Mac now, Carrie realized her grandmother was right.

Suddenly she was all too aware of being in her hotel room, a room holding a bed and very little else. Even if Mac was still yammering on about their plan of action, about business, he might stop talking at any moment, and then . . .

Then it was time to get them out of her room, Carrie decided. Thoughts of her parents and her birth had reminded her of what day this was. Which now gave her an idea.

She pushed herself upright and tucked her feet back into her shoes. It was harder to feel vulnerable with your shoes on . . . she hoped. She waited until Mac had completed a length of pacing and turned. Then she cut in, right in the middle of something about his "maybe getting more than one article out of this."

"Are you paying me overtime, Mac Kincaid?" she demanded, and discovered, with a sinking sensation, that he looked perfect even when he was gaping. It was definitely not fair.

"Paying you . . . ?" Mac blinked like someone just waking from a particularly deep sleep.

"I'm kidding," she said, taking pity on him. "But don't you think we could take a little time off from adoption? Even the word is beginning to make me sick."

He looked immediately contrite. "I'm sorry, Carrie. I guess I did get carried away. I swear, no more business tonight." He crossed the room to sit beside her. "What would you like to do?"

Several shameless suggestions darted through her mind, fueled by Mac's nearness, by the brush of his shoulder against hers as he sat down, by the warm masculine scent of him and the golden glint lighting his brown eyes as he faced her. Firmly she dragged her thoughts back to sanity.

"Promise you won't sneer," she said.

"I seldom sneer, Carrie Prescott. An occasional smirk, a leer or two—" he wiggled his brows up and down "—but almost never a real honest-to-nasty sneer. So...?"

"I'd like to go to Disneyland."

"Disneyland!" The glint in Mac's eyes was replaced by disbelief, disbelief not at all diminished by Carrie's affirmative nod. Clearly, the Magic Kingdom had not been high on his list of places to go this evening. "I had something like dinner and dancing in mind, somewhere quiet, with candles and soft music...."

Oh Lord, Carrie sighed to herself, thinking of dancing with Mac Kincaid, being held in his arms—closely, for he wouldn't be an old-school proper-distance type of dancer. He would hold his partner close, close enough for their bodies to touch occasionally as they moved to the music.

"I like Disneyland," she declared. "And we're just a monorail ride away."

Mac didn't keep his sigh to himself. "Do you suppose the hotel rents children to use as an excuse for being there?"

"Who needs an excuse? Don't you like Disneyland?"

"I did the last time I went...I was about ten, I think." His implication was clear.

Carrie ignored it. "You haven't been since you were ten years old? Well that's enough of an excuse for going, right there."

"Not for me," he said stubbornly, picking imaginary lint from the knees of his slacks.

"Well, how about this one?" she urged. "I've wanted to go to Disneyland on my birthday for as long as I can remember, and never have. And today is my birthday."

Mac twisted to look at her. "It's your birthday today?"

Carrie nodded, embarrassed at admitting it. But Mac smiled, that wonderful warm smile of his.

"Disneyland it is then," he said. "A birthday is a good enough excuse for anything—even that. But—" he paused and did his best to glower intimidatingly "—if you ever tell Libby or anyone else at the paper about this..."

Carrie laughed. "I know, Marquis, it's the rack or the iron maiden or worse..."

"Probably the 'or worse,'" he threatened inexplicitly, leaving her free to fill in the details with only his wiggling eyebrows as clues.

She did, graphically, and felt a hot blush staining her cheeks.

Mac watched Carrie flush candy-apple red and grinned. "I think I'd probably like your idea better than any of mine," he teased. "Want to tell me about it?"

Carrie stretched to her full height and jutted her chin upward. "We'll start with Tomorrowland, since that's where the monorail will drop us. Then a walk down Main Street, of course, and on to Adventureland." She ticked the stops off on her fingers. "New Orleans Square after that—we can have dinner in the Blue Bayou Restaurant before tackling Frontierland and Bear Country. We'll save Fantasyland for last, since I doubt you'll be in the proper spirit for the Mad Tea

Party, Peter Pan's Flight and Dumbo the Flying Elephant until then...."

"Dumbo!"

"And the King Arthur Carousel, Sleeping Beauty's Castle and..."

"There won't be time for all that," Mac said hopefully. "Surely the park closes at—"

"Midnight," Carrie filled in, smiling sweetly. "So you won't have to miss a thing."

Mac groaned.

A TRUE CALIFORNIA GIRL, Carrie had been to Disneyland numerous times. As a wide-eyed toddler, she'd screamed when a larger-than-life Mickey Mouse had tried to shake her little hand. At seven, she'd stayed up till midnight for the first time in her life one balmy summer night at the amusement park. As a giggly thirteen-year-old, she and a friend had stood in the long lines for the Matterhorn Bobsleds twelve times, hoping each time to be paired in the four-person sleds with two boys—any two boys over the age of thirteen. Her high school class had traveled all day on yellow buses smelling of diesel exhaust to spend the magic of grad night at the Magic Kingdom. Those times, and others, she'd loved Disneyland, at each age finding something special to enjoy.

But the park's magic had never been as potent as it was that night. If it was crowded, she never noticed. If the lines for the rides were long, she didn't care. There was still a world where adoption and searching were creating upheavals in people's lives, but that world was somewhere else, not here. Here there were fairy lights twinkling in the trees, music and laughter to foster enchantment, fantasies around every corner, and Mac to hold her hand. It was perfection from the moment they boarded the monorail at the hotel.

Despite Mac's earlier moans and groans, he seemed as susceptible as Carrie to the spell. He was the one who dared her to propel their rocket jet to the highest possible heights and who spun their giant-sized teacup faster and faster until the world became a kaleidoscopic blur. On the Jungle Cruise, he laughed as hard as she did at the corny jokes of the jungle boat guide. When they sailed in the wake of the Pirates of the Caribbean, he was the one who came out singing, "Yo ho, yo ho, a pirate's life for me!" It was impossible to tell who screamed the loudest as the Thunder Mountain mine train roller-coasted seemingly out of control beneath "tumbling" rocks and through a waterfall, or who jumped the highest when a shrieking ghoul popped up from behind a gravestone in the Haunted Mansion. And that made it all the more fun.

They ate dinner in the grottolike Blue Bayou Restaurant, where "fireflies" darted through the trees, "crickets" chirped somnolent tunes, and boatloads of "pirates" set off along the waterway leading to the place where "dead men tell no tales." They ate, talked of everything but business, and smiled at each other often and for no particular reason. When dessert came, Carrie's Black Forest cake had a single burning candle stuck in it.

"Happy Birthday, Carrie," Mac said, his eyes gleaming as brightly as the candle.

She couldn't believe it. "But how did you arrange this?" she asked. "When?" They'd been together every minute.

He shook his head, refusing to explain. "You are in the Magic Kingdom, after all" was all he said.

"Thank you, Mac," she whispered, her voice choked with the tears she was blinking from her eyes as she looked at him over the burning birthday candle. She was having the most marvelous birthday of her life, and Mac was the reason.

After dinner they rode the steamboat and the carousel, floated through the singing fantasy of a Small World and careened along Mr. Toad's Wild Ride. But when Mac said he wouldn't "object" if she wanted to try Peter Pan's Flight next, Carrie shook her head and hurried him toward the Skyway. At the entrance, though, she held him back, looking from the line of waiting people to her watch.

"What are you up to now, Carrie Prescott?" Mac asked curiously.

"Shh! You'll see," she told him. They stood there a few minutes longer before she said, "Now," and headed up the steps to join the line.

She'd timed it just right. At nine o'clock, she and Mac were in the small car sliding slowly along the tramway cable strung high above the park when the evening's fireworks display filled the sky. Sunbursts of color exploded overhead, outshining the stars, a dazzling show for which Carrie and Mac had the best seats in the house.

Only Mac wasn't watching the display…his eyes were on Carrie. Her face was tilted upward and a faint smile was turning her lips into a cupid's bow. A breeze blew a strand of her coppery hair across one cheek, and she reached a hand to casually brush it away.

Earlier, they'd ridden both the Matterhorn and Space Mountain, and Carrie had squealed like a little girl at the wild dips and twists and turns of the high-speed roller-coaster-type rides. But Mac had been all too aware of her, sitting between his legs in the tiny bob-sled and narrow space capsule. Her back had nestled against his chest and her hips between his thighs, and his arms had settled naturally around her waist. And then the little cars had taken off and their bodies had swayed and pressed and rocked together, and he'd found himself short of breath, his heart pounding, and his jeans growing far too tight in one specific region—reactions having nothing to do with the ride's excitement.

But those feelings were nothing compared to what he felt now, just looking at her. The graceful movement of her hand, the tilt of her head, the unconsciously sensual parting of her lips, the pure joy he read on her face—all sent an unexpected shiver of desire rippling through him. They had sat on opposite sides of the small car when boarding, but now, as he looked at Carrie, that situation suddenly didn't suit him at all. Smoothly and quickly, he crossed the space between the seats to sit beside her. And when she turned to him, her mouth opening in surprise, he put his hands on her shoulders, drew her to him, and kissed her.

The fireworks left the sky to explode within Carrie as Mac's mouth claimed hers, boldly, as if there was no doubt at all about his right to do so. She was surprised, and yet not surprised, by the kiss. It was sudden, but in a way it seemed they'd been moving toward this moment all evening...all day...since the day they'd first met. As her lips parted eagerly beneath his, she realized that choosing the playfulness of Disneyland over the romance of dinner and dancing had been a futile exercise. Futile, because anywhere she and this man were together was going to be romantic, sensuous...heavenly.

Heaven was being in Mac's embrace, his hands sliding tantalizingly up and down her arms, then massaging erotic little circles down the length of her spine to the swell of her hips. Heaven was the warm, melting feeling filling her as he gently urged her closer to him, molding the softness of her breasts against the firm planes of his chest and deepening their kisses. Their legs pressed together, thigh to thigh, and she felt the telling twitch of his muscles. Deep inside her, something quivered excitedly in response.

Mac nibbled the sensitive lobe of her ear and little sparks scattered delightful fire through Carrie. His fingertips teased the wide V-neck of her cotton knit sweater, then tickled their way beneath the material, brushing across the tops of her breasts, then sliding lower, and lower. Each tiny spark became a conflagration of need, snatching her breath, until Mac's hand slid still lower and he was cupping one breast, exploring its pleasure-tightened contours, its swollen peak. Moist heat flamed through Carrie . . . heavenly.

Heaven . . . heaven. . . .

Hell . . . when the skyway car dipped suddenly and, with a grinding of gears, clattered into the light and bustle of the terminal.

Mac swore softly as they broke apart. His eyes followed the hasty smoothing movement of Carrie's hands as she straightened her sweater. The still-aroused tips of her breasts showed through the soft material, and his fingers burned with the need to touch her again, to caress her, to kiss her mouth and once more taste her sweetly eager response. And his fingers weren't the only parts of him burning. He felt as though the world's biggest Band-Aid had just been ripped off his soul—raw and ragged and filled with a longing like nothing he'd ever felt before in his life.

Carrie heard Mac's oath, and silently echoed it. As she tugged her sweater back into respectability, she saw his eyes move, saw them linger intimately, and a tremor shook her. Then Mac looked up and their eyes locked together, flashing with their mutual yearning.

More than anything in the world, she wanted to take Mac's hand and lead him to the nearby monorail, back to the hotel, to her room, into her bed. Images of them lying together, melding together, whipped searingly through her mind. Her body pulsed with wanting him.

But there was more, more than wanting the physical sensations he could create within her with a touch of his hand. She thought of the moment at the Blue Bayou when she'd looked at Mac over the birthday surprise he'd arranged for her, of the comfort of Mac's arms in the hotel courtyard when she'd been upset by Janice Sedgewick's remarks, of Mac's concern for a little boy missing his teddy bear, and wondered. Was she falling in love with Mac Kincaid? Was she? It was so soon, so very soon, and she hardly knew him. She certainly didn't know if he felt anything similar for her. And she needed to know.

She could give in to the wanting tonight, and appease the needs of her body. She could quench her desire and the reflection of that desire burning in Mac's eyes. But what about her heart? Her heart had needs, too. Needs, and fears. Her heart wasn't ready. Not yet.

Mac stared into Carrie's eyes, those beautifully revealing eyes, as the small tram car came to a jolting halt inside the terminal. He saw her dampen the fire of her desire, and knew she'd done so deliberately, regretfully...but not completely. There was still a spark there in the green depths, ready to be fanned to flame again. He hadn't imagined her responses; they'd been as strong as his own to her. So he knew, without any sense of conceit, that he could coax that spark into life. If he asked her to go back to the hotel with him now, to bed with him, she would go. Willingly. But with some slight reservation.

With another woman, at another time, he might have done it, might have used a little friendly persuasion to get what he knew they both wanted. But not with Carrie.

He wanted her in his bed—God, how he wanted her in his bed! But not until she wanted, without the slightest reservation, to be there. Because he realized he wanted more from her than a few pleasurable moments. Much, much more.

The Skyway attendant pulled open the door of their car. Mac stepped quickly out, then reached a hand to help Carrie from the swaying car. He felt the Kincaid diamond, sharp and cold, dig into his palm, and the trembling of Carrie's slim fingers. Turning her hand, he twined his fingers with hers and squeezed reassuringly. After a small pause, Carrie squeezed back.

The attendant gave them a friendly nod as he sent the car on to pick up other passengers. "You were just in time for a great view, weren't you?" he said pleasantly. "Did you enjoy the fireworks?"

"Yes," Mac and Carrie answered him in unison—looking only at each other.

LATER, BACK AT THE HOTEL, Carrie sat on the end of her bed, silently waiting until she heard the shower come on in the adjoining room. Only then did she slip out of her sweater and slacks and into a shower of her own.

Where she shivered. And smiled.

CHAPTER NINE

A WEEK LATER, Carrie was tucked into the window seat in her bedroom, staring out at the raindrops trickling down the glass. She'd spent the morning there, a lap quilt over her legs and Pandora curled against her slippered feet while she caught up on her column.

She liked the Bay in all its guises—sun-speckled, wind-whipped, touched by mists that came on little cat feet or heavily shrouded in pea-soup fog, even roiling with a storm's fury. But there was something extra special about spring-shower days. She loved watching puffball clouds scudding across the sky, swallowing patches of blue and casting wraithlike shadows onto the dimpled surface of the water below. She loved the sound of rain fluttering against window and roof. She loved using the grayness outside as an excuse for a fire inside. Showery days were wonderful for tucking in somewhere, for cozy indolence and for thinking.

It was thinking that was keeping her huddled in the window seat, even though she'd finished her self-alloted amount of work some time ago. While reading, sorting and answering letters to Dear Carrie, she'd come across the one she'd been reading the day of her precipitous first meeting with Mac Kincaid. The sheet of powder-pink paper with its perfumed purple ink had fallen from a file folder into her lap, and Carrie hadn't even had to pick it up to recall its questions. One in particular.

"How will I know when a guy is really right?" Spinster had written.

Oh yes, Carrie remembered the question very well. She just hadn't found an answer yet, for Spinster, or herself.

And she should have. A week ago, at Disneyland, she'd asked herself if she was falling in love with Mac Kincaid. Between then and now, she'd spent a good portion of her time either in Mac's company or being reminded of him by something—or someone. Surely this week should have brought her closer to answering the question. Surely by now she should know... was Mac her Mr. Right?

A sea gull swooped by the window, looped around and, wings outspread, drifted down to perch on a wooden piling. There it fluttered its gray and white feathers, shaking off raindrops, before folding its wings neatly over its back. Carrie watched the bird, but her thoughts were moving back over the past week, searching for the answer she knew should be there... somewhere.

Mac had dropped her at her houseboat Sunday afternoon. He was heading for his house in Stinson Beach to finish an article on medical malpractice suits due in to Libby soon, he told her, but would see her Tuesday night—and not for work, if that was okay. It was, definitely, and Mac had kissed her goodbye as if the one kiss was going to have to hold him for two months, not two days.

Robin had immediately begged for every detail of the weekend. Carrie had been completely candid about the workshops, the people she'd met and stories she'd heard, and her confused reaction to it all. But when it came to the rest, she'd hedged. No, she and Mac hadn't gone dancing. Yes, they had talked a lot, about nothing in particular. No, of course they hadn't shared a room! Yes, Mac was...fun to be with. But nothing happened. Well, nothing worth mentioning.

Robin had listened intently, smiled one of her enigmatic smiles, and said, "That ring fits like it was made for you, doesn't it?"

The ring. Carrie had tried to give Mac back his ring on the plane that morning. He'd refused to take it.

"It's better if you hold on to it, Carrie," he told her. "We'll be going to Triangle meetings and who knows where else. The people involved in the illegal aspects of searching are going to be suspicious of anyone new at first anyway. Forgetting your ring just once could blow the whole investigation."

His reasoning made sense, and Carrie had nodded, telling herself to simply accept the ring as the prop it was, nothing more. That was obviously what Mac considered it.

But when she'd reluctantly nodded her agreement and slipped it back onto the appropriate finger, Mac had taken her hand and brushed a kiss across her knuckles.

"And besides," he'd murmured, his breath warm against her hand. "I like seeing my ring on your finger."

She'd been stuck with his ring. And, afraid of forgetting it at some crucial point, or worse, of losing the Kincaid family diamond, she decided the only safe place to keep it was on her finger. Where, unfortunately, its brilliance couldn't be missed by Robin, or Eddie...or Eugenie Brindle.

"Is that an engagement ring on your finger, Carrie Prescott?" Eugenie had caught Carrie on her way to do a little grocery shopping Monday morning. "Fast worker, that spiffy young man of yours!"

"No, Mrs. Brindle, I'm just…keeping it for him for a while…it's part of the work we're doing together."

Eugenie Brindle had smacked her wrinkled lips. "Nice work if you can get it," she'd cackled.

Eddie had seen the ring Monday night, at Carrie's belated birthday dinner of *Boeuf Bourguignon*, buttered noodles, crusty French bread and a well-aged cabernet. But he hadn't mentioned it. He'd asked her about her trip, about the progress of her work with Mac, about her birthday, all casual questions. When the meal was finished and the dishes done, he'd put a finger beneath her chin, tilting her face up toward the light. He'd looked long and hard into her eyes, then nodded. "I don't think you're walking so wounded these days, darlin'," he'd said softly. That was all.

That was enough. With a start, Carrie had realized he was right—she wasn't one of the walking wounded anymore. She supposed the hurt Doug Bannerman had dealt her had been fading gradually all along, like a summer tan through the winter. It had taken Mac, though, and the feelings he stirred in her, to complete the healing.

But what feelings were those, Carrie asked herself now, hugging one of the window seat pillows to her chest. Passion? Certainly passion, she admitted, her senses stirring at the mere thought of Mac's touch. But passion didn't equal love, she knew quite well. She let her thoughts drift back again.

Tuesday morning Mac's sister, Beth, had called, suggesting they get together for lunch. As Carrie had hesitated, wondering what to reply, she'd heard a shout in the background at the other end of the phone, and then Beth's giggle.

"All right, I'll tell her," Beth had yelled back at the shout before returning to her phone conversation. "Carrie? Mac informs me I forgot to mention that he's explained about the article he's doing on...search, and how you're helping him with it." There was another shout, and another giggle. "He also says I should warn you it probably won't save you from my 'incredible snoopiness,' but I hope you'll have lunch with me, anyway."

Carrie felt a ripple of happiness, knowing Mac had told Beth the truth. But she still hesitated over what to answer.

"I'd love to," she said finally. "But I promised to go with a friend, Robin, to the...obstetrician for her checkup. Her appointment's at eleven-thirty, and his office is on Geary, so we were going to head over to Sacramento Street for lunch and a little shopping...would you like to join us?"

Her hesitation in issuing the invitation stemmed from what she knew of Beth's situation, and Robin's condition. Her first thought was that Beth would not enjoy the company of a pregnant girl when she wanted, and couldn't have, a child of her own. But then Carrie remembered Beth worked in a preschool, and decided she obviously wasn't hiding from reminders of children. And something told her Beth and Robin would get along.

They did, even better than Carrie had expected—at times, to her chagrin. She wasn't subjected to any of Beth's probing questions; instead Beth and Robin simply discussed the relationship between Carrie and Mac as if she wasn't there, which was much worse. The two of them agreed it was a match made in heaven. Carrie and Mac were perfect for each other. And obviously something more had gone on over the past weekend than either of them were admitting to, since Mac looked head-over-heels to Beth, and Carrie, according to Robin, was lost on cloud nine. They kept on until Carrie intervened, threatening to borrow one of Mac's old tortures to use on both of them. After that, the talk switched to other things, like Robin's painting and Beth's work at the preschool. When Robin expressed an interest in the Montessori-type teaching, Beth invited her to visit the school one day.

Beth and Robin had changed subjects, but Carrie was still thinking of their earlier remarks. Were she and Mac "perfect" for each other? Was he "head-over-heels"? Was she on "cloud nine"? And was love mixed up in there anywhere?

She supposed she had been somewhere in the vicinity of cloud nine later that night. Mac had taken her to dinner and a Civic Light Opera production of *West Side Story*, and it hadn't taken a Magic Kingdom to put magic into the evening. They'd eaten in one of San Francisco's intimate little French restaurants, offering superb cuisine, elegant service, and candlelit privacy. Carrie, stuffed on chicken in the most wonderful white wine sauce she'd ever tasted, and had refused dessert. Mac had ordered chocolate mousse and insisted she taste just one spoonful—which had turned into two, three, more. And there had been something decidedly provocative about sharing the sensuously rich mousse with Mac, about the meeting of their eyes as he held out another spoonful of the dessert and she leaned closer to take his offering into her mouth. Later, at the musical, Mac had held her hand all through the show, and when she'd shared Maria's tears over her beloved Tony's death, he'd tilted her face up toward his and dabbed at her wet cheeks with a white handkerchief, whispering, "I had a hunch you'd need this."

It had felt like love then. Then, and after the show, as they'd sipped Irish Coffees at the American birthplace of the whiskey-laced drink, the Buena Vista Cafe. Then they had strolled along the grassy terraces of Aquatic Park, gazing alternately at the moonlit Bay and the strings of lights limning the buildings and pointy-topped clock tower of Ghirardelli Square. The chains of tiny white lights had reminded Carrie of Disneyland, and when Mac had stopped and taken her into his arms, she'd gone willingly, anxiously, not wanting the moment to ever end. Love?

What else but love could have made Mac's presence beside her at the Triangle meeting on Wednesday night so comforting, so reassuring?

The meeting had turned out to be surprising in more ways than one. The first surprise was that Robin asked to go along.

"We'd be happy to have you," Carrie answered, unable to resist a question of her own. "But I'm curious—just why do you want to come? Are you thinking about adoption for your..."

"Oh, I just think the meeting might be interesting," Robin replied, as uncommunicative as usual on the subject of her baby.

Robin couldn't have known what the evening's topic would be, Carrie told herself later. She couldn't have known, but nevertheless, the meeting turned out to be tailor-made for her. Even Mac had raised an eyebrow in surprise when Peter Millheiser smilingly opened the door of his Berkeley home to them, introduced the others there, and announced the subject for the meeting—new trends in adoption.

The meeting was, in many ways, a condensation of the conference. The same gamut of situations and concerns was discussed, many of the same opinions were expressed. But there were several important differences. First, Triangle was an educational organization, and its main emphasis seemed to be on improving the adoption experience rather than in criticizing it. Secondly, as Peter had told them, Triangle included members from all three sides of the adoption triangle—not just adoptees and birth parents, but also adoptive parents, who were trying to understand the whole process and how it would affect their lives and the lives of their adopted children. Their inclusion eliminated the tendency Carrie had sensed at the conference, to talk about the adoptive family almost as the enemy, as part of the wall standing between the adoptee and the birth family.

There were four speakers for the evening, two social workers specializing in adoption and two adoptive mothers, all giving their opinions of the change in adoption practices, especially what was known as open adoption, where the traditional secrecy was minimized, or even eliminated entirely. Names and complete information were being exchanged between birth mothers and adoptive parents, they said. Some birth mothers, and occasionally birth fathers, were even meeting the parents who would adopt their children and making agreements to continue contact through the years. There would be no need for these adoptees to search, though it was possible there would be other problems created by this new type of extended family.

Several times during the discussion, Carrie looked at Robin, sitting cross-legged on the floor, her fingertips occasionally tracing light little circles on the bulge of her stomach. Was she considering relinquishing the baby she carried? And if she was, how could she sit there looking so... serene, Carrie wondered. Whatever Robin was thinking, however, her expression didn't begin to give it away.

At the end of the talk, Robin and Peter wandered off together, talking earnestly, while Mac and Carrie were cornered by Janice Sedgewick.

Facing Janice was the part of attending the meeting Carrie had dreaded most, and as the woman walked toward them, she really appreciated the comforting arm Mac slipped around her shoulders.

Her greeting was typical. "I have to admit I'm surprised you came," Janice said, her small eyes on Carrie. "After the conference, I thought you would probably...well, I hesitate to use the words chicken out, but that's what happens to some searchers, you know. They start, and then...." She sniffed.

Carrie first felt herself bristling, and then felt the gentle, calming squeeze of Mac's arm. But still, she couldn't resist asking, "Don't you think an occasional person decides searching isn't a good idea, after all? Aren't there people who realize they're satisfied with their lives as they are?"

"They may tell themselves that, I suppose." Janice's smile was condescending. "My search workshop meets on Mondays... if you're still interested, that is."

Mac answered for them, which was a good thing, since Carrie doubted she could have gotten a yes out. Janice then suggested a few preliminary steps they could take.

"Contact the county agency that handled your adoption and ask for an appointment with a social worker familiar with your file. We'll be talking about the kinds of questions to ask on Monday, in fact," she said. "And send to the State Department of Social Services requesting adoptee background information from the state file. It will be basic, nonidentifying stuff, and probably will duplicate what you'll get from the county, but you never know when a clerk will slip up and include something useful. Also, ask for waivers of confidentiality for you and your adoptive parents to sign— if you think you can con them into it."

"What are waivers of confidentiality?" Carrie asked.

"A fairly recent California law established a state registry. Supposedly, if waivers of confidentiality are signed by the adult adoptee, the birth parent and the adoptive parents, then a meeting may be arranged between the parties. Of course, the operative word is 'may.'" Janice's sniff was louder than usual. "The people in Sacramento claim that if the waivers are there, and the addresses are current, and the county or agency that handled the adoption in the first place acts on the information properly, a meeting will be offered. But strangely, very few meetings are being arranged. And why the adoptive parents should have to agree to a meeting between an adult adoptee and his or her birth parent . . . ! By the way, Carrie, are your adoptive parents totally opposed to your search?"

"No, not at all," Carrie said firmly. "I certainly wouldn't have to con them into signing a waiver."

"Well, lucky you." Sniff. "That will make some things easier, anyway. Oh, and you should sign up with Soundex, too. They're a private nationwide reunion registry supported by most search groups, and do make some matches based on data supplied by the involved parties. Of course, it only works if the other party has signed up, too, so... But it's a place to start.''

Yes, Mac's reassuring arm around her had definitely helped at the Triangle meeting. And Carrie hadn't even minded that it had been tightest when Peter had come up to Carrie, offering to help her with her search in any way he could, asking her to please call him if there was anything at all he could do. Carrie smiled as she remembered the scowl on Mac's face as she'd told Peter thank you, she might do just that. She hadn't minded Mac's jealous reaction at all—it had made her feel warm and happy and...loved?

But, as she knew all too well, jealousy didn't necessarily mean love. Then what did?

Time spent enjoyably together? She and Mac had certainly had that this past week.

They'd spent a delightful day Thursday, acting on Janice Sedgewick's suggestions and then going to the San Francisco zoo. They'd shared sticky cotton candy, laughed at the antics of spider monkeys, fed apples to the elephants and snuck a quick kiss under the curious, huge eyes of the bush babies in the darkened nocturnal center. Friday she'd gone with Mac into Mill Valley to interview a woman—a birth mother—who'd been found and was very bitter about the intrusion of a stranger into her life. The interview had been difficult, but on the way back to Carrie's, Mac had stopped for two huge deep-dish pizzas to go, which they'd shared with Robin and Eddie that evening while watching an old Thin Man movie on television, laughing, joking and having a wonderful time. Last night, Mac had taken her dancing.

She'd bought a new dress for the occasion. Made of soft silk shimmering with the colors of tropical seas at sunrise, it had a full gathered skirt and belled three-quarter length sleeves. The bodice had a high square-cut neckline and smocking at the shoulders, but clung in womanly perfection everywhere that counted. The back dipped in a provocative V almost to the waist, while tantalizing rhinestone buttons ran down the rest of the length.

She'd loved the dress on sight, but it wasn't until Mac said she was the most gorgeous woman he'd ever seen, that she felt really beautiful in it. Beautiful, and filled with champagne, all bubbles and giggles and drunk with joy.

Mac had danced as she'd expected him to, with a graceful style and a lover's embrace. They'd moved together perfectly, their bodies brushing intimately, the movement of his every muscle telegraphing messages of longing to hers. His hands had caressed the bareness of her back exposed by the low-cut dress, his fingers had toyed with the rhinestone buttons. The thin silk of her dress had offered no protection from the feel of his hard chest against her breasts, the grazing of their thighs, the touch of his lips as he bent his head to drop a kiss against her shoulder. At times, she'd felt he was making love to her right there on the dance floor, and it had been marvelous. Would being in his arms, or just being with him, have felt so marvelous if she wasn't in love with the man, Carrie asked herself.

The latest rainshower had dwindled to a fine mist, which drifted down like scarves of thin gauze being waved in front of her window by the sea breeze. Carrie tossed aside the pillow she'd been holding and picked up Spinster's letter once again. And sighed.

She still couldn't answer the question, not really. She knew she...liked Mac Kincaid. Very much. She was undeniably attracted to him emotionally, as well as physically. And the more time she spent with him, the stronger her feelings were growing, the more she found to...like about him. He was warm, thoughtful, understanding, romantic, sexy...oh yes, definitely sexy... considerate, fun. In short, everything she'd ever admired in a man. He was coming over this afternoon so they could gather any papers she might have concerning her adoption and set up a search notebook in preparation for tomorrow's meeting with Janice Sedgewick's group. Then they would go out for a casual dinner. Mostly work, nothing special, and yet Carrie felt a warm glow at just the thought of seeing him soon. And that glowing, glimmering, feeling felt an awful lot like love.

But Carrie couldn't quite bring herself to say it, to say she loved Mac Kincaid. She couldn't quite give in to the feelings that kept trying to overwhelm her. Something was holding her back.

And she knew what that something was. She was afraid. Afraid of loving him. Afraid of the commitment loving him would mean. Because there were still moments when she knew he was holding something back, moments when his comments about the people at the Triangle meeting or the conference or searching, grew a touch too ascerbic for comfort. She'd realized from the start that Mac was very committed to his article on search, and at first it hadn't bothered her. From his other work, she knew he was always strongly committed to his subjects. But this time, was he too committed, too vehement? And was his interest in her, perhaps, only a reflection of the part she was playing in his very important investigation? When the task was done, would his feelings for her evaporate?

She was afraid.

Doug Bannerman had made her afraid.

Carrie leaned her head against the window, the glass wonderfully cool against her forehead. And she thought, about Doug.

She'd met Doug in her last year of college and been swept off her feet. Doug had been handsome, beautiful almost, with the flashy smile and winning personality suited to his career designs. He was going to be an actor. No, a star! Carrie had believed he would succeed with all her heart.

She'd even believed him when he decided he was too good for the Hollywood rat race; they should go to New York. He should be on the stage.

To her parents' despair, she'd gone willingly with him, and just as willingly got a very junior editorial position in a small publishing house to support them both while Doug attended classes, auditions and "events," the parties and galas where he felt he should be seen. Carrie had attended many of the gatherings, too, at Doug's insistence. She was good for his image, he decided. People—he meant men—liked her. He wanted her there.

Carrie had especially hated the parties. There were too many drugs, too much alcohol and too many men making passes. But she'd gone, even though she was often exhausted from work and the parties tended to last until all hours. She'd gone until one night an important producer, who was at the moment casting his next Broadway production, had made a very physical pass. She'd responded by disgustedly shoving him away—and just incidentally into the nearby stand of thorny rose bushes.

Doug had been furious—with her. He hadn't come right out and said she should have gone to bed with the producer, but when he didn't get the part for which he'd auditioned, he did blame the failure on her "outraged-virgin act."

She should have seen then that he was using her and had been all along. But when, after a few days of sulking, Doug had brought her orchids and champagne and apologized over and over again, she'd believed him—because she'd wanted to.

She'd refused to go to any more parties, however, but it hadn't mattered because Doug had got a small, but decent, part in another production, and was happy, for the moment. He was busy evenings, too, which left Carrie with a lot of free time. She started writing.

She didn't tell Doug about the novel until it was finished. Then she told him, sure he would be proud of her accomplishment and as supportive of her hopes as she was of his.

He wasn't. He saw her "scribbling" as a waste of time, which she could have been spending helping him with his career. The play had closed and he was looking for another "break." Why couldn't she help him instead of frittering away her time on something so mediocre?

The worst thing to remember now was how she'd meekly accepted Doug's verdict of her work—at first. But several people at the publishing house had known she was writing, and when she finally gave in to their requests to see the finished manuscript, they'd insisted she try for publication. Finally, Carrie had reluctantly agreed to send it to a publisher who dealt in young adult material.

What would have happened, she wondered, if the editor she worked for hadn't been friends with the editor at the other house who'd read, and loved, her book? Would she have given up writing? Would she have gone back into the mold Doug had wanted her to fit into; that of acolyte, admirer, assistant?

Carrie doubted it, but even now she couldn't be sure. She would never know, either, because one editor had talked to the other, and eventually she'd found out Doug had destroyed her letter from the publisher, because, he said, he didn't want their lives to change. Didn't she see he'd only done it because he wanted what was best for both of them?

She didn't. She'd left that night, returning first to her parents' house, then moving into the houseboat a short time later, where she'd met Eddie, and he'd called her one of the walking wounded.

Only she wasn't wounded anymore, Carrie thought, turning her head so her cheek pressed against the cool window glass. As she'd realized the other night, it didn't hurt to think of Doug and his selfishness anymore. Not really. But she was still afraid. Afraid of her own judgment. She'd misjudged Doug and even her feelings for him; she'd let her infatuation with him blind her for so long. And now she was afraid, afraid of letting herself fall in love until she was absolutely sure of Mac, and of his love. But when would she be sure? What would make her sure? How could she tell if the "guy is really right?"

Another cloud slid across the sun and raindrops started splashing against the windowpane again. At Carrie's feet, Pandora rose, stretched her scrawny body, and scrambled over the hill of Carrie's knees to land on the papers in her lap. Carrie reached down to scratch behind the cat's ears.

"What do you think, Pandora?" she whispered.

Pandora only blinked . . . and purred.

CHAPTER TEN

"DON'T YOU EVER throw anything away?" Mac grumbled as he pulled another cardboard box from the shelf of Carrie's walk-in closet.

"I don't suppose you save mementos," she challenged from her cross-legged spot on the floor beside her bed. They were supposed to be gathering any of her pertinent adoption documents before going out to dinner; the only problem was that Carrie didn't know exactly where her pertinent documents were.

Years ago, her parents had given her some papers concerning her adoption, she remembered. She also remembered glancing at them, deciding they weren't of much interest or import, and tossing them into a box. She just didn't remember which box.

Having Mac Kincaid in her bedroom wasn't helping her memory at all, either. As she dragged a dog-eared autograph book, a tear-blotched book of poems and a diary with a tarnished golden key from a box, she wasn't seeing any of the mementos that had once been so important to her. She was seeing the ripple of Mac's shoulder muscles beneath his knit shirt as he reached for another box, the sexy undulations of the back pockets of his cords as he bent to set the box on the floor beside her, the teasing glint in his eyes as he grumbled about her pack-rat propensities.

"Why would I keep stuff like this?" he was saying as he crouched down beside her, poking a finger into the collection filling one box. "If something's memorable, I remember it."

Carrie pursed her lips. "You don't save anything?"

Mac shook his head cockily.

"No sports trophies on a shelf? No high school yearbooks tucked away somewhere? How about the award certificate for your article on teenage gangs in the suburbs?"

It was the final one that wilted his cockiness. "Well . . . I might have saved one or two things. But I don't keep them mixed up with important papers."

Carrie laughed, and Mac joined her. But as he laughed, he leaned forward until he was gazing deeply into her green eyes.

"You're very beautiful when you laugh, Carrie Prescott," he said tenderly, the words like a caress.

And Carrie reacted as if it actually had been a caress. Her mouth was suddenly desert dry, there was a strange prickling in her fingertips and an even stranger ache in the center of her body.

"Mac, I . . ." she began breathlessly, then stopped, not knowing what she wanted to say.

"Yes, Carrie," he whispered, making it just barely a question. Sparks were dancing in the brown depths of his eyes, sparks of desire.

"I . . . I've just remembered where the papers must be," she exclaimed, and leaped to her feet, turning toward the closet to escape the longing in his eyes that was calling up the longing within her.

Carrie disappeared into the closet and Mac sank back against the bed, stretching his legs out in front of him.

There was a skylight over Carrie's bed, which at the moment was framing a patch of sky reflecting the first glimmerings of the approaching sunset. The morning's clouds had given way to a clear sky filled now with a golden light that suited the room, just as the room suited Carrie. It was feminine without being frilly, done in apricot and Wedgwood blue. In the wall facing the water, a bay window cradled a well-pillowed window seat, where, at the moment, her scraggly cat was studiously washing herself and keeping one wary green eye on him. Another wall held a small tiled fireplace. The queen-sized brass bed was centered beneath the skylight and covered with an old-fashioned quilt.

Mac had always liked skylights; there was one over his bed in the Stinson Beach house. The last several nights, though, lying there awake, staring up at a star-speckled, midnight—or two or three A.M.—sky, he hadn't liked it quite as much as usual. He'd kept imagining gazing up at the night sky with Carrie pressed close beside him, of turning from the sky stars to the stars in her eyes, of bending over her, pressing into the softness of her...and such thoughts didn't make for comfortable nights. Of course, the daytime hours, except for those he'd spent with her, hadn't been much better.

Carrie came out of the closet with a small green record case. "Voilà!" she pronounced, sitting down beside Mac and flipping open the lid. Inside was a collection of old forty-fives and a single manila envelope, folded to fit the box.

Mac shook his head as she unfolded it. "Is this how you always deal with important papers?"

"I never considered these important," she answered. "If I had, they would be with my other important papers...."

"I know, in the Buster Brown shoe box," he cut in, grinning as he jerked his head toward the box on the bed, which Carrie had taken from the sun room desk earlier.

Carrie slapped the manila envelope against Mac's outstretched leg. "Here, you can have the papers. I have more important things to look at." She started sorting through the records, every one a love song linked to a memory.

There wasn't much in the envelope, Mac discovered. A petition to adopt, a final decree of adoption, and a single sheet of paper listing some biographical information about Carrie's birth parents. The biographical information was sketchy and nonidentifying, giving only their ages, ethnic background, general health and educational levels. The petition and the decree were typical legalese. All three papers were imprinted with a lawyer's name, Charles A. Wieland. It was only when Mac started to put them and Carrie's birth certificate into the file folder that was going to be part of their official search notebook, that something struck him as unusual.

He pulled the papers out again, comparing them, "Weren't you adopted as an infant, Carrie?"

Her affirmative "Um-hmmm" became part of the love theme from a silly tear-jerker movie, which even on TV and cut by forty-five minutes of commercials had the power to bring tears to her eyes.

"But this petition to adopt wasn't filed until you were about two and a half, with the final decree being issued six months later."

Carrie stopped humming. "That can't be right," she said, scooting closer to him to peer at the papers he held. "I was just a baby, I'm sure. My parents have pictures of me with them at eight or nine months of age."

But Mac was right. According to the dates on the documents, she'd been almost three years old when her adoption had become final.

Carrie's eyes swept over the final decree, reading the words she'd found unimportant years before. "For all legal intents and purposes, it shall be the same as if the child, hereafter to be legally known as Carrie Ann Prescott, had been born to Oliver S. Prescott and Helen J. Prescott, in lawful wedlock, according to the prayer of the petitioners herein." And then came the date, the date that didn't fit at all with what Carrie knew of her past.

As it had the other night when she'd studied her birth certificate, a peculiar feeling shot through Carrie, a mixture of curiosity and uneasiness. She might have felt this same way, she thought, if the floor beneath her had suddenly turned a little soft and unsteady.

"Could there have been some hitch in the adoption?" Mac asked. "Something that held it up for a while?"

"I'll have to ask my parents," she said, taking the papers from Mac with trembling hands. "I wonder what they're doing tonight?"

"So, THE PLAN is to go through the typical search procedure, step by step," Mac told Carrie's parents that evening. "Using Carrie's background to make us look genuine, I'm hoping to connect with someone in the underground network who will offer us the information we're supposedly searching for, for a price. The most likely place to make the connection is through one of the search groups, like Triangle.''

"You don't actually want to be successful in your search then, do you?" her father asked.

Mac shook his head. "Absolutely not. We have to seem desperately anxious, and totally unsuccessful. Our urgent desire to marry—that's why we're posing as an engaged couple—will explain our anxiousness; hiding any information we come across that might actually lead to the truth will assure our failure. Then, we just have to be lucky.''

"There's a lot of legitimate searching going on, too, though, isn't there? It seems to me I recently read an article on the subject...."

Carrie looked across the table at her mother, and the two of them smiled conspiratorily at each other.

It seems to me I recently read an article on the subject...how many times as she'd grown up had Carrie heard that phrase, she wondered? Hundred, thousands? No matter what topic came under discussion in the Prescott household, Oliver Prescott was always interested, he always asked appropriate questions, and he had always "recently read an article on the subject."

Once upon a time, Carrie had hated the phrase. She'd just started dating, and whenever a boy came to pick her up, her father would engage the poor young man in conversation. And no matter what turn the conversation took, her scholarly father had always "read an article" about it, and proceeded to inundate the prospective boyfriend with his knowledge.

"The guys think they've stumbled into a classroom!" Carrie had wailed to her mother after one particular episode—about basketball, if she recalled correctly. "It's so embarrassing!"

"Carrie, your father's a professor and the most widely read man I've ever met. He's not exaggerating when he says he's read something about whatever it is—he always has," her mother had patiently explained. "I know it's hard, but you have to accept him the way he is. Someday you might even learn to love him for those qualities you now find so embarrassing. I do."

"How can you? Doesn't it drive you crazy?"

Her mother had shaken her head. "Not at all. A long time ago, when Oliver and I were first dating, it might have, just a little. But then one night your father drove me up to the local lovers' point...."

"Mom!"

"Never mind—" she'd flushed prettily "—we were up there, and your father started talking about how we'd been seeing each other for several months now and since his feelings for me were growing deeper all the time, he thought it was time to make a more permanent arrangement. And then he pulled a ring out of his pocket, dropped it into my hand and said, looking straight out the window, 'I know there must be a better way to put this, Helen dear. In fact, I know I recently read an article about the subject of proper proposals...but at the moment the whole damned thing's gone straight out of my head.' I've loved the phrase ever since."

From then on, Carrie had loved it, too, and each time Oliver Prescott used that particular phrase, she and her mother smiled at each other, sharing the wonderful secret.

Sharing a smile with her mother now eased a little of the tension Carrie had been feeling ever since she'd called, inviting herself and Mac to dinner. All during the drive south down the penninsula to the older, ranch-style house tucked away in the hills above Stanford University she'd been nervous, wondering how to best explain Mac's article, her pose as his fiancée and her sudden interest in her adoption. She remembered assuring Mac at the conference that telling her parents and enlisting their help wouldn't be a problem. But somehow, finding the discrepancy between her memory of the facts of her adoption and the dates on her adoption papers had made her less confident. Was there something about her adoption she didn't know? Something that had held up the final papers until she was nearly three years old?

Added to her nervousness over the adoption issue had been another worry. What would her parents think of Mac Kincaid—the man with whom she might be falling in love?

The latter worry had been put to rest before the first. Shortly after they arrived at the Prescott home, her father had put on the wire-rimmed eyeglasses he needed to see across the room but refused to wear in "company," and her mother was urging Mac to have just a little bit more of her Stroganoff—sure signs of approval.

Which left only the adoption questions to worry about, and so far Mac was handling that, Carrie thought, as she stirred sugar and milk into her tea. They had moved from the dining to the living room and the oak-framed sectional facing the slate-front fireplace. Insisting they leave the dishes for later, Carrie's mother had set out pots of tea and coffee, and settled back to listen to Mac explain his projected article and how Carrie was going to help him. And now her father was finishing up his description of the article he'd recently read on searching, and it was time for Carrie to join the discussion.

"Two of the steps in the search procedure are going over any documents you have," Carrie said, hoping no one noticed the slight tremor in her voice, "and writing down any information, stories, comments, you can remember about your adoption." She paused and, not quite ready to ask about the inconsistent dates, looked at her mother. "The first thing I'm putting down is the fingernail polish story. I was telling Mac about how, when I was a baby, I stopped crying the moment you first held me because of your fire-engine-red nail polish. That story's always been so important to me."

Helen Prescott was a blue-eyed redhead—though the red was dimmed with gray now—and had the milk-white complexion to match. Which meant she'd never been able to hide even slight discomposure. She couldn't now, either. Her cheeks were the same shade as the ripe strawberries they'd had for dessert.

"But you do know that story wasn't exactly true, don't you, Carrie?" she asked hesitantly.

"It wasn't?" Carrie could barely get the two words out past her suddenly constricted throat.

Her mother shook her head. "Oh, I was wearing bright red polish sometimes—it was fashionable, then. And you always loved grabbing for those red nails. But it didn't actually happen that way the first time I held you."

"No, you cried for some time after we got you," her father put in. "In fact, the doctor wanted to put you on sedatives, but your mother wouldn't let him. She said you'd stop when you realized you were safe and loved here with us . . . and you did."

"But Mom, you told me...."

"When you were small, I guess I embroidered the story a little," Helen admitted, her eyes on her daughter's face. "It started out as just a way to expose you to the idea of being adopted, but you loved it so much, you made me repeat it and repeat it, until we all knew it word for word. But I never realized you thought it was the absolute truth."

"Well, no, I didn't think that..." Carrie murmured, feeling like something precious had just been stolen from her, but too conscious of her mother's worried frown to admit it. "I was just a baby when you adopted me, though, wasn't I? Because we noticed a strange thing on the adoption papers—the dates indicate I was almost three before the adoption was final."

"That wasn't our doing," her father answered. "It was your biological aunt and uncle—they delayed signing the papers."

"My...aunt and uncle?"

"Yes, you see they had adopted you first," her mother said. "Oh, it's so complicated, which I guess is the main reason we never talked about it—that, and the fact that you've never been interested before. But your biological mother planned on giving you up for adoption from the very beginning. She didn't want a...reminder of her unhappy love affair. But she was living with her aunt and uncle—I guess they'd be your great aunt and uncle, really, who hoped she would change her mind after a time. So when you were born, they adopted you. But after six months or so, they realized your mother would never...do that, and they were too old to take on the job of parenting permanently, so they had to give you up. They didn't want to, though—so even after we had temporary custody, they hesitated over signing the relinquishment papers.''

Carrie was stunned by this wrinkle in the story of her beginnings. She knew her mother was waiting for her to say something, but she couldn't. All she could think of was that much of what she'd always believed about her adoption wasn't true. It didn't matter that she'd been adopted twice; knowing she'd had a great aunt and uncle who had cared about her didn't change the way she felt about her parents or anything else . . . but it was disturbing.

''So I lived with an aunt and uncle for six months before you got me?'' she finally got out, and Mac heard the nervous quiver in her voice.

''Nine months actually, before the temporary custody was arranged and we went to pick you up,'' her father said.

''Did you see . . . the house . . . where I was?''

''You mean the aunt's and uncle's house?''

Carrie nodded, but her mother was shaking her head.

''No, we didn't. We picked you up at the lawyer's.'' She hesitated, thinking. ''Though we did have one picture that showed part of the house—it was the first picture they sent us of you. You were in a baby swing sitting in a big hallway and I remember there was a huge curved stairway in the background with the most beautiful carved bannister. It looked like a large and elegant house.''

''Do you still have the picture?'' Carrie asked, barely above a whisper.

''No, we . . . well, we didn't keep it.'' Helen looked at Carrie. ''We probably should have, I guess, but at the time, we didn't want a reminder of the time you hadn't been ours. I didn't think that someday you might want it...."

Carrie shook her head, thinking of her dream of the house with the staircase leading to the room where she was crying. Was it a real house, a real room where she'd actually been as a baby? Where she'd cried?

Mac filled in the silence by asking her parents if they had met Carrie's birth mother or her aunt and uncle.

"No, we never wanted to," Oliver said. "It was all handled by the lawyer. He handled some legal stuff for us and knew we were hoping to adopt a child, and he knew the mother, too, I think."

"Was that Charles Wieland?"

"Wieland, right. I'd forgotten his name. He used to practice up here but I think he's moved down south now, to Santa Barbara or around there somewhere. Do you know Santa Barbara, Mac? I've always thought it sounded like a nice little town. I read an article about it once...."

"I think I'll get some hot water for the tea," Helen said, snatching up the still half-full pot and heading for the kitchen.

Carrie looked after her, her own personal worries dissolving. In all her years, she doubted she'd ever heard her mother interrupt her father before. After a moment, she stood and followed.

Her mother was standing in front of the stove, where the kettle was making fussy little heat-up noises. She was just standing there, doing nothing except waiting for the water to boil, which wasn't any more natural than her interrupting her husband.

Carrie moved to stand beside her. "Mom, did my questions about the adoption bother you?" she asked.

Her mother shook her head. "No, I understand about Mac's story and all, really I do," she answered. "And anyway, your father and I always felt that if you ever wanted more information you deserved all the help we could give. We promised ourselves we wouldn't take it personally if you decided to search. Of course, in my heart, I always thought that no matter how well I'd be able to intellectually accept your searching for another mother, I'd never be able to accept it emotionally. I was sure I would be heartbroken...."

"Oh, Mom!" Carrie threw her arms around her mother, pressing her cheek to the translucent whiteness of the other woman's. "I didn't want to hurt you, not for anything."

"I know that Carrie," she said, hugging back. "But you didn't let me finish. I wanted to tell you that all these years I've thought that if you did search, my emotional hurt would be the worst part—but now it turns out I'm afraid of something else. I'm afraid you'll be hurt. Dredging up the past, looking into things this way, even in pretense, might lead you to something that will hurt you."

A shiver of apprehension slid through Carrie, and she leaned back to look into her mother's blue eyes. "Like what, Mom? Is there something you haven't told me?"

"Oh no, Carrie, I swear there isn't," her mother quickly assured her. "Your father and I didn't really ask that many questions. Years ago you didn't ask. If I were doing it all over again now, I probably would demand a lot more information, for your sake. But then, we just wanted you. You were our baby—that was all that mattered. Believe me, there's no deep dark secret I've been keeping from you. But delving into the past does mean opening old wounds, raking up unpleasant memories—and not necessarily just for you. I've often thought of your...mother. On your birthday especially, I always wondered how she could have stood giving you up and wished I could send her a note, just to let her know how much we loved you and how happy and well you were growing up." She took her arms from around Carrie to reach for a dish towel and dab at her wet eyes.

"You're wonderful, Mom," Carrie said. "And don't worry. How could anything I might find in the deep dark past hurt me when I have you and Dad and all your love? I love you both so very, very much."

Yet for all her brave words, Carrie was subdued and thoughtful when, a short while later, she and Mac left her parents' house. The scene with her mother, the alterations in what she'd always believed about her adoption, had left her feeling strangely unsettled.

Mac noticed Carrie's preoccupation, just as he'd earlier noticed the glimmer of tears in the eyes of both her and her mother when the two woman had returned from the kitchen—without the teapot. And it worried him.

"Carrie, I know Libby said you were perfect for this research because you don't have an ax to grind," he said, breaking the unnatural silence that had filled the car for the past fifteen minutes. "And I know you've said your adoption doesn't bother you. But are you sure that's true?"

"Of course I'm sure," she said automatically.

"You never felt the sense of alienation from your adoptive family that so many people at the conference talked about? You never felt you were missing your roots or whatever?"

Carrie smiled. "Maybe I didn't pay enough attention in biology class, but I never felt I wasn't actually a part of my family just because I had a different set of genes."

She thought back. "When we had to do a family tree in school, I didn't have the least qualm about supplying my mom's and dad's ancestors. In English class when we were supposed to write about a family tradition or story, I wrote about my great-grandfather—my mother's grandfather—a Dutch cigar maker who had to leave Holland because he was too politically outspoken. It never entered my mind that I might not be entitled to claim him as an ancestor. And when I was eighteen years old, my mother gave me the seed pearl lavaliere that her mother had given her on her eighteenth birthday—and I will pass it on to my daughter someday, and it won't matter at all that I wasn't physically born to my mother."

An image of an older Carrie, giving her daughter her grandmother's pearl lavaliere, flashed into Mac's mind, making him smile. She would have a few fine lines around her eyes by then, he supposed, and some around her mouth, carved by her frequent smiles. The bright cinnamon of her hair might have mellowed just a bit, the youthful firmness of her body might have eased to a softer curvaceousness. But she would still be beautiful, he knew.

It was all he could do to drag his thoughts back to the discussion at hand, to what he needed to ask her. "But even if your adoption itself isn't a problem, Carrie, what about the searching? Is going over all this stuff and dredging up the past going to bother you?"

Mac reached out, putting a hand softly on her neck to rub at the stiffness he'd known he would find there.

"Because if it is, let's forget your search," he told her. "I'll get the information I need some other way. I don't want you to be hurt."

Mac had unknowingly echoed her mother's words of concern, and Carrie, looking at him, felt a surge of love so strong, so undeniably real, that it was terrifying. She knew how very important the story was to him, yet he was offering to write off the work he'd already done and the cover they'd established, and start over—to protect her from hurt.

He cared about her first, the story second.

And she loved him. As if this one moment had obliterated all the fears and uncertainties in one swift stroke, Carrie knew she loved Mac Kincaid, wholeheartedly, passionately, for always. And knowing, being absolutely certain, she discovered, was even more frightening than not knowing had been. Carrie stared at Mac and was petrified.

So she did what she'd done all her life in moments like this—she started talking. She answered Mac's question: no, continuing with the search wouldn't bother her at all, she was certain. And went on from there. Talking, about anything, barely knowing and not really caring what she was saying, just so long as there weren't any long silences that she might end up filling by blurting out that she loved him. She truly loved Mac Kincaid.

CHAPTER ELEVEN

THE NOTE WAS TAPED to the slatted double half doors leading to the kitchen, almost as if Robin had known Carrie would invite Mac in for coffee when they returned to the houseboat and so be heading that way. Almost as if the girl had wanted to make sure Carrie had issued the invitation before she discovered her "chaperone" wasn't home.

Robin had decided to spend the night with a friend, she wrote. They were going sailing the next day, too, so Carrie shouldn't expect her back until late in the afternoon. And in case that hadn't made things clear enough, she'd added a postscript.

> p.s.   Give the gorgeous hunk a kiss
> for me, Carrie...and enjoy!
>   Love Robin

Carrie could almost hear the girl's giggle.

"I'd better get the coffee started," she said hastily, crumpling the note in one hand. She pushed through the white doors, asking if Mac would like cream, sugar or a dash of Irish Cream in his coffee, but the doors swung shut before he could reply.

Mac grinned. He'd stood beside Carrie, unabashedly reading over her shoulder and watching an appealing rosy blush spread across her cheeks. Robin's opinion of his relationship with Carrie evidently had a lot in common with Beth's, he thought, recalling a few of his sister's more pointed hints at how his love life should be progressing. And he didn't disagree with either of them.

Carrie was standing at the kitchen counter. She'd started to spoon coffee beans into a grinder, getting as far as holding the filled spoon in midair when her thoughts wandered down several interesting garden paths. What did she want to happen next? Pinpricks of desire stabbed through her, offering the obvious answer. But was it the right one? The paths were knotting into a maze, and Carrie didn't hear the kitchen doors swing open at all.

"Irish Cream," Mac said softly, his breath feathering the hair behind her ear.

Beans flew all over the counter and floor, landing with startled little plink-plunks. Carrie's heart was doing similar things.

"Mac! You scared me to death!" she gasped. "What . . . what did you say?"

"Irish Cream," he repeated, smiling as he took the empty spoon from her hand. "You asked what I wanted in my coffee . . . I answered. Now, where's the broom? One of us better start sweeping, unless you usually feed coffee beans to your cat."

"Pandora!" Carrie followed Mac's pointing finger to the cat who already had one bean between her pointy teeth. Directing Mac toward the broom closet, she scooped up the animal and began trying to pry open its jaw. But it was the broom's appearance that made Pandora surrender her prize in exchange for the freedom to jump to the only safe place her old bones could still manage—a chair beside the table. From there, her sea-green eyes warily followed Mac's every sweeping movement.

"I don't think that creature likes me," Mac said.

Carrie rinsed her hands and returned to coffee making. "It's not you. Pandora's just a little old lady, part tyrant and part grouch."

"How old is she?"

"I don't really know. The vet guessed sixteen or seventeen." And she told him Pandora's story, in undoubtedly more detail than he had wanted to know. But it filled the time while her mind tried to find its way out of the maze.

"You make picking up strays a habit, don't you, Carrie?" Mac observed, leaning on the broom. "Robin, Pandora . . . are there others?"

"No . . . not really," she answered, but couldn't help thinking that there had been something of the stray in Mac Kincaid on the day they'd first met, when he'd asked her to help him; when he'd held her hand and said he needed her. She smiled, imagining his reaction if she told him that.

Mac was watching Carrie as the smile spread across her face, and a fine heat spread through his body. God, she was beautiful, he thought. And desirable. And lovable. And that smile did unbelievable things to him. . . .

He propped the broom against the wall. A few steps and he was touching a finger to the petal-soft center of her lips. Her swift intake of breath was like the brush of butterfly wings against his fingertip, and her green eyes widened into bottomless emerald pools to drown happily in. Reverently, he cupped the side of her face, her skin silk against his hand. His thumb sketched the high sweep of her cheek, then dipped down to rub softly across her mouth again.

Hot and cold sensations flooded through Carrie and her hands itched to reach up to Mac's face, to trace the full line of his lips, to feel the slight roughness of the strong jaw that hadn't been shaved since morning, to touch the small triangular scar beside his mouth. She turned away, setting the coffee grinder on the counter and pushing a button to start its shrill whine.

"How...how did you get that scar?" she asked, pouring the rich-smelling grounds into a filter cone and reaching for the kettle of boiling water.

"Researching," Mac said, rubbing at it with an index finger. Which gave at least one of his suddenly empty hands something to do. "I was doing an article on criminal recidivism, and one of the individuals I was interviewing objected to my questions."

"You mean someone did that on purpose?"

"Actually, he meant to carve a W, for Willy—but I persuaded him otherwise. Willy's back in prison now, for armed robbery, not this little thing. But he sends me a card every Christmas, just signed with a big childishly printed W."

"That's so...horrible, Mac." Thinking of what *could* have happened, she shivered. Coffee began dripping into the glass pot beneath the filter cone, filling the room with its aroma. "Have you done many investigations that turned out to be so hazardous?"

"Not many," he replied lightly, "and none as hazardous as trying to answer questions from a bunch of crazy teenagers."

"Crazy? Why do you think teens are crazy?"

"Because I was, way back then. It's all those hormones and wild emotions banging around inside. It starts on your thirteenth birthday, and you grow out of it somewhere around . . . well, I used to think I'd grown out of it around the age of eighteen, but lately. . ." Mac's eyes grazed over Carrie, sparks snapping in their brown depths.

"Well, umm . . . teenagers may be crazy by your definition, but I still wouldn't call answering their questions hazardous." She opened a cupboard and took out two glass mugs. "Though admittedly, some of the questions are tough."

Mac grinned. "I know the ones you mean. The ones about s-e-x. And that's ninety-five percent of them, right?"

"Wrong!" she declared, laughing. "Actually, although the kids don't always seem to recognize the fact, many more of their questions have to do with love, with how to find it, how to keep it, and how to know when it's re . . . real."

Carrie couldn't help it. As she tripped over the word, thinking of Spinster's letter and her own questions about loving Mac, she couldn't help looking at him. She knew her eyes might give her away, and yet she couldn't stop herself.

Mac gazed into Carrie's eyes. And he knew. He knew the reason for all the chattering, for the stammered words, for the fevered flush in her cheeks. He knew.

"And you answer all the letters yourself, Carrie?" he asked, his voice rich and slow and sweet, like chocolate melting in the sun.

She nodded, unable to look away. "Though not all the answers go into the column. And there are some I can't answer definitely yes or no. But I just tell the writer why I'm not sure, and that seems to work out."

Her cheeks were flaming, the fire spreading from there through her, everywhere.

"My sisters tell me you do a great job, even with the tough ones."

"Well, I . . . try. . . ."

"Then will you try one for me, Dear Carrie?"

"Sure!" she said, trying to sound flippant. She failed.

"Dear Carrie," Mac began, moving closer to her, until Carrie could feel the heat of his body reaching out to hers, little electric waves lapping against and around her.

"Dear Carrie," he said again, "when are we going to quit all this chattering that's just a smoke screen to hide what we're really feeling—that we both want to make love so badly it hurts. Signed . . . Frustrated."

It was like being tumbled out of the hammock and having all the breath snatched from her again. But this time it felt somehow different than on that first day. When she breathed again this time, it was with wonderful relief, as if a monstrously heavy weight had just been lifted from her chest.

Carrie breathed, and turned and set down the coffee mugs she was holding. Then she put out her hand and gingerly, carefully, touched Mac's face.

"Dear Frustrated," she said softly, as anticipation and longing spun heated webs within her. "Now could be a good time, I think. Now."

IT WAS HARD to take it slowly when his body was on fire, and yet Mac wanted to. He wanted to savor every moment, every taste and touch and feel of it . . . of her. They stood in the velvety darkness of Carrie's room, mouths and hands not needing the light to find their way, their bodies knowing instinctively how to press together, to move together, to create the most swiftly moving whirlpool of sensation, the strongest current to sweep them away.

Mac kissed her, his lips devouring the sweetness of hers, then moving to nibble the sensitive spot at her temple, the hollow below her ear, the column of her throat. His hands slipped from the silken tangle of her hair, raining tempestuous caresses down her back, her waist, then womanly roundness of her hips. Carrie sighed, a soft moan of growing hunger, and Mac felt the answering sting of yearning.

He sank down on the end of the bed and drew Carrie toward him, into the cradle of his spread legs. The outer curves of her legs brushed against his inner thighs, denim against cords, and his hands slid around the backs of her thighs, pulling her yet closer. His mouth pressed into the fine-knit weave of her sweater where it covered the flatness of her stomach.

His hands on her legs held her firmly against the moist heat of his mouth, and she arched into the bewitching contact that was weakening her knees and sending brightly colored rainbows through her mind. His fingers massaged the softness of her thighs, rubbing up and down the hard inner seams of her jeans, and the warm moistness was inside her, flowing from her. Then his mouth was nuzzling the bottom edge of her sweater upward, exposing a line of skin to his tonguing exploration.

"Oh Mac..." she whispered, her voice lost somewhere deep in her throat. Her fingers reveled in the softness of his hair and teased beneath the collar of his shirt.

His hands slid up, over the luscious curves of her bottom to span her waist, then shifted forward, easing the sweater farther upward until his knuckles grazed the luxurious fullness of the undersides of her breasts. The chill of the air sent goose bumps across Carrie's bared stomach, but Mac licked them away, his tongue tickling into the hollow of her diaphragm. She giggled, huskily, and writhed within the V of his legs.

Mac sucked in a breath and his thighs tightened against hers. His fingers moved to the front of her jeans. He popped the snap open with a flick of his thumb, then the zipper was rasping downward, slowly. And his mouth was following.

Need was a whip lashing through her and Carrie's fingers clenched in Mac's hair. She started to sink to her knees, but he stopped her, his hands going to her waist again. Gently he raised her sweater, slipping it slowly up, letting his fingers graze her ribs and the already-sensitized tips of her breasts before he lifted it over her head. His own shirt swiftly followed hers to the floor, and then he was leaning backward into the softness of the bed, taking her with him, down against the hard length of his body. Their mouths came together again, fire to fire.

Carrie pressed into Mac, learning him, reveling in the feel of his body responding to the movements of hers, in the concurrent responses of her body touching his. Her hands roamed the roughness of his jaw, she brushed her breasts tantalizingly against the muscles of his chest. Her hips ground against his yearningly.

Mac made a growling sound and his arms tightened around her. But he supported her weight tenderly, gently, like a cherished treasure, as he eased her over onto her back. He loomed over her, blessing the silvery glimmer drifting through the skylight that enabled him to see her aroused and unbelievably arousing beauty, as his hands gently eased her jeans and panties from her body. He stood, slipping hastily from the rest of his own clothing, and then he was coming back to her, bending to taste the sweetness of her breast, slipping a knee between the powdery softness of her thighs.

"I love you, Carrie," he whispered against her wildly pounding heartbeat. "I think I've always loved you, through all my yesterdays and for all my tomorrows. Forever."

The everyday, ordinary world exploded into a thousand glittering pieces. Then Carrie moved, opening anxiously, hungrily, to Mac, and they melded together, perfectly, sublimely. And together they refashioned a brilliant new universe made up of only him and her, and love.

"Go 'way, you damned animal," Carrie mumbled, her face buried in a pillow. She reached back with one hand to brush at Pandora, whose parade up and down her spine was drawing her from sleep. And from the most marvelous dream.

"I wasn't that bad, was I?"

The huskily drawled comment reached her ears just as she touched, not the cat she expected, but another hand. A warm hand and fingers dancing sexily down her bare back.

Carrie flipped over, and the dream became reality. Milky morning light was filtering in through the skylight, and Mac Kincaid was sitting on the edge of her bed, wearing only his cords and balancing a breakfast tray precariously on his knees. That sight, and the lovely scent of omelets, toast and coffee tickling her nose, finished the job his fingers had started.

"Mac..." she sighed, smiling as memories of the night before flooded pleasurably over her like warm bathwater. It hadn't been a dream. She loved Mac Kincaid, he loved her, and she had just spent the most wonderful night securely, sensuously, nestled in his arms. And the world was a beautiful, heavenly place.

"Come on, lazybones, breakfast is served," he said, his voice thick with feelings engendered by the sight of her. Her hair was sleep-tousled, her eyes were passion-dark, and the bedsheet was tangled low around her hips, offering her rosy breasts, slim waist and the tantalizingly pearly skin of her abdomen to his hungry view. And she was smiling that perplexingly familiar smile, that half-shy, half-sexy, nymphet smile....

"The mermaid!" Mac exclaimed, the answer flashing into his brain, so obvious that he couldn't believe he hadn't recognized it long before.

Carrie's slumberous eyes blinked in confusion. "The mermaid...?"

"On the gate." He was grinning. "Your smile seemed familiar from the first time I saw it, but I couldn't figure out why. But just now, I realized... you were the model for the mermaid on the gate."

Magenta rushed to Carrie's cheeks and she snatched the sheet up to her chin. "No," she said.

"No?" Mac balanced the tray even more precariously with one hand and lifted an edge of the sheet with the other. He made a production of peeking underneath. "Well, you don't have a fish tail, obviously, but..."

Carrie slapped the sheet down tight against her legs, but that only pulled the top edge down from chin level to the tips of her breasts.

Mac skimmed a finger across the exquisitely sensitive skin just above the white cotton. One brow arched doubtfully. "No?"

"Well, not exactly," she was forced to amend, pushing away his hand and yanking the sheet upward again over her taut, tingling breasts. Every part of her was blushing now; she could feel the prickly heat everywhere. "I mean it is my face... I did pose for the face, and for... well, the position of the body... but not for... the..."

It was so simple, really, and totally innocent. Eddie had asked her to be the model for his gate carving and she'd agreed, not realizing the extent of dishabille he was planning for his mermaid. After posing fully dressed, she'd been stunned when she saw the completed carving for the first time.

"But Eddie..." she'd stammered then, too. "It's beautiful, of course, but I didn't pose like... it isn't... they aren't... oh, Lord, Eddie, where did you...?" She'd pointed.

"I still have imagination, don't I darlin'?" Eddie had replied, smiling.

Far too much imagination, in Carrie's opinion. But fortunately, not many people had known she was posing in the first place, and the mermaid's long hair helped disguise the source of Eddie's inspiration, if not much else. Few people recognized Carrie as the model. It was just her luck that Mac had.

But suddenly Mac's grin was fading as the thought of Carrie posing for the mermaid struck him in a different way. Carrie had posed for it... had smiled that smile . . . for the artist . . . who had undoubtedly been male. Suddenly, he wasn't finding that idea at all amusing.

"You must know the artist quite well, then," he said, shifting plates and cups around on the tray he held.

Carrie had watched the change in Mac's expression, not knowing what to make of it, until his comment. Then it was her turn to grin.

"Oh yes," she said, deciding turnabout was perfectly fair play. "He's a very close friend, and such a darling. He's a gourmet cook, too, as well as a successful artist. And so handsome. He's always taking me to the nicest places, too. I just love Eddie."

The silverware on the tray rattled like sabres.

"He sort of watches over me, too," Carrie continued expansively. "You know, he lets in a repairman if I can't be home, or takes care of a package someone might want to leave for me, things like that. And Eddie just loves pizza and Thin Man movies. . . ."

"Thin Man movies . . . ?" Mac was frowning. "Eddie . . . you mean Eddie from the other night? That nice old guy . . . he's the artist?"

"Eddie is not old at all," she defended, grinning. "But he is the one who did the gate—using primarily his imagination, I might add."

"You might have added that, and a few other minor details, a bit sooner," Mac grumbled.

"Why? I liked watching you maul the breakfast things."

Mac glanced down at the disarranged tray, then back up at Carrie, at her beguiling smile, and the muscles of his stomach tightened. "Didn't anyone ever warn you it's dangerous to tease, mermaid?" he asked, his voice velvety. He bent to set the tray on the floor, then sat back up, putting a hand on either side of Carrie's hips and leaning forward. The sheet she was clutching to her chest pulled taut as his thumbs began sketching lazy circles at the tops of her thighs. "It seems to me you're really asking for it."

Carrie looked into Mac's eyes, then let her gaze drop down his tanned chest, across his flat, hard stomach, to the undone button of his cords. "Yes, Mac Kincaid, I think I am," she whispered, and let go of the sheet.

CHAPTER TWELVE

CARRIE THREW OPEN the door and was immediately swept into the haven of Mac's strong arms.

"God, I missed you," he whispered across the millimeter separating their lips. And then closed the millimeter.

"You only left here three hours, fifty-two minutes and thirty-seven seconds ago," Carrie said when she could breathe again.

Mac laughed and his hands slid down her back to the swell of her hips. "Much too long, mermaid," he told her, his caressing fingers saying the same thing.

Carrie smiled her agreement. It did seem much too long since Mac had left the houseboat. Earlier, they'd fixed brunch together, replacing the abandoned breakfast that had grown decidedly cold. But after eating, they'd each reluctantly admitted they had things to do before the search group meeting at Janice Sedgewick's that night—Mac had needed fresh clothes and a shave, for one thing. So he'd left—after several interesting delays, she recalled with a blush. But the houseboat had seemed unbearably empty without his presence, even after Robin had returned from her sailing trip, lightly sunburned and grinning cheekily.

The girl was bestowing the same grin on Mac at the moment. "Mermaid?" she queried curiously from her cross-legged perch on the couch. She was surrounded by skeins of baby-fine blue wool and a rainbow of crochet hooks, but her eyes were on Carrie and Mac.

"Private joke!" Mac said, grinning back.

"Hmmph! I never would have left you two alone last night if I'd known you were going to start keeping secrets. What a rotten deal!"

"Fortunes of matchmaking, I'd say." He winked, and let his hand close tightly around one of Carrie's. "Are you ready, love? We'd better get going. Wouldn't want to be late. Ms Sedgewick might be—" he paused and sniffed loudly "—insulted."

Carrie sighed. She wasn't looking forward to the meeting, but she supposed it was unavoidable. And the sooner they got on with the investigation, the sooner it would be over. *That* she was looking forward to. "Ready," she said.

"Have fun," Robin called, as Mac ushered Carrie out the door.

"Don't wait up," he called back.

Robin giggled. "Right...."

"I JUST CAN'T LIVE with not knowing who I am, with staring at strangers' faces and always wondering—is that my mother, my father, my brother...? It haunts me constantly, and always has. I tell myself—and everyone else tells me—that it doesn't matter, I should stop dwelling on the past, but I can't. I can't find any direction to my life, can't form lasting relationships. I don't feel...real...and I know I never will unless I learn the truth about myself. I have to find out. I just have to."

The young woman's voice broke over her last words and something twisted sympathetically within Carrie.

She and Mac weren't the only newcomers at the search group meeting, and Janice had suggested they all introduce themselves and explain why they were interested in searching. Carrie, listening to the others' explanations, was once again struck by the certainty that though she might never really understand why some people felt this desperate need to know, the need itself was genuine, deeply ingrained and linked in some way with various other personal problems. A majority of the searchers had been in therapy at some time; two of the women adoptees had been unwed mothers who'd relinquished children of their own; Peter Millheiser's marriage had ended in divorce, he believed, because of his insecurities brought on by his feeling of "rootlessness."

But Janice Sedgewick's story was the most startling. She'd been abused as an adopted child. As a teenager, she'd had two abortions and tried to commit suicide three times. She'd been married and divorced three times, too, always blaming herself for the failures. All her life, she said, she'd considered herself worthless and unlovable—until she'd heard about Triangle and searching. Only then had she realized she needed to exorcise the ghosts of her past before she could learn to respect herself. And even though her search had not ended in total success...yet, she added...making the decision to search had changed her life. Which was why she was so involved now in the adoption movement. She wanted to help others as she had been helped.

Janice told her story flatly, with her usual abrasive sniffing as punctuation. But still, Carrie felt tears welling in her eyes. She was hurriedly blinking back those tears when Janice called on her for her story.

All the various stories had shared the same basic sentiments, and Carrie had intended to parrot something similar with innocuously vague details when her turn came. But for some reason when she began speaking, what came out was not that vague little speech.

"I'm Carrie Prescott and this is my fiancé, Mac—Ashley MacAllister, actually," she began. "And I never thought I would be searching. You see, I have a wonderful relationship with my parents...."

"You mean your adoptive parents, Carrie?" Janice interrupted.

"Well, I guess for clarity's sake, I do," she answered, "though they've always been just my parents to me...no qualifiers necessary. Anyway, I was never interested in searching at all, until I happened to come across some...inconsistencies between what I had always believed about my adoption and the facts. All little things and unimportant really, but they made me feel...funny, out of kilter somehow, a little unsure of myself. And I started wanting to find out the rest, too, to get everything back in order, to make sure I wouldn't someday stumble across another surprise. And...well, here we are."

"And we're going to be married as soon as we're done with this search," Mac added. "So, as you can well imagine, I sure hope it isn't going to take long."

Everyone laughed, and the meeting soon progressed to the evening's subject: how to get the most from an interview.

"You never know which way an interview will go." Peter Millheiser began the discussion, smoothing his chestnut-colored beard. "Some people are very sympathetic to searchers and will stretch the rules a long way to give you what you need. Others are totally opposed to searching and will put obstacles in your way, even lie, on the principle that you shouldn't be doing this in the first place."

"The latter's a lot more common than the former," called out one veteran searcher grimly.

"Probably," Peter agreed. "Things are changing, however slowly, but we'll all run into the type who treats a searcher like a five-year-old having a temper tantrum...."

"Or tells you what you really need is a shrink," Janice added. A lot of heads in the room wagged up and down.

Peter smiled. "Well, there are different ways to approach each type, different ways to put your questions to even the most obnoxious, condescending person, to get the most from them."

As Peter went on, Mac leaned close to Carrie, his arm slipping tightly around her shoulders, drawing her to his whisper. "Congratulations, mermaid," he said softly. "You're really getting to be a pro at this—your little speech almost had me convinced of your sincerity. They'll be giving us the information we want in no time if you keep it up."

Carrie looked at Mac, and he winked conspiratorily. His fingers were kneading a sensuous promise into the softness of her upper arm, he shifted his leg so it was pressing against hers, he smiled happily.

And Carrie had the sudden urge to get up and run out of Janice's living room and never return. She wanted to be back at her houseboat, in the cozy shelter of her bed, in the safe, marvelous world of Mac's arms. She looked at Mac's confident smile and prayed he was right about their investigation being over soon. Very, very soon.

"Look, I know you're anxious," Peter was saying.

The group meeting had ended a short while before, but Janice—at Peter's instigation, Carrie suspected—

had invited her and Mac to stay after to talk. They'd gone over Carrie's search notebook and then Mac had broached the subject of their eagerness to complete Carrie's search. Peter was replying.

"Everyone who finally decides to search feels the same way—we all wanted to know *now*. But you have to realize it may not happen now, or tomorrow, or next month. The availability of information, the attitudes of the people you'll contact, your own determination and available time to spend on it, and of course, luck, all play a part, the latter probably most of all. One person lucks out right away and it's over in weeks. Others search for years."

"Years!" Mac looked absolutely horrified, and he reached over to take Carrie's hand. "Peter, Carrie really wants to complete her search before we get married, and I sympathize with that. But we don't want to wait years! There must be something we can do to hurry things along."

Peter glanced at Mac's hand clasping Carrie's, then at her. "Well, as I told Carrie before, I'm willing to help any way I can," he said. "And you could hire a private search consultant or a detective."

Carrie remembered the detective at the conference with his claims of finding anyone, for a price. Obviously, not all detectives and consultants would be the same, but still.... "No," she said, with a shudder of revulsion. "I'd rather do this on my own."

"That's really best anyway, and what we recommend," Janice said. "You see, you'll find the search itself becomes important as you go along. Because what you're searching for is yourself, really. That's why all searches end well."

Mac's fingers tightened on Carrie's. "Surely you don't mean all searchers get a happy ending?"

"That's exactly what I mean," Janice declared, tossing her mane of red hair. "No matter what they find, it's better than secrecy. The favorite argument of people opposed to searching is that the searcher may find out some horrible thing about his background. What they don't seem to understand is that no truth is as hard to deal with as an unknown, as always wondering and imagining the worst. And even those who never find, or who find names but are refused contact, still have a kind of success because they've dared face up to the unknowns in their lives. They learn something about themselves in the process . . . and that's success, too."

"I see . . ." Mac pursed his lips thoughtfully.

"And in your case, Carrie, you have a great start," Peter said. "Your adoptive parents are cooperating, you have some unusual details—the great aunt and uncle and your first adoption—which always makes things easier, and you have the name of the lawyer who handled the adoption. You said you'd written to him—have you heard back yet?"

Carrie shook her head. "It's only been a few days."

"Well, you might want to go to see him in person, if you can. You know, court adoption records are sealed by law, but most other records, such as those of hospitals, lawyers and agencies, are only closed by policy. Policy, though, makes it easy for bureaucratic minds to refuse a written request. But refusing a pretty young woman, who might even have tears in her eyes as she asks for help, is another thing entirely."

"Are you saying Carrie should go in person and put on a good act for Charles Wieland?"

Peter stroked his beard. "As I said earlier tonight, asking the right questions in the right way is the name of this game."

"Doing whatever it takes to get the information, you mean?"

"Within limits, of course."

Mac's smile was stiff. "And if that doesn't work?"

"When you've exhausted all the regular avenues, we can start considering some of the less regular ones," Peter answered.

"Like what?" Letting go of Carrie's hand, Mac leaned forward.

Peter only shrugged. "Oh, we'll think about that if the time comes. For now—" he paused and reached out to Carrie, patting the hand Mac had just relinquished "—just hang in there, okay? Don't get discouraged. And call me anytime...for information, encouragement, or just to talk...okay? We're all in this together; we understand what you're going through."

Guilt flooded through Carrie, and she had to swallow several times before she could form a smile. "Okay," she said. "And thanks, Peter."

BACK AT CARRIE'S there was a bottle of wine and two wineglasses on the redwood-burl coffee table, a fire laid in the small fireplace, and a nest of pillows from Carrie's bedroom window seat arranged enticingly in front of the stonework hearth. Only the dim hall light was on, and Robin's door was firmly and conspicuously shut.

Carrie stood looking at the carefully set scene and shaking her head.

"Boy, I don't know what I'd do if we weren't..." she began, then broke off, embarrassed. But Mac, coming up behind her, slipped his arms around her waist and pulled her tight against his body.

"I don't know what I'd do, either," he murmured against her hair as his fingers splayed wide across her stomach. "I was getting awfully tired of cold showers."

Carrie leaned back against Mac, feeling the perfect fit of their bodies, the security of his very masculine strength supporting her, the tiny, erotic movements of his fingers on the soft cotton of her full skirt. It all felt wonderful.

But when her eyes drifted closed, she was seeing the people at the meeting telling their stories.

"Mac, what did you think of tonight's meeting?" she asked, her voice low and carefully even.

"It was great," he answered enthusiastically. "I never thought things would move as quickly as they are. We'll be making the illegal connection in no time. It's a shame we have to bother going to see Charles Wieland, but we'd better. Peter and Janice will want to know all the details, I'm sure."

"But Mac, what if Wieland just tells us what we want to know about my...adoption?"

Mac shrugged, releasing Carrie and moving to the fireplace. "Then we'll have to lie. But cross your fingers that old Charlie isn't a cooperative type; it'll be a lot easier if we can stick to the truth." A long fireplace match rasped into flames and he poked it here and there among the kindling. "Are you free on Thursday? I was thinking we could take a leisurely drive down the coast route to Santa Barbara, see Charlie Friday and have the rest of the weekend to ourselves."

Mac paused and turned to Carrie, the burning match still in his hand. His eyes on her, he pursed his lips and blew it out. "How does that sound?"

"Lovely," Carrie said, at the same time kneeling beside the low table and reaching for the wine bottle and corkscrew. "But what I wondered about the meeting," she said, carefully applying herself to opening the wine, "was what you thought of the people—and their reasons for searching?"

Mac tossed the wooden match into the fire and sat on the edge of the hearth. "Quite a crew, aren't they, with all their poor-me stories? Every bad thing that's ever happened to them is due to their being adopted, of course, and every problem will be solved if they can only complete their searches."

Carrie smiled faintly. "Mightn't there be some basis for their feeling that way, though?"

"Like what?"

"Oh, I was thinking of what we heard at the conference—that psychological and emotional problems are more common among adoptees than in the general population." The cork came out of the bottle with a soft pop, and she started to pour the wine. But her hand was shaking and she had to steady the bottle rim against the edge of the glass. "If that's so, Mac, there must be a reason for it. And if the reason has to do with their lack of information about their pasts, then finding that information might . . . well, it might actually help some of them, don't you think?"

Mac leaned forward to take the glass she held out to him. "It might, if what they really wanted was information, but it isn't," he said, taking a swallow of the ruby-red liquid. "Oh, plenty of these people start out saying they just want the basic facts of their background and biological heritage. But give them that and they also want to know the circumstances of their relinquishment. Give them that, and they won't feel complete without names. But names aren't enough either—they need to see their birth mothers and fathers, talk to them, touch them, be acknowledged by them. It's never enough unless it's the whole thing, because what they're really after is a confrontation with the woman and man who gave them away."

"Confrontation is an awfully strong word," Carrie said softly.

"But that's exactly what a lot of them want," he insisted. "To confront their birth parents and demand to know why—why they were given away, why they weren't wanted, why, why. They're angry and insecure and looking for a way to undo the rejection of their relinquishment. Why do you think Janice Sedgewick is willing to badger a woman who has refused to see her and to barge in on a very sick old man and his suffering wife? To ask where her red hair came from? She may loftily claim her search has already been successful, but you notice she's still trying for the confrontation."

Carrie stared at the flickering firelight through the blood-red prism of her wine, thinking of Janice's story, of what the woman had suffered through. "And you don't think there's some justification for wanting that...confrontation? That for some people, their need to know is so strong that searching becomes truly necessary?"

"First, I think this need to know is really a self-indulgent excuse these people use for not dealing with their problems, for sidestepping responsibility," he said. "And secondly, even if I'm wrong and the need is genuine, it doesn't justify hurting other people, invading other lives. Not in my book.''

"What about the argument that often birth parents want to be found? Certainly the number of joyful reunions you hear about lends some credence to that.''

"Some do, certainly," Mac nodded. "And I have no quarrel with registries where each party can sign up indicating a willingness to be 'found,' and an intermediary arranges contact between matchups. I would support a single nationwide registry, even, to make it easier. But searchers don't wait for registries, do they? Remember how Janice suggested you sign a waiver of confidentiality and put your name in with Soundex? But she certainly wasn't advising you to sit and wait to hear whether or not your mother wanted to see you, too, was she? Because searchers don't care whether the person they're searching for wants to be found or not. That doesn't count. Nothing and nobody else does.''

Carrie lifted the wineglass to her lips, but then had difficulty swallowing the liquid she took into her mouth. There was a lump in her throat, and a tear was gathering at the corner of each eye. She couldn't argue with what Mac was saying; she'd felt the same many times over in the past few days, she admitted to herself, thinking especially of her reaction to Janice Sedgewick's description of her visit to the home of her ailing birth father. She couldn't argue with Mac, yet for some reason she wanted to. She wasn't even sure just what point she wanted to argue. But he sounded so sure, his answers were so pat. Too sure? Too pat? What was bothering her?

"Hey, what's up?" Mac had lowered himself from the hearth to the pillows below, and he was leaning toward Carrie, staring into her face. He shifted to one side, and firelight turned two tiny tears into drops of gold. Setting his wineglass on the table, he touched a knuckle to her cheeks, and gold trickled down his fingers. "Tears? Why?"

"Oh, I've always been a sucker for a sad story," Carrie said quickly, forcing a smile. "And you have to admit, some of the people tonight told some very sad stories. Of course, a couple of little tears is nothing. You should see me on reruns of *Love Story*. One glimpse of Ryan O'Neal on that bench and I'm awash. And remember the old Disney movie, *Old Yeller*? Well, I've been known to sob for forty-five minutes after that poor old yeller dog gets it.... Even books have been known to do it to me. The worst was...."

"I've got a really sad one for you, Carrie Prescott," Mac interrupted, taking the wineglass from her hand.

Carrie's brows arched into her bangs. "You do?"

Mac nodded. "Yep. You see, there was this man, a nice, normal American male, not too bad looking, reasonably personable, presentable enough to take home to mother. And this poor presentable guy was in love with a mermaid." He put her glass down on the table beside his. "And they were together one night in the most romantic situation imaginable and all he wanted to do was take her in his arms and make mad passionate love to her. But what did she want to do? Talk business and old sad books! Can you imagine what that did to the poor guy's libido? He was even starting to think of cold showers again, and..."

Smiling, Carrie put her palms against Mac's chest and pushed him backward into the nest of pillows, following him down. She reached for the buttons of his shirt. "I'll stop talking if you will, Mac Kincaid," she whispered.

"Deal," he said huskily. And sealed it with a kiss.

CHAPTER THIRTEEN

CARRIE AND MAC left so early Thursday morning that Eugenie Brindle hadn't even made it out to her rocker yet. But as they walked by her houseboat, Mac carrying Carrie's suitcase, a window slid open and a voice called out, "More work, huh, Carrie?" And Eugenie laughed gleefully.

Carrie flushed, but she laughed, too, more amused than embarrassed. Eugenie's innuendoes were cute now—now that she didn't care who heard them. She loved Mac, he loved her and, as the old saw went, all was right with the world.

Well, almost all. They still had the investigation to get through, and she wasn't looking forward to any part of that—except the being with Mac part. The rights and wrongs of searching and secrecy, illegal connections and her own pretense, were all mixed into a confused muddle in her mind, which only seemed to grow worse each time she tried to sort it out. So she wasn't going to try anymore—at least not today. Even if the reason for their trip to Santa Barbara was tomorrow's appointment with Charles A. Wieland, today was for her and Mac, and she was going to enjoy every minute of it.

It wasn't a difficult resolution to keep. California Highway 1, ribboning along the coast, offering one stunning view of the Pacific after another, was a million miles from everyday concerns. For the first part of the trip, gray veils of fog obscured the sun and turned little seaside towns into fantasy villages and the car into a cozy magic carpet for two. But by the time they stopped for breakfast in Carmel, sunshine was punching holes through the mists and promising a happily-ever-after blue-sky day.

They ate at the Tuck Box, a tiny tea room–restaurant in one of Carmel's fairy-tale cottages. They were both hungry, and a good portion of the omelets and jam-smeared scones were gone before either of them spoke. But when a young couple, the wife very pregnant, passed by on their way to a nearby table, Carrie was reminded of Robin and her plans for the weekend. She wondered if Mac knew.

"Did you know that Robin is spending the next few days with Beth?" she asked him, taking a sip of steaming honey-laced tea.

He nodded, lifting his cup of coffee. "Beth told me she'd invited Robin to stay with her since Stewart is going out of town on business. So the two of them will have hours and hours to discuss the future of our love life."

Carrie groaned. "Which will undoubtedly result in more questions and more not so subtle notes from Robin."

"Oh, well, I don't mind her notes..." Mac drawled, his eyes twinkling. Beneath the white tablecloth, his leg rubbed suggestively against Carrie's. She blushed and he grinned. "But I suspect we'd better be prepared for a full-scale meddler's marathon when we get back," he added. "Those two are going to make a dangerous pair."

Carrie shook her head woefully. "And I introduced them!"

But even though she'd arranged that first meeting, Carrie had still been surprised when Robin had told her not to worry about being away for the weekend because she was staying with Beth.

"Beth Abramson? Mac's sister?" she'd asked, disbelievingly. As far as she'd known, Beth and Robin had shared one lunch together. But Robin explained otherwise.

"I visited her preschool last Friday and we went shopping on Tuesday," she said. "I really like Beth. She's so sweet, and she has so much love to give—you could see it in the way she is with those kids at the school. It's sure a crummy deal that she can't have children of her own when she wants them so much." Robin was crocheting and an ever-increasing blue wool rectangle rested on the ever-increasing bulge of her stomach. The crochet hook stilled in the blue wool for a moment as she looked down, then it started flashing in and out again. "Life's unfair a lot of times, don't you think?" she said.

There wasn't an answer to that question, Carrie knew, and Robin didn't seem to expect one. But it did provide an opening she had been looking for.

"Robin, I don't want to pry, but have you made any plans . . . for the baby, I mean?" she asked hesitantly.

"Sure," the girl nodded, turning the blue rectangle and starting a new row. "I want a Lamaze birth. In fact, I was going to ask you to be my birth coach. There's a class starting next week—would you have time to go with me? I signed up for one of the family-centered birth rooms at the hospital, too, which means you could stay with me the whole time, for the birth and all, if everything goes smoothly." Robin paused, and the crochet hook was still again.

"Would you stay with me, Carrie?" she asked, and for the first time looked like what she was—an unmarried, pregnant and very young girl.

Carrie had assured Robin she would be happy to act as birth coach. But when she'd tried to turn the discussion back to plans for after the birth, Robin had somehow managed to change the subject. Again.

The problem of Robin's baby was another of those things Carrie didn't want to think about at the moment, though. She looked at Mac over the rim of her china teacup, and it was easy to forget everything but him. He was wearing a chamois shirt in a dark coffee color that matched his hair and eyes. The shirt was open at the neck and the soft material snugly hugged his chest and shoulders. Imagining how it would feel to run her hands over the almost downy softness of the chamois, over the firm muscles beneath, she smiled.

Mac had a forkful of omelet halfway to his mouth when Carrie smiled, but suddenly he forgot all about breakfast. Setting the fork on his plate, he reached for the check.

"Let's get out of here," he said.

THE TRAIL WASN'T VISIBLE from the road and there were no other cars parked in the unmarked turnout Mac pulled into south of Big Sur. On the ocean side of the highway Mac indicated a steep path and a tunnel. The tunnel, he told Carrie, had been cut through a sheer rock cliff in the 1880s and led to a rocky cove, once a landing for the shipping of lumber and tanbark. Taking two beach towels from the trunk, he guided her instead to the trail heading east, across a wooden footbridge and into a redwood-filled canyon.

The path followed a swiftly flowing creek cutting through the canyon. The music of water splashing over and around huge mossy boulders and fallen trees mixed with the twitter of birds. Gauzy streamers of sunlight filtered down through the branches of tall redwoods, to touch on the green lace of ferns and miner's lettuce and add a hint of warmth to the misty air. Fallen needles muffled the sound of their footsteps, and the world outside the canyon faded away.

They stayed on the trail until it switchbacked away from the creek to climb the hillside. Then Mac led Carrie in the opposite direction, off the path.

"There's something I want to show you," he said.

They scrambled over boulders and ducked under the thin branches of saplings struggling to grow in their parents' long shadows, leaving the trail farther and farther behind. Twice Mac carried her across the gushing stream, its twists and turns sharpening as the canyon narrowed, its walls rising higher and steeper. The second time, even after they were across the clear burbling water, he didn't set her back down. He held her, cradled in his arms, as he edged around a steep rocky outcropping, pushed through a screen of feathery bushes—and into paradise.

The creek had divided near their crossing, one section still following the main canyon, this second part veering into the beautiful seclusion of a small U-shaped gorge. Long shafts of sunlight spilled onto a grassy bank beside the stream. The high rock walls on two sides were dotted with emerald-green moss and tiny purple wildflowers, but on the third side, at the head of the gorge, a waterfall cascaded gloriously down over the silvery rock it had been sculpting and polishing for years.

"Oh Mac," Carrie sighed. "It's so gorgeous. How did you ever find it?"

Mac eased her to her feet on the grassy bank, but his arms stayed around her waist, his thumbs hooking into the wide leather belt she wore over her loose-fitting artist's shirt. She pressed backward, against him, as they stood gazing at the rainbow-tinted veil of water.

"I've known about the canyon trail and the cove for some time," he said. "But a couple of years back I decided to see how far up along the creek I could go. I came around that big rock and here it was."

His hands left her waist to slide caressingly up her arms, over the billowy sleeves. "The minute I saw it, I knew this was a special place. A place I would share with the woman I loved, a place where I could make love to her and spin a memory to last the rest of our lives." He paused, then slowly and gently turned Carrie until she was facing him, until he could look deep into her green eyes.

"I had the place, but I didn't have the woman," he said, his fingers releasing the metal clasp of her belt. "Until you, Carrie. Until you."

THURSDAY WAS A MARVELOUS DREAM. Friday was closer to a nightmare. Thursday evening, when she and Mac arrived in Santa Barbara, Carrie took an instant liking to the small city tucked onto a narrow shelf of land between mountains and ocean north of Los Angeles. It was a fascinating blend of seaside resort, university town and wealthy suburb, with a strong dash of Spanish heritage thrown in for color and spice. They were staying in a cozy bed-and-breakfast inn near the beach, and from the private balcony of their room in the Tudor-styled bungalow, they could watch a captivating waterfront parade. Surfboard-carrying Volks-wagens jockeyed with Porsches for cruising position on the palm-lined street. Gaggles of teenagers toting monster radios and elderly couples holding hands strolled the boardwalk, breeds apart. Though every passing body, young and old, seemed to be sporting a T-shirt, the ones emblazoned with trendy slogans—mostly obscene—seemed designed to contrast with the knits bearing discreet little designer logos on their pockets. As far as Carrie could see, Santa Barbarans shared a passion for only one thing—the ubiquitous southern California suntan.

They ate fresh seafood in a restaurant overlooking the harbor as the sun slid into the sea, walked along the beach until the salt-damp breeze grew too chilly, then returned to their room to make love to the rhythmic melody of the waves.

The next morning was their appointment with Charles Wieland.

The lawyer's office was located in a pseudo-adobe building, and his waiting room was furnished to match. Heavy, dark wood pieces stood against stark cream walls, on which framed old photographs and maps of early Santa Barbara hung in precise arrangements. And Carrie had time to study each picture and map, because Mr. Wieland was keeping them waiting—a very long time.

As she finished another circuit of the small room, the secretary behind the huge Moorish-styled desk looked up worriedly. Anna Verlatti had apologized for her boss's tardiness several times already. She did so again now.

"I can't understand what's keeping him, Miss Prescott," she said as Carrie stopped in front of her. "I am sorry." She was a young woman with a friendly smile and a habit of shifting the picture on her desk a fraction of an inch this way one moment, then back again a moment later, as if she just couldn't resist touching it. The picture was of a little boy in the arms of a man.

Carrie smiled, shaking her head. "It's not your fault."

"He's usually so prompt," the woman said. "But he did seem a bit...upset this morning."

From his spot on the black leather couch across the room, Mac chuckled, and Carrie knew just what he was chuckling about. Charles Wieland had been a bit upset on the phone, too, earlier in the week, when Mac had called for an appointment. At first the lawyer had tried to discourage them from coming. But when Mac would have happily given up, figuring the aborted attempt was as good as or better than an actual meeting for their purposes, Wieland had changed his mind and instead been most insistent they come. Which made as little sense as did his keeping them waiting for forty-five minutes this morning.

And Carrie was getting very annoyed. She was normally a reasonably patient person, and she and Mac weren't in any real hurry. But the delay was so obviously deliberate—even the man's poor secretary couldn't figure it out. Mac's amusement wasn't helping, either. She knew he was pleased that Wieland was turning out to be one of the "uncooperative types," and that she should be feeling the same...but she didn't. She told herself she simply wanted to get the appointment over with, however it was going to turn out...and wasn't sure that was true, either.

"I wish there was something I could do," Anna Verlatti said. "Perhaps I should buzz him again...."

"You did handle my adoption?"

"Yes. But beyond that, there's nothing I can tell you."

"Nothing you can . . . or will tell me? Legal files are open to the parties involved, aren't they? Surely I count as one of the parties in my own adoption?"

"Miss Prescott, you're a pretty young woman. You've got a nice-looking young man. What you should do now is marry him, have some children of your own, and forget all this adoption nonsense . . . for your own good."

Carrie couldn't believe what she was hearing. Resentment flared in her like a Roman candle. "I don't need you to tell me what is or is not for my own good, thank you. I'm not a child, Charles Wieland!"

The lawyer reacted as if Carrie had reached out and slapped him. His florid face lost all its color, he jerked backward in his chair and his protruding eyes bulged. For one moment, Carrie was afraid he was going to have a stroke.

But then he seemed to recover himself. Closing his eyes, he squeezed the bridge of his nose between thumb and forefinger for a few seconds. When he looked at her again, the mud brown of his eyes had frosted over.

"If you're not a child, quit acting like one, miss," he said. "Quit bothering yourself and others about things that can't possibly matter now."

"They matter to me."

"Then you should be looking for a psychiatrist, not a mother!" He grasped the edge of the desk as if he were going to push to his feet, but he didn't move; his knuckles just whitened. "You need to face your problems instead of hiding behind a fantasy and dwelling on the past. It's over, done with. Why would you want to create difficulties for other people now?''

"I don't. I just want to know a few things about my birth and—"

"You want to snoop into a stranger's life! The woman who gave you up for adoption was promised secrecy, not just for a few years, but forever. Her pregnancy wasn't a pleasant time for her. She gave up... a lot because of one mistake. But she was finally able to put it all behind her, to finally forget it ever happened. So what right do you have to barge into her life now, twenty-six years later, and bring it all up again?''

"Do you really believe a woman can truly forget giving birth to a child?'' Carrie demanded, remembering her mother's words. "Can she really stop wondering what has happened to that child, no matter how many years pass? Maybe she would like to know me, or at least something about me. Maybe she'd like to know how her decision worked out for her child.''

"She wouldn't.''

"How do you know that?''

Charles Wieland did push to his feet then. "If I had the information, I wouldn't give it to you,'' he said harshly. "And now you'll have to excuse me. I have other appointments.''

"CARRIE...''

"Who the hell does he think he is!'' Carrie didn't slow her march down the street. She'd stormed out of Wieland's office, only refraining from slamming the door because Mac was behind her. But he hadn't been close enough; she was halfway down the block before he caught up with her.

"Carrie..."

"How dare he tell me I need a psychiatrist! How dare he assume he knows what I want, what I need, while he sits there knowing things about my past, about me, and refusing to tell them to me. Of all the rude, supercilious bast—"

Mac grabbed her arm, cutting off her words along with her fury-propelled forward progress. "Carrie Prescott," he said, pulling her around to face him, "our car is the other way."

Carrie's eyes widened, and the bubble of her anger burst as if pricked by a pin. "Oh, Mac," she breathed, sagging against him. "I'm sorry. Wieland just made me so damned mad...."

"I noticed," he said dryly, a grin in his voice. Pivoting, he slipped a supporting arm around her shoulders and they started back the way they had come. "In fact, the people in the next office probably noticed, and everyone along this street, maybe even a few down at the beach—"

"All right, all right, I get the idea," she interrupted. "But I couldn't help myself. He was so condescending...and did you see the way he kept looking at me, as if I was something under a microscope he wished he didn't have to see? He deliberately kept us waiting all that time, too, just so he could tell us off. Didn't he make you furious?"

"Not really," Mac shrugged. "He was annoying, but he did exactly what we hoped he would—refused to give you any information. So we'll have plenty to complain about at the next search meeting. Which is just what we wanted, right?"

Carrie stumbled and would have fallen if Mac's arm hadn't been tightly around her. "Oh...right," she said.

"Of course. I guess I just got caught up in the whole...act."

"You sure did. You were spouting the party line like a pro," Mac told her. "But as for the way he was looking at you...I noticed it, too. And you know what I think? I think your birth mother was more than just a client to Charles Wieland."

Carrie hadn't considered the idea before, but instantly she knew he was right. Charles Wieland had known her birth mother, and not just as a client. That explained his extreme reaction to her questions, his strange expression as he'd looked at her, his vacillation about seeing her in the first place. He'd known her birth mother. But how? In what way? And how well?

Even as Carrie asked herself those questions, a possible answer popped into her mind, one she definitely did not want to consider. But it was there, and she couldn't unthink it. Coming to a dead stop, she looked up at Mac in dismay.

"Mac, you don't...you don't think Charles Wieland could be my..." She shuddered, unable to finish the question.

"Your birth father?" Mac laughed. "No, I don't. That look of his wasn't fatherly. No, it was something else...." The back of his neck prickled with curiosity. "It would be interesting to know just what, though, wouldn't it?"

Carrie nodded weakly, relieved at Mac's assessment, but still feeling sick with dismay. Because for the first time in her life, she was wondering who her birth parents were—not in some vague, abstract way, but specifically. She'd thought of one specific man and wondered if he had fathered her. Which had led inevitably to wondering about the one specific woman who had given her birth. So now, even if she could believe Charles Wieland wasn't her birth father, she couldn't help thinking that somewhere there was a man who was, just as there must also be a woman who had given birth to her. Two real people. Two individuals with likes and dislikes, strengths and weaknesses, habits, hopes, desires. Two people whose union had given her life.

And she didn't know who they were. She would never know.

"Hey, don't look so worried," Mac said, putting a finger under her chin to tilt her face upward. He grinned down at her. "Even if the old goat was the one, it wouldn't matter a bit to me. I'd love you, anyway."

He was just teasing, trying to jolly Carrie's frown into a smile. So he couldn't understand why Carrie suddenly threw her arms around his neck and hugged as if she was afraid to ever let go. Or why she sounded so fiercely serious when she whispered. "You're right, Mac Kincaid. It doesn't matter. It doesn't matter one damned bit!"

CHAPTER FOURTEEN

CARRIE SWIPED at the steamy bathroom mirror with a corner of the towel she was using to dry her freshly washed hair. Her face—sun-pinkened by the afternoon she and Mac had spent lazing on the beach—appeared in the cleared circle and she leaned closer to the misty glass, studying her reflection.

Wide green eyes with dark lashes stared back—her best feature, she thought. Her hair was stick-straight, but a lovely rich reddish-brown color even when wet. Her nose was small, but a shade too pointed. Her mouth was okay; and though the upper lip wasn't quite full enough to balance the lower, her smile somehow made up for the defect. Altogether a passably pretty face—one she'd looked at day in and day out and never wondered if there was another similar face somewhere, a mother's or a father's. She'd never asked herself if she'd inherited this from one, that from the other. It had never mattered.

And it didn't matter now. Carrie turned away from the mirror, letting the steam swallow her reflection again, and reached for her blow-dryer.

Her hair was only half dry and she was still wearing only a not-quite-long-enough towel when the bathroom door opened slightly. Mac's head poked around the edge and she switched off the roar of the blow-dryer.

"I knocked," he said, his eyes roving appreciatively. "But I think I'm glad you couldn't hear me."

Pins and needles of delight tickled through Carrie, and she refused to give in to an incipient attack of shyness. "Am I taking too long? I thought our dinner reservation wasn't until eight."

"There's plenty of time...but you have a phone call," he told her. "It's Mrs. Verlatti, from Wieland's office."

"Anna Verlatti?" Carrie's eyes were wide. "But what could she want?" She dropped the dryer and her brush onto the counter, and clutching her towel tightly around herself, scooted past Mac. As she sat on the bed and picked up the receiver, she realized there were all types of pins and needles, some not quite so delightful. Did the lawyer want to see her again, she wondered. And if he did, should she agree?

But Anna Verlatti wasn't calling on behalf of her boss; instead she was calling without his knowledge, as she hesitantly told Carrie.

"I...I've never done anything like this before," she said, "and I wouldn't be now if you hadn't seemed so nice, and if Mr. Wieland hadn't been in such an...unreasonable mood after you left, and if I weren't adopted myself. It's just that I can imagine what you must be going through, even though I've never wanted to search myself...and, well, I know from what Mr. Wieland said that he wasn't willing to help you at all, although I'm sure he could have, and...I thought of something you might try...I'm not sure anything will come of it, but..."

The pins and needles formed a prickly lump in Carrie's middle. "I'd appreciate any suggestions."

"You could try Violet Durning." She spelled it. "She was Mr. Wieland's secretary for years and years, including the time when he was practicing in northern California. She's quite elderly and lives in a retirement home in Lompoc now, but there just might be a chance she'd remember something as special as your adoption must be, if it still upsets Mr. Wieland this way after all these years. I could give you the name and address of the home if you wanted to try talking to her...."

"Yes, please." Carrie grabbed a pen, not noticing how the movement affected her towel. Behind her, Mac stretched out on the bed, propping his head on an elbow.

"I hope you don't think I'm terribly disloyal," the secretary continued. "Mr. Wieland is really a nice man, but for some reason he's being unfair to you and I... well, I hope it works out well for you, Carrie."

"Thank you, Anna," Carrie said sincerely, knowing how difficult the decision to call must have been for the woman. Anna Verlatti would almost certainly lose her job if Charles Wieland ever discovered what she'd done, yet she'd been willing to risk that to help a stranger. "I appreciate this... more than you can know."

Putting down the phone, she stared at the name and address she'd written down. A name and address that might be a link to her past. The past that didn't matter.

Mac had been watching Carrie the whole time she was talking to Wieland's secretary, but he still wasn't sure what to make of the subtle changes in her expression. Admittedly, he had been distracted by the advances and declines of the scanty towel she was clutching around herself. How could he not be distracted when the snowy white terry cloth covered only the essentials—and those not very well. The sun-kissed rosiness of her skin, the softly rounded curve of breast exposed as she reached for a pen, the dewy line of moisture trailing intriguingly down her spine—oh yes, he'd been distracted.

But not so much that he hadn't noticed the wariness that changed to uncertainty that segued to a kind of excitement and then back to uncertainty again as she hung up. He just didn't know what it meant—not even after Carrie had twisted around to face him and explained Anna Verlatti's suggestion.

"There's no need to bother with that," he said. "We can just as easily leave this wrinkle out of our description of our unsuccessful trip when we talk to Janice and Peter."

"Mac, maybe we should talk to the woman," Carrie said, tucking her legs up under her on the bed. The two edges of the towel parted, exposing a long length of thigh and hip all the way to her waist.

He put two fingers on her knee and started tiptoeing up her thigh. "You're not still worrying about being related to the officious Charles Wieland, are you?"

She shook her head, seeming suddenly very interested in the weave of the bedspread. "No, of course not. But it would look good in our search notebook, wouldn't it, another page filled, another dead end uncovered, proving what diligent, desperate searchers we are. And Lompoc's on our way home, almost, isn't it?"

Mac looked at Carrie not looking at him, and frowned. Stopping in the little town of Lompoc on their way north tomorrow wouldn't require much of a detour—but enough to put a definite crimp in the plan they'd made earlier to travel leisurely back up the coast and spend the night in Carmel. And he wasn't quite convinced of her reason for wanting to talk to Charles Wieland's old secretary. Was she still worrying about the possibility that Wieland was her birth father? But she didn't care about that biological connection non-sense—did she? The back of his neck prickled and he wanted to cup her face with his hands and turn it up to his so he could see what was in those revealing green eyes of hers. But before he could put action to the thought, she spoke again.

"We don't have to if you'd rather not," she said, shifting position, easing over onto one hip. "It was just an idea; it's not important."

Carrie still wasn't looking at him. But as she moved, her towel parted further, revealing the full undercurve of her breast.

Mac forgot all about trying to read her eyes. As she'd said, whether they stopped or not wasn't important.

"We can stop anywhere you want, mermaid. As long as we can discuss it—" his fingers had followed the towel's opening all the way to the terry cloth corners she clutched in one hand "—later."

Carrie smiled. "Later," she agreed.

THE RETIREMENT HOME where Violet Durning lived was more like a pleasant old-fashioned hotel than the con-valescent hospital Carrie had been dreading. Seventeen elderly men and women boarded in the large old house, where meals, cleaning services and friendship were provided. The residents were unable or unwilling to live alone, but they weren't bedridden or seriously ill. A middle-aged husband and wife acted as "house par-ents," living in, and there were several daily aides, a cook and a housekeeper. The house was scrupulously clean and pleasantly homey, with an overall atmos-phere as cheery as the bright flowers blooming in the front garden.

Of course, any self-respecting home in Lompoc had flowers blooming in May. The small town, nestled in a narrow valley just a stretch of hills away from the coast, was known as the flower-seed capital of the world. Although the height of the season wouldn't be until June, already field after colorful field bloomed with flowers, forming a stunning patchwork carpet of pinks, purples and golds, filling the valley and scenting the wind with their fragrances. At the appropriate times the specially bred flowers would be harvested and their seeds sent around the world.

They had found Violet's home at the southern end of town and had been greeted there by "Mom," who'd warned them that Violet's mind did tend to wander, so they shouldn't expect too much—and definitely shouldn't press her if she didn't remember what they wanted to know. Then the woman had shown them to a sunny sitting room where Violet was waiting.

Violet Durning was a sweet-faced woman in her seventies, with eyes to match her name and snow-white hair pulled tightly into a bun circled by a tiny garland of daisies. She seemed pleased to have visitors, but her blue-violet eyes really lit up when Mac, explaining their reason for coming, mentioned Charles Wieland's name.

"Charles is such a dear," she said, astonishing Carrie. Charles Wieland, dear? It didn't seem possible, but Violet quite definitely believed it.

"He still visits me, you know," she enthused. "Once a month, without fail. And it's his generous pension that allows me to stay here. I worked for Charles for twenty-three years, you know."

"We know," Mac said. "That's why we're here. Carrie needs some information about an adoption that Charles handled years ago, and he wasn't able to help us. So we wondered if you might remember something about it."

It wasn't quite a lie, but it made Carrie realize that Violet Durning might not be so willing to talk to them if she knew of her "dear" Charles's true feelings in the matter. Mac, with his reporter's instincts, had obviously realized the fact much sooner.

But as it was, Violet was happy to talk. And she definitely did remember.

"The adoption, of course," she declared, waving a small, wrinkled hand, its nails painted an incongruously schoolgirlish petal pink. "How could I forget? It was the only one Charles ever did—and he only did it because it was for that girl, the one he loved."

The yellow and white sitting room was toasty-warm with late afternoon sunshine. But all at once Carrie felt very cold. Crossing her arms, she rubbed at the gooseflesh pebbling her skin.

"Yes, that girl," Violet repeated. "She just appeared at the office one day, without an appointment or anything, but Charles looked like Christmas had come early when he saw her. And he kept his next two appointments waiting while they talked. But when they came back out of his office, he was miserable.

"'She's pregnant, Vi,' he told me, later that day. He was always confiding in me, you know. 'Pregnant and not married,' he said, 'and she wants me to help her give away her baby.'

"Oh yes, I remember...he told me all about her. They'd met years before while he was doing his graduate work—"

"You mean they were at college together?" Carrie asked, and then regretted the interruption because it seemed to confuse Violet.

"Were they? I didn't know that...." She stared off into space for a while, but finally blinked and went on. "But I knew he loved her, though she only wanted him as a lawyer."

Violet's pink nails fluttered as she waved her hand again, and sighed. "Ah well, Charles was never much to fuel a young girl's dreams. He was a plodder, good-hearted, but dull, I guess you'd say. He still visits me, though, and always brings me chocolate-covered cherries, my favorites." She looked at Mac a bit petulantly, as if she was wondering why he hadn't brought her candy, too. "I've told him not to bother with an old woman like me, but he says we survivors have to stick together. His wife died in a car accident years ago, you know. Along with both his children. That's when he moved to Santa Barbara. It was dreadful—poor man. Though I don't think he really loved his wife—he only married after that adoption thing."

Carrie was thinking about Charles Wieland, loving her birth mother and not being loved in return. No wonder he had reacted so defensively when she'd come to him, bringing up the past that hurt him so badly. And he was still trying to protect the woman he had loved— and possibly still loved.

So it was Mac who asked the next question. "Violet, do you remember the girl's name? The pregnant one?"

"Oh yes, of course."

Carrie felt as if her heart had stopped beating. She stared at Violet, waiting for the name to come from the old woman's lips, thin lips, which Violet was smacking as if the thought of the name was as tasty as her favorite chocolates.

"Caroline," she said. "Caroline, one of my favorite names, you know. My sister's first girl was Carolyn, with a 'y.' I liked this other Caroline better; it's so sweetly old-fashioned. It caused me no end of confusion when I was typing the adoption papers, though. I kept spelling it Carolyn and having to do it over. Charles was always a perfectionist about documents, you know. There was one time..."

She rattled on while Carrie sat very still, stunned. Caroline...Carrie...was she named for her birth mother? Though her amended birth certificate said Carrie, not Caroline, could she once have been Caroline...for the Caroline who had carried her?

She leaned forward. "Violet, do you remember Caroline's last name?"

"My sister's girl? Why would you want to know Carolyn's last name? It was Andrews, but then she married some Greek fellow and I never could pronounce his last name...Papadopo-something."

"No, Violet," Mac said gently. "Not your sister's Carolyn. Charles Wieland's Caroline. The one he did the adoption for. What was her last name?"

"Oh, that—you know, there were two adoptions, actually."

"Two?" Carrie looked sharply at the woman. Could she be so mixed up that she was confusing cases? Could the name Caroline, which was richocheting so painfully through her mind, mean nothing at all. "Two adoptions?" she prodded.

Violet nodded. "Yes, for Caroline's baby. She gave it to her...her sister and brother-in-law...or was it an aunt and uncle...to some relatives, anyway. Later, they came back to have Charles handle giving it away again. I wonder if the couple who took it then, kept it...strange giving away babies like unwanted parcels...."

"But do you remember Caroline's last name...or that of her relatives, Violet?" Carrie pressed.

Violet blinked her eyes, suddenly looking horribly confused. "Her last name. I...I should remember...." She patted ineffectually at a tiny wrinkle in her skirt. "I forget things sometimes, you know, and feel so foolish. I don't mean to be difficult...."

Carrie looked at the small hand with its pale-pink nails, fluttering nervously, and at Violet's bluish eyes, filling with tears. And she reached out, taking the woman's hand and squeezing comfortingly.

"Don't worry about it, Violet. I shouldn't be bothering you with this. It really doesn't matter. Not at all."

Outside the rambling white house, Mac pulled open the door of the car for Carrie. But before she could slip inside, he took her in his arms and kissed her thoroughly.

"What was that for?" she asked breathlessly, when she could. "Not that I'm complaining, mind you...."

"Oh, just for being you, Carrie Prescott," he said. "For being so sweet to Violet, for caring more about comforting her than your questions." He kissed her again.

Carrie flushed. "Well, she just looked so unhappy," she murmured, ducking into the car.

Mac shut her door, then walked around to climb behind the wheel. "That's what I mean," he continued. "You cared that she was unhappy. And that reminded me of the difference between you and a real searcher. Can you imagine Janice Sedgewick or any of the others caring about the feelings of an old woman who had the name they wanted?"

"I'm sure they would," she answered, thinking of the various members of the search group—and then of others.... "At least, most of them would."

"Not," Mac added his own ending to her sentence. "But you do, and that is thing number six-hundred and eighty-two I love about you, you know. Remind me to tell you each one of the others sometime."

There was a huge lump in Carrie's throat, which, she told herself accounted for the hoarseness of her voice when she said, "I love you, too, Mac. Very, very much."

CHAPTER FIFTEEN

DURING THE NEXT FEW WEEKS, it seemed to Carrie that she was constantly busy with one thing or another, some pleasant, some not. But either way, there wasn't time to sit around thinking, and for that she was grateful.

There was work to catch up on for her column, and notes to make on the character for her next book, who had popped into her mind one dawn, demanding immediate attention. There were Lamaze classes to attend with Robin, where she marveled at all she learned about the magical process a woman's body undergoes giving birth. She marveled, too, at Robin, now in her eighth month and still completely serene and, as far as Carrie could tell, completely without plans for her future or that of her baby. Eddie had asked Carrie to pose for another mermaid—this one a small statuette in redwood—and while he did the preliminary sketches, she told him her concerns about Robin. He advised her not to worry.

"She's got plans, Carrie," he said. "She just isn't ready to tell us about them yet. She'll let us know when the time is right and until then, all you can do is relax."

Mac agreed with Eddie.

"Robin knows you're there if she needs you, Carrie," was his opinion. "But I'd bet she's known from day one how things were going to work out with her baby. Sometimes, looking at her, I even believe she

knows how everything is going to work out for all of
us."

She and Mac were spending as much time together as
the two of them could manage, and Carrie fell more in
love with him with every passing day. They went sailing on the Bay and hiked at Point Reyes. They had dinner in the Carnelian Room high atop the Bank of
America Building, with a spectacular sherbet-hued
sunset for dessert. They enjoyed just being together at
her houseboat or in his small redwood bungalow, with
the skylight over his bed and Stinson Beach just outside the front door. They made love, and each time was
better than the last.

They also went to a Father's Day backyard barbecue
at his parents' home in the East Bay hills, and it turned
out wonderfully, despite Carrie's severe case of meet-
ing-the-parents-of-the-guy-you-love jitters, and the
news Mac gave her on the way there.

"You could have worn the ring, you know," he said
as they crossed the graceful silver span of the Bay
Bridge. "I told my parents all about you."

"You...you told your parents all about me?"

"Well, not all...." His brows wiggled up and down.
"But enough. So you could have left the ring on."

Today, for the first time since he'd given it to her,
Carrie had taken off the Kincaid diamond, hiding it in
the toe of a woolly sock buried beneath her underwear
for safety. She'd been hoping Mac wouldn't notice its
absence.

"I just thought...well..." She shrugged. "They
know about the investigation, then?"

Mac sobered. "They know, but it would be better not
to bring it up."

"You mean because Beth and Stewart will be there?"

"Because they won't be there, Carrie," he said, his hand going to the gearshift. One finger began skating round and round the plastic knob. "I told you Beth and my mother argued about the . . . adoption thing."

"But Mac, surely Father's Day is reason enough for them to make it up."

He shook his head. "Both my mother and Beth have stubborn streaks a mile wide, and their argument was a bad one. They're both hurting, but neither will give in."

"But Mac, that's so . . . wrong."

"Right . . ." he said grimly. There was a long silence and his finger circled the gearshift knob faster and faster. And then words seem to burst from him.

"It is wrong, but dammit, it never should have happened in the first place."

"What shouldn't have happened?" Carrie asked, startled by Mac's vehemence, by the anger that seemed to leap from him like some wild thing slipping its leash.

But a moment later it was gone—or maybe only leashed again. "Oh, just the argument," he said far too casually.

Mac had turned all his attention to the road ahead, leaving Carrie free to look at him. She felt an urge to touch him and beg him to tell her whatever it was that was bothering him, whatever it was that he'd been holding back since the very beginning. But his face was set, and he wasn't drawing patterns on the gearshift anymore—his fist was clenched tightly around the knob instead. And she couldn't ask, not now.

She'd expected to feel awkward meeting the Kincaids, but she wasn't given the chance. Mac's youngest sister, twelve-year-old Tessa, pounced on Carrie the moment they pulled up in front of the two-story house with the horse paddock and barn in the back. How did

Carrie do her column, she wanted to know. How many letters did she get and how did she come up with such great answers? By the time Tessa's lively curiosity was satisfied, and she'd met Mac's four other sisters, Laraine, Andi, Deborah and Kelly, and their three "communal" horses, Carrie's initial nervousness had disappeared.

She liked Mac's father immediately and inevitably, since he was so much like Mac—the same eyes, same dark hair, same warming smile. And, like his son, Joseph Kincaid seemed to take instantly to Carrie.

It took a few minutes longer with Victoria Kincaid. Mac's mother had short curly hair and a slender figure, like Beth's, and her hazel eyes, noting her son's arm curled possessively around Carrie's waist, were as appraisingly curious as Beth's had been at the airport. But there was a natural warmth and friendliness about the woman, too, as if she just couldn't resist mothering anyone who came within her reach—and that very quickly included Carrie.

It was hard to believe such a woman could be estranged from one of her daughters, and it became even harder when, after the barbecued ribs and corn on the cob were finished, Joseph began opening his presents. One was a box wrapped in paper that had been decorated by tiny hands dipped in red, blue and yellow paint—Mac had brought Beth's and Stewart's present. As Joseph worked on the ribbon with shaking hands, Victoria asked Mac how Beth was doing.

"Fine, Mom," Mac said into the silence that had fallen over the table. "Though she misses you, and being here...."

"I miss her, too," Victoria Kincaid said, then abruptly and firmly changed the subject. But there were tears in the woman's eyes.

In spite of that moment and the obvious absence of one Kincaid daughter, the party was enjoyable, and Carrie, an only child, was in turn astonished and delighted by the rowdy, loving atmosphere of Mac's huge family.

Not everything went as smoothly.

On her return from the trip to Santa Barbara, Carrie had tried for days to forget that she might be Carrie, named for Caroline. But she couldn't help thinking that she must have had a name, must have been called something during the first six months of her life before her second adoption—ideas she'd never considered before her visit with Violet Durning. And then her Adoptee Background Information form, filled out by some unidentified person at the State Department of Social Services, arrived in the mail.

Information from Carrie's adoption file, originally supplied by her birth mother, had been filled in on the standard form in dry-as-dust prose. There was nothing remotely identifying, but what was there was still...well, spooky was the only way she could describe it.

Her birth mother had been twenty years old at Carrie's birth, and unmarried. Health good, of English-French descent, with no specific illnesses running in her family—those were details Carrie had always known. But there were other details she hadn't known. Her birth mother was five foot two and a half inches tall—she'd added the half inch, just as Carrie always did. Her hair was auburn, her eyes gray-green, and her favorite hobby was writing, though at the age of twenty, when she'd presumably filled out the paperwork, she'd never had anything published.

Spooky. As was one particular aspect of the few notations included about her birth father. He'd wanted to be an actor, and had ended the relationship and gone to New York after getting a part in a Broadway production. He hadn't known about the baby because the birth mother, knowing he wouldn't want the encumbrance, hadn't told him she was pregnant.

Carrie's birth father had been a selfish, would-be actor—like Doug Bannerman!

Carrie read the form over and over again, read the parallels and similarities between herself and her birth mother, and wondered—was there one more similarity? Had she been named Caroline after the woman who gave her birth? Was she Carrie for Caroline? Finally, she had to ask her mother.

Half-reluctantly, Helen Prescott told Carrie she had originally been named Gayle Caroline. They hadn't realized Caroline had been her birth mother's name, though, but the aunt and uncle had called her Carrie. So when the Prescotts adopted her they kept Carrie, dispensing with Gayle Caroline and adding Ann, her "new" grandmother's name.

The way a little girl, on a whim, changes her dolly's name, Carrie thought, and then, horrified, tried to erase the dreadful thought from her mind. But her mother must have seen something of it on her face, because she said, as if in explanation, "We just wanted to make you more ours, Carrie."

"I'm sure glad you did," Carrie forced lightness into her voice, at the same time putting her arms reassuringly around her mother. "I don't look a bit like a Gayle Caroline!"

That remark to her mother came back to haunt Carrie later that week, when she went to U.C. Berkeley—Charles Wieland's alma mater, according to Anna Verlatti—to look through yearbooks on the off chance that Caroline and the lawyer had met at college. For three hours, she and Janice Sedgewick, who had volunteered to help her, pored over page after page in the books covering the appropriate years. Janice made lists of the names while Carrie stared at pictures of one Caroline after another. Then, considering the confused states of Violet Durning's mind, they added Carolyns, Carols, Caroles and even Gayles. But the pictures were of women younger than Carrie was now, the hairstyles and makeup were totally different. And not one of them made Carrie think this, this is my birth mother.

That night, as she soaked exhaustedly in a hot bubble bath, Carrie decided that had she really been searching, the day would have been one of the most discouraging of her life. She and Janice had talked about the large number of discouraging days a searcher typically suffered through, Janice being extremely sympathetic and Carrie discovering it was getting easier all the time to understand how the people at Triangle could get so worked up about being denied the truths of their pasts.

The Triangle meetings were getting easier to sit through, too, though she was feeling worse and worse about her deception—primarily because she was growing closer to the members of the group. There were still times when their one-sided view of searching infuriated her, there were still a few people whose self-centered outlooks continued to put her off. But it was hard not to grow to like people who helped each other, supported each other, and were always ready to lend a shoulder to cry on when the disappointments came in. Even Janice, with all her irritating ways and attitudes, had willingly spent hours helping Carrie with her supposed search and sympathized with her impatience over the lack of success. So when one of the group, Allyce, was reunited with the twin sister she'd been separated from at birth, Carrie joined the celebration lunch at Maxwell's Plum in Ghirardelli Square, truly happy for the woman.

Mac was in Sacramento, interviewing people in the State Department of Social Services and the Attorney General's office about the illegal underground, on the day of the luncheon. But he stopped by Carrie's that night on his way home to Stinson Beach, surprising and pleasing her. She fixed him a snack, since he'd skipped dinner, "To get back to you sooner," he said. He ate, they indulged in some light-hearted necking, looked at Robin's latest painting and talked. But when Carrie started telling Mac about the lunch, he cut her off abruptly.

"Why would you want to waste your time that way?" he demanded, and a cold shiver shot through Carrie.

"It wasn't a waste of time. I enjoyed it."

"How can you enjoy celebrating something so ridiculous!"

"Mac, Allyce isn't one of the fanatics," she explained, wondering why he hadn't realized that on his own. "You were at the meeting where she described her search. She never hurt anyone. She used records and signed up with registries and such. And when she finally located her sister, she had an intermediary contact the woman first, to scout out the situation and make sure she wouldn't be intruding at a bad time. You can't think there was anything wrong with that."

"I . . ." Mac leaned his head back against the couch cushions and rubbed at his eyes with his fists. "I guess I'm just tired, Carrie. I didn't get much from the people in Sacramento—they admit illegal access might be happening, but refuse to consider how it's being done or who might be behind it. They aren't really interested in stopping it. To them, it's small change, hard to prove or prosecute. But to the people affected and hurt by this, it isn't small at all—that's what they don't understand."

Carrie understood, and told Mac so. He took her in his arms, and everything was all right again. For a while.

THE FOLLOWING MONDAY, Carrie had an appointment at the county agency that had handled her adoption so many years before. Not long after she and Mac entered the office of Irene Orrock, a social worker with the agency, she decided the meeting was a replay of their encounter with Charles Wieland. A replay, only worse.

As before, she and Mac were kept waiting, but without the ameliorating presence of Anna Verlatti. And when they were finally shown into an austere gray-walled office, Irene Orrock, standing behind a large gunmetal-gray desk, didn't bother apologizing for the delay.

"Miss Prescott? Mr. MacAllister? What can I do for you?" She sounded impatient, like a schoolteacher trying to control too many unruly children, and she used the capped fountain pen she held like a pointer stick, waving them into the chairs facing the desk. She sat down as they did.

"As I wrote when requesting this appointment, I would like some information about my adoption," Carrie answered.

Ms Orrock dipped her head slightly to peer at Carrie over the steel rims of her bifocals. "What type of information?"

"Anything," Carrie replied evenly. "Everything."

The woman smiled thinly. Probably in her early fifties, she was wearing an officious navy-blue straight skirt, navy blazer and primly bow-tied white blouse. On her desk, stacks of smoke-gray plastic trays formed fortresslike towers, while paper clips, rubber bands, blank labels in various colors and rubber stamps were segregated in little smoke-gray cups. Carrie imagined each tray and cup was neatly labeled.

"Of course you're aware that I can't tell you everything," the woman said, taking a file folder from the top of one tower. "But let's see what there is."

Irene Orrock began thumbing through the contents of Carrie's file. Slowly. Suddenly she had all the time in the world. She turned a page, read every word written on it, then turned another page. Occasionally she would pause, uncap her fountain pen, make a notation on a separate sheet of paper, then recap the pen before going on. Other times, she paused to glance up over her bifocals at Carrie again, make a little humming sound and then return to her leisurely perusal of the file.

Earlier this morning, before Mac had picked her up, Carrie had lectured herself on how casually she was going to go through this meeting, on how it was part of Mac's investigation, and nothing more. Whatever happened, it didn't matter to her personally, she'd told herself sternly, resolving to remain detached and calm.

But watching Irene Orrock's infuriating performance, Carrie felt her resolve slipping. The woman was reading details about Carrie's past, was learning things Carrie didn't know about herself and might never know. And if she looked up over those ridiculous glasses and hummed one more time, Carrie thought she would scream.

The social worker flipped the folder closed and smiled her thin smile. "As I thought, there's very little I can tell you."

"But there is something." Carrie made it a statement.

"Miss Prescott, I see that your adoptive parents have given permission for our disclosure of non-identifying information to you, but have you really considered how unfair to them you're being?"

"I don't believe I'm being at all unfair to anyone."

The woman jabbed her pen in Carrie's direction. "You're searching, aren't you?"

"Well..." Carrie wasn't sure how to reply. Peter had advised the searchers to never give searching as their reason for wanting information. It closed too many doors, he said. Genealogical research was a better excuse for questions in most instances, but didn't work at an adoption agency, for obvious reasons. For them, he suggested expressing concern about health problems, especially in connection with childbearing and inherited diseases. But since Carrie was only pretending to search, following Peter's advice now meant using one lie to cover up another lie. It was all getting too confusing, and she wasn't sure anymore which lie to tell at the moment.

"Yes, Carrie is searching," Mac filled in. "She's very anxious to know about her past before we marry."

Ms Orrock nodded smugly, as if she'd known all along. "Sadly, this dwelling on the past has become the 'in' thing to do," she said. "But few of these searchers consider how unfair they're being to the parents who took them in, cared for them, provided for them—"

"Loved them?" Carrie interjected sarcastically, but didn't wait for a reply. "Look Ms Orrock, my parents are wonderful people and I love them very much. If I've decided to find my birth parents, it's a separate thing entirely and no reflection on that love. They understand that."

"So they know exactly what you're doing?"

She might as well have said "what you're up to." As if Carrie were a child sneaking a cookie before dinner.

"As it happens, they do," Carrie said. "Though I don't see what possible difference it makes. I'm twenty-six years old. An adult, responsible for my own actions and decisions."

"But not for the actions and decisions of others, Miss Prescott. Which all you searchers seem to forget. There are others involved here. Your birth mother, birth father and your adoptive parents. They all matter."

"Well, of course they do. I wasn't suggesting they don't matter...."

"We've always felt that the best interests of all involved are best served by keeping identifying information secret. That hasn't changed just because searching has become the fashionable thing to do among adopted children."

"I think it's more fashionable among adopted adults," Mac said dryly, barely stressing the final word. But it was enough to bring color to Irene Orrock's pale cheeks.

Carrie flashed him a grateful smile.

"All right, Miss Prescott, Mr. MacAllister," the social worker said frostily, drawing toward her the sheet of paper she'd written on during her study of Carrie's file. "This is what I can tell you."

Carrie had thought the minimal information included on her Adoptee Background Information form from the state was dully phrased. Irene Orrock's recitation was worse, and contained less. When the woman finished, Carrie tried asking a few questions. After referring to the file again, Ms Orrock answered a few. But mostly she claimed she couldn't—even on a couple of questions to which the state form had already supplied the answers.

"This is pointless, isn't it, Ms Orrock?" Carrie said finally.

The woman smiled. "I thought you understood that at the beginning."

Carrie stood. "May I have those notes?" she asked, pointing to the sheet of paper in front of the social worker.

Pursing her lips, Irene Orrock studied the paper for a moment, obliterating a line here and there with sweeps of her fountain pen. "I guess so," she said at last, snapping the cap back on her pen before handing the paper to Carrie.

Carrie stared at it, at the words the woman had written there in tight little block letters, in black ink that had a strange greenish cast to it. There were three lines obscured by solid greenish-black boxes; the rest said almost nothing.

Years of her mother's training in proper manners made Carrie say thank-you. But it didn't keep her from nearly choking over the word.

CHAPTER SIXTEEN

"Ms Orrock sounds like one of the old school," Peter said. It was after the Monday night search group meeting, and Carrie and Mac had related the unsuccessful results of their appointment with the social worker to Janice and Peter.

"They refuse to believe there could ever be a justifiable reason for searching," he went on. "To them, every request for information is an insult to the whole traditional system of adoption. Years ago, the theory was that all adoptees were going to grow up contentedly in the homes the social workers found for them, all birth mothers were going to forget completely the babies they signed away and everyone was going to live happily ever after. Thousands of adoptions were arranged and files were sealed on that basis. Some people still want to believe it's all worked out that way and don't like evidence to the contrary."

"But she wouldn't even give me as much information as was included on the state form," Carrie said.

"Typical," Janice put in, sniffing. "There are a few social workers who are sympathetic enough to stretch the rules a bit to help, but fewer still will circumvent the sealed-records policy."

"Circumvent it how?" Mac had been ruffling a corner of his notebook ever since the four of them had settled on the two facing love seats in Janice's living room.

Somehow Peter and Carrie had ended up sitting together, leaving him the space next to Janice. And from there he had watched Peter drape his arm across the back of the love seat, just half an inch above Carrie's shoulders that were bared by her buttercup-yellow sundress. That's when he'd started ruffling pages with his thumb. But his finger stilled now as his attention shifted to Janice.

"Oh, they might 'need' to leave the room for a few minutes during a meeting with an adoptee, 'forgetting' the file on the desk. Or they just happen to let a crucial name or place 'slip.' Things like that."

"Well, Ms Orrock didn't let a thing slip," Mac said.

"Which leaves you with Charles Wieland and Violet Durning," Peter advised. "They're your best leads."

Mac shook his head. "We'll never get anything out of Wieland, and Violet Durning . . ."

"I don't want to press Violet," Carrie put in. "It isn't right." Actually, she wouldn't press Charles Wieland, either, not even if she was really searching. Knowing what she did about him now, she couldn't. He had reasons for his silence, whether she believed he was right about them or not. And besides, she never wanted to see his mixed look of fascination and revulsion again.

"Carrie, you can't be so squeamish about these things," Peter said. His arm moved and he gave her shoulders a comforting squeeze. "You have to keep in mind that these people are denying you your rights, your biological heritage. That's wrong; getting the truth isn't."

"No matter how you get it?" Mac said sharply, his eyes on Peter's hand, on the dimples his fingers were pressing into the soft flesh of Carrie's upper arm. Mac's thumb scraped across the corner of his notebook again, and the paper hissed. "No matter who you trample in the process?"

Three surprised faces turned to stare at Mac, and Carrie's especially told him how badly he'd just blown it.

"I wouldn't put it quite that way," Peter said, taking his arm from Carrie's shoulders at the same time.

Mac rubbed a hand back and forth across one side of his face, like an eraser over a bad drawing, then sketched in a smile. "Hey, Peter, I apologize. This whole thing, the delays and all...well, it's getting to me. I know you warned us it might take a while, but we were hoping.... Anyway, Carrie doesn't want to talk to either Wieland or Violet Durning again, and I don't blame her. We've tried all the other obvious avenues, and even more farfetched ones, but we're getting nowhere fast. And, hell, we want to get married! I think we're ready for those less regular ways of finding information you once mentioned."

Peter looked from Mac to Carrie, then nodded slowly. "Let me think what might work in your case."

"How about a blanket search for the hospital where she was born?" Janice said. "We're pretty sure it's in the Bay area."

"Worth a try," Peter said, then added an explanation for Carrie and Mac. "A blanket hospital search is simply writing all the hospitals in an area requesting the medical records of say, Gayle Caroline, born on such and such a day, etc. It's time-consuming, and the chance of getting a positive response, even if we hit the right one, is only fifty-fifty, but we are talking long shots here."

"What about contacting some search buddies in New York?" Janice offered another suggestion.

It was a new term to Carrie. "Search buddies?"

"They're people involved in the adoption movement all across the country who are willing to help others by researching some detail in their area," Janice explained. "Maybe we could ask someone to look into what Broadway productions were going on just prior to your birth. Do you know if Equity keeps records that far back, Peter? Any chance of locating Carrie's birth father by finding out which new young actors in small parts were from California that year?"

"What about the illegal underground?" Mac interrupted before Peter could answer Janice, and once again everyone was staring at him.

Janice sniffed. "Where did you hear about that?"

"At the conference, I suppose," Mac said, shrugging. "Or in some article I read. Is it true? Is there a nationwide network of people getting information from sealed adoption records for a fee?"

"I've heard of it, yes," Peter replied guardedly. "But getting involved with it is, as far as I'm concerned, a definite last resort—and for some people, not even that."

Carrie shifted on the couch to face him. "What do you mean?"

"Just that for some, using an illegal connection is going against the grain. No matter how a person might feel about his or her right to the information contained in the adoption records, illegal is still illegal. For some, the need to know is enough to justify the illegality, but for others, nothing quite eliminates the guilt over doing something dishonest." Peter was looking at Carrie. "I think you might be one of the latter."

Mac was watching her . . . them . . . and he saw Carrie's eyes widen, saw the green darkening with guilt at Peter's comment.

"But what if we wanted to do it anyway?" he put in quickly.

"I'd still warn you there are risks simply because it is an illegal activity," Peter answered. "Everyone involved is necessarily committed to secrecy, so it's difficult to be certain that the information you get will be accurate—or even that you'll get anything at all. And it isn't cheap."

"You mean somebody is making a lot of money off this?"

"Not a fortune. But even though I like to think that most of those involved do it because they disagree with the policy of sealing records, logic tells me where there's money involved, not everyone is being altruistic."

"How does it work?"

"As I understand it, an intermediary will contact a person who's expressed an interest in such means, quoting a price. If the searcher agrees, the intermediary makes the contact with someone who has access to the appropriate records. The money and the name are exchanged, and hopefully all is well."

"But Peter, couldn't anyone get information from government files that way?" Carrie asked, frowning. "Not just those in adoption search who maybe are entitled, but other people wanting information for the wrong reasons. Couldn't this illegal underground be opening the door for a lot of other problems?"

He nodded, stroking his beard. "That's one of the reasons I hesitate to condone it as a method. I don't think it's . . . well, I'm not sure I can say it isn't right, because I think keeping birth information from adult members of the adoption triangle is so very wrong in the first place. But I do believe legal search is still the best way, along with fighting to have the outdated laws changed so that adoption records will be open to those involved."

"It might be best, but it sure isn't fast," Mac declared, and flipped his notebook closed.

"I DIDN'T KNOW you were going to do that tonight," Carrie said later, when they were in the car heading for Sausalito. "Bring up the illegal underground, I mean."

"That's because I didn't know I was going to do it, either, until I did," Mac admitted. "But as I sat there, listening to Peter Millheiser's suggestions for our future search steps, I had a vision of you and me, still running around pretending to be searchers two or three years down the road. And I don't want to wait that long to nail these people."

"Nail them?" Carrie twisted around as far as the seat belt would let her. "Mac, what are you talking about?"

Oncoming headlights flashed on Mac's set features and on his hands clenched tightly on the steering wheel. "The people like Peter who are involved in this illegal underground crap, that's who," he declared.

"Peter! How can you think Peter is involved? He told us the underground wasn't the best way to go, that other search methods are better."

"You mean the methods that are just a little 'unusual' instead of out-and-out illegal?"

"Well, there is a difference."

"Oh, come on, Carrie, weren't you listening back there? He and Janice were talking about 'stretching' and 'circumventing' the law, 'sympathetic' doctors, social workers who let things 'slip'—the only difference between slipped information and the illegal kind is semantics, and how much you have to pay for it.''

"But I'm sure Peter and Janice and most of the others at Triangle are only acting with the best of intentions.''

"And their good intentions are putting other people through hell!''

"Mac!''

"Well, what would you call it when a stranger appears at a woman's door and says, 'Hi, Mom, remember me?' Or when a birth mother contacts her child, who never even knew she was adopted?''

"Sometimes it works out,'' she said softly.

"And sometimes it doesn't!'' he nearly shouted.

Carrie knew Mac was right. Even before beginning this whole investigation mess, she'd suspected searching could cause trouble, and in the past few weeks she'd heard plenty of stories to support that suspicion. But she'd also heard from people whose searches had ended happily, changing their lives for the better. So where was the answer in that?

"Obviously there's a problem with searching. But there's a problem with the secrecy, too, maybe even with the whole traditional approach to adoption. That's what Peter's trying to change.''

"Peter Millheiser's just as bad as all the rest,'' Mac stated flatly. "For all his talk of improving the adoption experience, he still believes searching is some God-given right, that the one searching, be it birth parent or adoptee, is always bathed in some golden glow of righteousness. And I think he could very well be the illegal connection we're looking for.''

Carrie shook her head. "He couldn't be; he discouraged us...."

"Don't be naive. Do you think we're the only ones capable of pretense? He's probably making the contact with someone who can get access to your records right this minute. He'll be telling us how much your birth mother's name is going to cost us one day very soon, I'd bet anything—and I can't wait!"

Carrie looked at Mac. They'd been halted by a stoplight, and a red glow splashed eerily over his face. But it was more than strange lighting that made her suddenly feel she didn't know him at all. Oh, she knew he liked black coffee and hated tea. She knew he had a heart-shaped mole on his right shoulder blade, he fidgeted with anything handy when he was worrying, and he was a passionate, caring lover. She knew so many things about him, including the fact that she loved him more than she'd believed she would ever love anyone. But at this moment, he seemed like a stranger.

"I thought we were doing an unbiased article on adoption search, not an exposé," she said, her voice light. "I didn't realize we were supposed to be finding villains to crucify."

"That's not what I'm doing at all, Carrie!" he snapped.

The light changed then and he gunned the car forward. The roar of the engine almost drowned Carrie's next words.

"Are you sure about that, Mac?"

He didn't reply.

IT HADN'T BEEN an argument, Carrie tried to comfort herself as she walked slowly along the dock toward her houseboat. Not quite. Just close enough.

She didn't even really understand how it had happened. All she knew for sure was that now she was going to be spending the night alone, instead of in Mac's arms.

She'd be really alone, too, she remembered, pulling her fringed white shawl closer around her shoulders. Robin was staying at Beth's again, even though Stewart wasn't out of town this time.

Normally, Carrie wouldn't have minded being alone. But she'd expected to be with Mac tonight, and since she wasn't she felt lonely—already.

But when she reached the houseboat, she heard soft music coming from inside and more than just the porch light was burning. For a moment, panic pumped adrenaline through her veins, and she was fervently wishing she hadn't so cavalierly dismissed Mac at the Mermaid Gate. But then logic took over and she realized neither burglars nor ax-murderers turned on lights and played music while engaged in their respective nastinesses.

Carrie peeked into the living room to find Robin chewing the end of her paintbrush and studying the canvas on the easel in front of her, while Pandora sniffed at tubes of paints in the box on the floor.

"Hi, Carrie, be done in a sec," she said without turning. The painting was one she'd been working on for weeks, of children on a merry-go-round. Blurs of brilliant color somehow conveyed an impression of actual movement, bright smiles and wide eyes expressed sheer joy. Carrie had thought it was perfect days ago, but Robin wasn't satisfied. She kept adding a dash of cadmium yellow here, a spot of cobalt blue there. Tonight her brush was tipped with white.

"I thought you were going to Beth's," Carrie said.

"Oh . . ." Robin leaned forward, touching the brush to one child's eye; suddenly the child was giggling with excitement. "I decided to stay here instead."

"Want some tea?" Carrie offered.

"Camomile?"

Carrie nodded, heading for the kitchen, Pandora on her heels.

By the time the cat's demands for an evening snack were satisfied, the water came to a boil and Carrie returned to the living room with the teapot, mugs and a pot of honey, Robin had cleaned up her painting things and was sitting on the floor in front of the couch. Her legs were bent, the soles of her bare feet were pressed together and drawn in toward her stomach, and her gauzy rose-red dress was spread out around her like the petals of that flower. Ever so gently, she was bouncing her bent legs up and down, her knees dipping closer to the floor with each bounce.

"You're stretching the muscles of the pelvic floor," Carrie announced to prove she'd been paying attention at Lamaze class. Setting the tea tray on the redwood-burl table, she knelt on the floor beside Robin. "Want to try some breathing while the tea brews?"

"Okay . . . stage one, early labor," Robin replied, leaning back against the couch and stretching her legs out straight.

Like a good coach, Carrie reached for a small pillow and tucked it behind Robin's back. Glancing at her watch, she grasped Robin's lower leg and squeezed gently. "Contraction begins," she said.

Robin began the series of slow even breaths she would use during the early stages of labor, at the same time consciously relaxing her body. Carrie counted forty-five seconds, the length of a typical early contraction, then released her hold on Robin's leg.

"Contraction over," she said. Robin took a deep cleansing breath and smiled.

"Good, another one won't be due for twelve minutes," she declared. "Time enough for you to tell me what's wrong."

"How did you know...?" Carrie started to ask, but realized Robin's clear, cornflower-blue gaze was as much answer as she was likely to get. Had the girl known she would need a friend tonight? Was that why she had decided to stay at home instead of going to Beth's? Carrie didn't have the faintest idea—and didn't really care. She was just glad Robin was there. She needed to talk it out.

She did. They sipped soothing camomile tea while she told Robin about the meeting with Janice and Peter, and about her near argument with Mac and her doubts about his objectivity when it came to searching.

"He can't be entirely objective about it, Carrie," Robin said, putting down her teacup. "No matter how much he may have intended to be, or even wants to be, he can't."

Carrie stared at Robin. "Why can't he?"

"Because of Beth, and his mother...and a woman named Priscilla." She leaned back against the couch again, and told Carrie what Beth had told her, the story of how Victoria Kincaid had been "found."

"At the age of seventeen, Victoria had an illegitimate baby and gave her up for adoption. Later, when she met and married Joseph Kincaid, she told him about it, but for various reasons, they decided not to tell their children. So none of them knew, until a few months ago, when Priscilla arrived on the scene and presented herself as Victoria's illegitimate daughter.''

Carrie clutched the warmth of her mug with both hands, thinking of Mac's close, loving family, of Victoria Kincaid. Already, her heart was aching.

"That alone would have created a difficult situation. What made it impossible was that Priscilla presented herself first not to Victoria, but to Beth.''

"To Beth? But why on earth...''

"Priscilla had been searching for some time, and when she finally discovered Victoria's whereabouts, Victoria and Joseph were off in Palm Springs, celebrating their thirty-fifth wedding anniversary. But Priscilla didn't intend to wait. Telling a neighbor she was a relative from out of town, she got Beth's address and went directly there, arriving just minutes after Beth had returned from the doctor, who had confirmed the irreversibility of her infertility and had suggested adoption as the only alternative. So Beth, miserable and confused, first heard of her mother's deep dark secret when she opened the door to a stranger who said, 'I'm your sister.'''

"Oh, no!" Carrie cried. "But why would Priscilla do that? Why confront Beth?''

"Anger, I think, and vindictiveness. Beth didn't say this outright, but I gather Priscilla is not a happy person. She told Beth she'd had several emotional breakdowns and two divorces, and her third marriage was on the rocks, all of which she blamed on being, as she put it, abandoned like an unwanted kitten. She'd been searching a long time, too, and had finally paid for her birth mother's name, quite a lot of money....''

Full understanding struck Carrie like a fist. "You mean she used an illegal connection.''

"Right. And she painted a very grim picture of the kind of woman who would make such a thing necessary by carelessly and callously discarding her own flesh and blood. But she didn't stop there. Somehow, Beth ended up admitting her infertility problems to Priscilla, who then claimed Beth was paying for her mother's sin."

Carrie felt herself pale. "No," she whispered, but Robin nodded.

"At some other less emotional time, Beth probably could have handled the whole thing better. But that was the wrong day, and she was too upset about her own disappointment to look at things rationally. All she could see was that she wanted a baby so very much and couldn't have one, yet her mother had 'casually' given *her* baby away. Her barrenness, her mother's actions and adoption in general, got all mixed up in her mind, until, angry and confused, she called Victoria in Palms Springs and repeated Priscilla's accusations word for word. Victoria, shocked and hurt, got angry as well, they argued bitterly, and haven't spoken since. And the rift in the family is tearing them all apart, especially Mac."

So much came clear—Mac's lying to Beth about what they were working on at first, Beth's aversion to adoption and her absence from the Father's Day gathering. And most especially Mac's attitude toward adoption search.

"But the really ironic twist was that Priscilla had the wrong information in the first place," Robin added.

Carrie's brows shot up into her bangs. "You mean, she wasn't—"

"She wasn't Victoria's daughter, after all. The illegal connection had given her the wrong name, and she just hadn't bothered to check out all the details before contacting the Kincaids. But by the time the mistake was discovered, the damage had been done." Robin stretched out one arm, making it stiff and clenching her fist, while relaxing the rest of her body—another childbirth exercise. "So you see why Mac finds it difficult to be objective about searching."

Carrie did indeed see, almost too well. She remembered the notes Mac had given her in the beginning and knew one of the cases he'd written out as background for his article was his mother's. She remembered him, on the way to his parents' house, saying, "Dammit, it never should have happened in the first place," and understood his vehemence, his anger. Beth and Stewart might never have the baby they both wanted, the relationship between Beth and Victoria might be irreparably damaged, the whole family was suffering. And all because of a stupid mistake and a careless, selfish woman... who'd been searching.

No wonder he was angry. No wonder he found it difficult to be objective about the subject.

Difficult, but not impossible, Carrie told herself. Mac Kincaid would always be able to put aside his personal feelings in order to be fair in his work.

Wouldn't he?

Carrie tossed and turned most of the night, wondering about Mac's anger and his article, about their investigation and their argument. Wondering especially when she would see him again. The first glimmerings of dawn were creeping into the sky before she finally slipped into an uneasy sleep. And then, what seemed like only minutes later, the phone rang, jolting her awake.

Her gritty eyes snapped open and her first thought was; it might be Mac!

Sky rockets exploded in her mind as she quickly shifted Pandora, who had curled up against her stomach. Rolling over, she grabbed for the jangling instrument.

"Good morning, darlin'," Eddie said in answer to her hopeful hello, and Carrie felt overwhelmingly disappointed. But only for a moment.

"I apologize for calling so early," Eddie continued, "but I thought you'd like to know that ever since six-fifteen a young man's been sitting out on your front deck, massacring a bunch of yellow roses. He's still got a few flowers to go through, but darlin', it's starting to rain."

Carrie barely heard the last part of Eddie's explanation. She was already throwing back the bed covers and reaching for her silky blue robe. "Thanks, Eddie," she gasped, then dropped the phone and ran for the door.

Mac was there, really, truly there. Carrie couldn't believe it, not even when she yanked open the front door and saw him.

He was sitting on the small bench on the deck, shoulders hunched, head bent. In one hand he held a bunch of long-stemmed yellow roses wrapped in green florist's paper; with the other he was nervously picking the flowers apart. He'd been at it for some time, too, because yellow petals formed a circle around his feet.

As Eddie had said, it was starting to rain. Already the shoulders of Mac's ecru windbreaker and the knees of his black slacks were speckled with raindrops. Damp locks of hair curled boyishly across his forehead and at his neck. As Carrie opened the door, he looked up, then at the rose petal he'd just plucked from its stem, then back at her. He shook his head sheepishly.

"I'm sorry, Carrie," he said. "For everything, including showing up here at this hour of the morning. But I got a call late last night—I'm going to have to fly to Washington, D.C., at ten today. A guy in the Federal Drug Administration claims he's got hot information about a high-level official who's accepting bribes from a certain pharmaceutical company. I'll probably be back tomorrow, but I couldn't leave without seeing you, without telling you..." Standing, he took a few hesitant steps toward her, as if very unsure of his welcome.

"About last night," he said, "I shouldn't have taken my bad mood out on you. It's not your fault that...well, anyway Carrie, I'm sorry." He thrust the poor bedraggled bouquet toward her. "Forgive me?"

Carrie looked at Mac and all her doubts and worries faded into nothingness. Of course Mac would be fair when it came to his article, she thought. Of course everything would be all right. It had to be. Because for the rest of her life, love was going to be a bunch of mutilated yellow roses. She pushed the door open wide.

"Don't you know enough to come in out of the rain, Mac Kincaid?" she said, taking the flowers, and his hand. And she smiled.

CHAPTER SEVENTEEN

IT WAS JUST EIGHT-THIRTY when Carrie's phone rang again.

Mac had left a short while before, insisting she stay in bed instead of dressing to walk him out to his car. It was raining still, he'd said. And besides, he wanted to "take away with me the picture of you just as you are this minute—all soft and sleepy eyed and beautifully naked beneath the blankets."

Alone, Carrie had snuggled deeper beneath the bed covers that still held traces of his warmth and the delicious scent of his body, and assured herself again that everything was going to be all right. She and Mac loved each other enough to make it all right, no matter what. Smiling, she'd fallen asleep. Only to be awakened a second time that morning by the telephone—and this time the call wasn't nearly so pleasant.

"Miss Prescott?" Groggy as she was, Carrie recognized the voice instantly, even before he added, "This is Charles Wieland."

"Yes, Mr. Wieland," she replied, sitting up, suddenly completely awake. "Is there something I can do for you?"

"There is. Stay away from Violet Durning, Miss Prescott. Don't bother her again."

It didn't take much thought to figure out what had happened. Violet had said Wieland visited her once a month. Obviously a visit had taken place recently, and he had heard about Carrie's and Mac's visit to the woman, either from Violet herself or from one of the staff.

"We weren't bothering her," Carrie said. "We just asked her some of the questions you wouldn't answer—"

"About things which don't concern you!" he snapped, and all the irritation Carrie had felt before in his office flooded back over her.

"But they do concern me, very much," she said coldly.

"You people will do anything, won't you, to get what you want? Even pester an old woman. It's disgusting."

"We weren't pestering Violet. We simply talked; I think she even enjoyed our visit."

"Well, she won't be enjoying any more visits. I've instructed the staff about you and Mr. MacAllister. They won't let you see her again."

"Are you related to Violet Durning, Mr. Wieland? Or perhaps you're her legal guardian?"

"I pay the bills at the home...."

"As I understand it, Violet's pension pays the bills there," she cut in furiously. "Which doesn't give you the right to tell her who she can or cannot see, does it?"

"Damn you, why can't you leave this alone!" he cried. "Leave *her* alone!"

Carrie's hand tightened on the receiver and her knuckles went white; Wieland wasn't talking about Violet now.

"I don't want to hurt anyone," she said softly. "There are things I'd like to know, but I don't want a...confrontation of any sort, truly. If you know where...she is, if you would simply let her know I'm interested, perhaps she'd be willing to talk to me, or write a letter..."

"No! Stop intruding where you aren't wanted, Miss Prescott."

"You can't know whether I'm wanted or not if you won't ask Caroline..." Carrie began. But Charles Wieland had slammed down the phone.

ROBIN PUSHED through the slatted half doors leading into the kitchen. She looked at Carrie, standing at the sink, beating something in a bowl with a wooden spoon.

"What are you doing?" she asked.

"Making pancakes," Carrie replied, the spoon slapping into the batter again and again.

Robin tilted her head. "It looks more like assault and battery to me."

"GO HOME, CARRIE PRESCOTT!" Eddie ordered, throwing down his sketch pad.

Carrie looked at him in surprise. He'd asked her to pose again this afternoon—the mermaid statue wasn't coming along the way he wanted. But she'd only been sitting on the big pillow out on the deck of his houseboat for a few minutes, and now he was telling her to go home.

"What's the matter?" she asked.

"You...you're the matter," he replied. "You're sitting there as tense as an overwound spring. And I can't make a mermaid from a spring. So, go home. Or go for a long walk. Or stay and tell me what's bugging you. But forget the posing for today."

"Eddie, I...I..." Carrie sighed. "I'll see you later, Eddie."

CARRIE WALKED. She walked into town, and then she boarded the ferry. She rode the ferry across the wind-whipped Bay to the touristy bustle of Fisherman's Wharf, and rode it back again to Sausalito. But it didn't help. And then Janice Sedgewick called.

"I've talked to someone who can get your birth mother's name for you, Carrie," Janice said that evening. "But it will cost fifteen hundred dollars."

For a long moment, Carrie just stood there, clutching the phone, stunned. Janice was the illegal connection. Janice, who ran Triangle's search group, who had spent hours poring through yearbooks with her, who had even suggested other search methods she and Mac could try. Janice?

"You mean you're the connection to the underground?" she finally asked. "Does Peter know?"

"No, and I don't want him to," Janice said. "He's uncertain about the whole idea, as you probably could tell."

"And you aren't?"

"Not at all. To me, it's just another search method, one we keep as a last resort, for times when other methods won't work, or as in your case, where time is an important factor. But I don't see anything wrong with it."

"It is illegal."

Janice sniffed. "Immoral is worse than illegal—and having some lousy bureaucrats tell us what we can and cannot know about ourselves and our backgrounds is immoral. It's their fault this is necessary."

"But Janice, what if you and your...contact are caught?"

"No one cares enough to do any catching. This is your basic victimless crime."

"What about the . . . the person whose name I get? If I contact someone who's been expecting anonymity all these years, she might consider herself a victim."

"Knowing your biological heritage is your right, Carrie. Your birth mother owes you that much. She has no reason to feel victimized."

"But still, she might—"

"Look, if you don't want to go this way, it's fine with me," Janice interrupted briskly. "I don't take any money for this, you know. I only do it to help in special cases, and you and Mac did seem interested in hurrying things along."

At the mention of Mac, all sorts of thoughts skittered through Carrie's mind. Mac . . . and his article . . . and his anger. Beth and his mother, and what had happened to them. And ending the investigation.

Finding the illegal connection would finish the investigation, Carrie thought. Mac would have what he needed for his article and she would have . . . well, she would have what Charles Wieland and Irene Orrock and some clerk in Sacramento all knew, but refused to let her know—her birth mother's name. Not that she intended doing anything with the name. But she would know it. And the investigation would be over.

"We are interested, Janice," she said. "Just tell me what we have to do."

THE INTERCOM ON HER DESK buzzed twice before Libby Sandowski, concentrating on a piece written by a promising new reporter, noticed its signal. She reached out absently and flipped a switch.

"Yes?"

"Mr. Kincaid is here to see you, Ms Sandowski," a sexy male voice responded.

"Send him in, Tim," Libby said, smiling at the square box on her desk.

Ah, women's liberation, she thought, not for the first time lately. She still wasn't used to having a male secretary. She'd left the hiring of a new secretary to the retiring old one, a woman who'd also been a friend with a sense of humor. The result was Tim. Tim with the sexy voice, the male model face, the cutest tush....

Her office door slammed lightly and Mac crossed the room to flop into the "hot seat."

"He's gay," Mac said, grinning at the unusual sight of Libby sitting there dreamy-eyed.

"Doesn't bother me a bit," she tossed back. "He's got the best skills of any secretary I've ever had, and he's a lot more fun to look at. And that voice..." She sighed.

Mac laughed. "You're a dirty old woman, Libby Sandowski, and I need fifteen hundred dollars."

Libby leaned back in her swivel chair, the dreaminess in her steel-blue eyes turning to sharp curiosity. "Your trip to D.C. must have been interesting."

"D.C.?" For a moment Mac looked totally blank, then he nodded. "Oh, that—no, that wasn't anything. The guy was a low level clerk with a high level grudge against his superior and a bunch of insinuations and unsubstantiated rumors. I did make a few other contacts that might result in something later, though."

"Then why do you want to rob the paper's piggy bank?"

Mac leaned forward and fished a paper clip from the Japanese teacup on Libby's desk. "For this adoption search thing. We've got the intermediary contact and she's promised us the name of Carrie's birth mother straight from the sealed files for fifteen hundred bucks.''

"Isn't the intermediary enough? Do you really need to go through with the deal?''

"Absolutely. I want the one who's actually taking the information from the files, and the money's my only leverage for getting at least something to work on.''

Libby watched Mac toss one broken paper clip into the trash can and reach for another. She'd hoped that by now some of the crusading fire would have left him, but it obviously hadn't. Which meant that one of her ulterior motives for throwing him and Carrie Prescott together had failed. She couldn't help wondering about the other.

"And how are you and Carrie getting along?'' She'd asked the same question a few weeks back when he'd brought in his finished article on medical malpractice suits, and gotten a gruff "Fine!'' for her trouble.

Today, Mac said the same thing. "Fine.'' But this time he couldn't stop a slow grin from spreading across his face. A big, wide, self-satisfied, heart-melting grin.

Well, well, Libby thought. *Score one for the old intuition.*

"Though she's far too soft to ever make a good reporter,'' he added. "She's let all these adoptees with their sob stories get to her.''

"I've known you to get a bit soft over a sad story, Mac Kincaid. But not in this case, hmmm?''

"Of course not. Granted, some of these people have real problems. But I can't feel too sorry for them when they keep blaming everything on one small aspect of their lives, and when the only solution they will consider is intruding into someone else's life. They seem to be saying the only way they can get rid of their problems is to load them onto someone else's back."

No, the crusader was still very much at work, Libby mused. And what, she wondered, did Carrie think about the crusade?

"How does Carrie feel about all this? Especially being so close to getting her birth mother's name."

Mac coiled a paper clip into a silvery snake. "She doesn't care about that."

Libby's eyes widened. "She doesn't care? Not even a little?"

"She doesn't care about ancient history. She told me so in the very beginning."

"And how about lately, Mac?"

He launched the paper clip snake into the basket. "What do you mean?"

"I mean what has she told you lately about her feelings?"

"Lately...?" Inexplicably, the back of Mac's neck prickled and several pictures flashed through his mind. Carrie, looking like a little girl who'd lost her favorite doll as her mother admitted her "adoption" story wasn't quite true. Carrie, furiously rushing out of Charles Wieland's office. Carrie, accusing him, Mac, of trying to find villains to crucify, and not quite looking at him last night as she told him about Janice Sedgewick being the illegal connection.

None of which meant a thing, he told himself. She was probably just as tired as he was of the whole mess, of dealing with people like those at Triangle, of having to keep up the pretense of caring about the facts of her adoption. That's all it was. And soon it would all be over, all except the magic between the two of them.

"Carrie's feelings haven't changed," he told Libby. "Not a bit."

A few minutes later, Libby watched Mac Kincaid heading out the door of the office, a requisition for fifteen hundred dollars in his hand. She shook her head.

She fervently hoped she was wrong, but she suspected Mac was heading for a rude awakening somewhere along the line—with his article, with Carrie, maybe with both. He was in love with Carrie Prescott, she was sure. But love was not nearly as blind as a man on a crusade. And, she thought, looking down at the empty Japanese teacup on her desk, any time Mac Kincaid went through a whole cupful of paper clips in fifteen minutes, he had to be heading for trouble.

She flipped a switch on the intercom.

"Yes, Ms Sandowski?" Tim's delightful bass answered.

"Tim, I'm going to need more paper clips in here," she said. "Before Mac Kincaid's next visit, please," she added, and sighed.

TWO DAYS LATER Mac and Carrie met Janice Sedgewick at a small Mexican restaurant in Berkeley, ostensibly for lunch. Mac and Janice ordered margaritas and full meals. Carrie asked for a plain dinner salad and a glass of water.

Over the margaritas Mac handed Janice a manila envelope containing fifteen hundred dollars in cash, and Janice handed Carrie a small white envelope, sealed. Carrie's hand shook as she took it.

Neither Mac nor Janice noticed. They were too busy, Mac probing, Janice fending off his questions.

"Where does the information come from?" he asked, gesturing at the envelope Carrie held by one corner.

"From Carrie's adoption file," Janice replied.

"From her state file, you mean?"

"Not necessarily."

"Then it's from the county agency's file?"

"Not necessarily," she said again. "Look, Mac, it doesn't matter where it came from, does it? What matters is that you've got what you want."

"I'd like to be sure we do," he said. "I don't want to end up with the wrong name."

Janice sniffed. "You don't have to worry. I've dealt with the . . . person who had access to Carrie's file before. The information has always turned out to be reliable."

"This person must work in the Sacramento office, then."

"Not necessarily."

"Then it must be someone in . . ."

Mac went on, but Carrie wasn't listening. She was staring at the white envelope. On the front of it was her name, Ms Carrie Prescott, in small block letters written in black ink. It felt empty; there couldn't be more than a single sheet of thin paper inside. But it only took one small piece of paper to hold a name . . . her birth mother's name . . . Caroline?

Ever since agreeing to go ahead with buying the information, she'd been asking herself what she would do when she actually reached this moment. But even now, with the envelope in her hand, she wasn't sure. She was torn between wanting to know and concern that knowing might somehow endanger her relationship with Mac. She stared at the envelope and wondered how such an innocent-looking thing could feel like a time bomb about to go off.

Mac was still trying to coax information about the illegal connection from Janice, without success. But Carrie stared at her name, at the small block letters, wondering if her birth mother's name would be written in the same way, in that same black ink with its peculiar greenish cast....

"It's Irene Orrock!" she exclaimed.

Janice's small eyes widened. "How did you know...?" she began, then bit off the words abruptly. But not fast enough—and she knew it. Lifting her glass, she downed half her margarita in one gulp.

Mac smiled. "Irene Orrock...of course. Must be a nice little sideline for her—refuse adoptees any information at the official meetings and then, through groups like Triangle, find out which of them are desperate enough to pay for that same information. What a racket!"

"Janice, how could she?" Carrie cried. "And how could you deal with a woman like that? She doesn't want to help searchers at all. She just wants to use us, and you."

"But she gets the information, Carrie," Janice replied calmly. "Not all my connections are as mercenary as she is, but even if they were, it wouldn't matter. I don't have to like them to take what they have to offer. And people like Irene Orrock are sometimes the only means of getting the truth."

Carrie looked at Janice and then at the envelope she held. She remembered the way Irene Orrock had peered at her over her steel-rimmed bifocals, smirking, lecturing her. And all the time she was involved in...this. It was so coldly, horribly calculated, and suddenly Carrie felt physically ill. Blindly jamming the envelope into a pocket of her shoulder bag, she grasped Mac's arm.

"Let's go, Mac," she begged. "Please."

"Carrie, I think you're overreacting," Janice said, sniffing. "You haven't even had lunch yet."

"I'm not hungry anymore," Carrie said, standing. Mac rose, too, and took her hand, but he was looking at the other woman.

"You won't mind getting the check, will you, Janice?" he said. "After all, you have money."

"How did you know it was Irene Orrock?" Mac asked the minute they were outside the restaurant.

"The handwriting and that strange ink. I remembered it from the paper she gave me...at the meeting...." Every detail of that meeting with the social worker was indelibly engraved on her mind, she realized now.

"Well, you were great! I wasn't going anywhere at all—and now we have the whole thing, including proof of the way the illegal underground operates. We should go somewhere and celebrate! Or maybe we should save the celebration for after the article is done, what do you think? I've already roughed out a good portion of it, so it should only take me a few days to finish up, especially with what we learned today to clinch things. Damn, this is going to be the best story I've ever done!"

Carrie looked at Mac, at the triumph glittering in his brown eyes. She thought of what had happened to his mother and knew he was hoping that somehow the article he was going to write would help heal the wounds between her and Beth. He wanted to make his family whole again, and she certainly couldn't blame him for that. She even hoped it would work out just that way. But he was so...excited....

"Mac, the article is going to be . . . well, it is going to cover all the aspects of searching, isn't it?" she asked hesitantly. "Not just the illegal underground? Because there's so much more to it, so much more involved that people need to understand. . . ."

"Of course it will deal with the whole thing," he said dismissively. "That's why I've spent weeks researching, why I've done all those interviews and so on. But it was the confirmation of the illegal underground I wasn't sure we could get. I knew all along that it had to be people in the adoption groups working with people in the appropriate government offices—hell, one of the guys I interviewed in Sacramento even admitted it had to be done that way! But proving it, even for just one group like Triangle and one worker like Irene Orrock, makes all the difference. Now I have enough to really draw attention to the scam. And I owe it all to you!"

Suddenly Mac's arms went around her and he was lifting her off her feet and swinging her round and round, laughing. "I love you, Carrie Prescott!" he declared, oblivious of the other people in the restaurant parking lot.

His laughter was the perfect chord playing somewhere deep inside her, Carrie thought, looking down at his smiling face. "Oh, I love you too, Mac Kincaid," she whispered fiercely.

WALKING OUT THE DOCK toward Carrie's houseboat, Mac said he wouldn't come in with her.

"If you don't mind, I'd like to just head on home," he said. "I'm in the mood for working, and the sooner I get busy, the sooner it'll all be finished and behind us. And then you and I can go away for a few days and really celebrate. How does that sound?"

It sounded wonderful to Carrie, especially the part about putting the whole thing behind them. And she understood perfectly how it was to be inspired and desperate to get the words in your head down on paper before they flittered away on the wings of some other thought. But thinking of the end of the investigation had reminded her of something else.

"I don't mind at all," she said. "But what happens now, as far as Triangle and Peter and Janice, and all?"

"Don't worry about that," he said, hugging her close against his side. "The pretense is over. You won't have to be Ashley MacAllister's intended ever again."

"Oh! That's right, I should give you back your ring." She hadn't been thinking of their "engagement" at the moment, and the ring had begun to feel very natural on her finger. Embarrassed, she started to tug it off, but Mac stopped her.

"Leave it for now," he said. "We can take care of that when I'm done with the article, okay?"

"Well..."

"Okay," he said firmly.

Carrie might have argued if her mind hadn't been busy with something else. "Mac, what about Peter and Janice? We'll have to tell them about the article now, won't we? I mean, it only seems fair to give them some warning."

He smiled at her. "You're a real softy, you know," he said. "But don't worry, I'll let them know what's going on. All you have to do is be patient while I finish up. Your part is over. Everything will be fine."

He sounded so sure, so confident, and Carrie wanted with all her heart to believe him. She wanted her part to be over. She wanted to have nothing more to do with searching and adoption and illegal connections and the envelope in her purse—the envelope Mac seemed to have forgotten completely. She wanted to put it all behind her, and go off with Mac somewhere, anywhere.

Carrie put her arms around his waist and pressed her face against his broad chest. "I'll try to be patient, Mac," she said softly, "if you'll try to hurry."

"Deal!" he said.

"Deal," she sighed.

LATE THAT NIGHT, Carrie sat behind her desk in the sun room. Her Buster Brown shoe box was open on the desk, while in her hand she held the envelope Janice had given her. The still-sealed envelope.

"It's over," she said, thinking she really should simply tear the unopened envelope into tiny pieces and throw them off the end of the dock.

But instead, she slipped it into the shoe box and closed the lid. And then she sat there, clutching the box to her chest, for a long, long time.

CHAPTER EIGHTEEN

THE ENVELOPE STAYED in the shoe box, unopened, for the next few days, and Carrie did her best to forget about it. Which wasn't as difficult as it might have been, since missing Mac took up so much of her thoughts. She hadn't realized before how much time they'd spent together during the past few weeks, but now it seemed that no matter how busy she was, there were great big holes in each day when there was nothing to do but miss him. And hope the article was going well.

But then one evening, something happened that brought the envelope very much to mind again.

She and Robin were doing their Lamaze exercises. Robin was sitting on the floor, leaning back against the couch, with several pillows plumped behind her back. Carrie knelt beside her, one hand on her leg, giving the commands for practicing the difficult transition-stage breathing.

"Contraction begins, getting quickly stronger, stronger," she intoned, squeezing Robin's leg harder and harder to match her vocal commands.

The girl didn't seem to notice the building pressure on her leg at all. She was taking shallow, quick breaths, speeding up as the "contraction" built.

"You feel the urge to push now, Robin, but it's not time. Pant-blow."

Staring straight ahead, Robin automatically started the rhythmic pant-pant-blow breathing that would keep her from trying to push too soon.

With the next simulated contraction, though, Carrie said it was time. "You can push, now, Robin."

Immediately, the girl changed position, raising her knees, tucking her hands behind them and leaning forward. Though she didn't practice the actual pelvic pushing, she did change her breathing. Taking several deep breaths, she then held one, as she would during those real moments when she was "pushing" the baby from her body. A dewiness broke out across her forehead.

They practiced several more "expulsion" breaths before quitting. As Robin sank back against the pillows, she smiled at Carrie.

"Thanks, coach," she said. "We make a pretty good team."

Carrie smiled, too. It was strange how exhilarating just the exercises were, and how draining. She couldn't begin to imagine how the actual birth was going to be.

"It won't be too much longer now, will it?" she said. "Which reminds me, how was your checkup today?"

Beth had taken Robin to her doctor's appointment this morning, and afterward they'd gone baby-clothes shopping, according to Robin. But for some reason she hadn't mentioned, she'd left her packages at Beth's.

"Fine. I'm fine, he's fine..." she paused, patting her stomach. "All systems are go at six weeks and counting. There is just one little change of plans I should mention, though—Beth and Stewart are going to be with us for the delivery."

"Beth and Stewart? Why would they...?" Carrie stopped, realizing what Robin might...must...mean.

"Are you telling me Beth and Stewart are going to...to...?"

Robin nodded. "We decided today—they're going to adopt my baby. So I thought they'd like to be there when he's born."

Which explained the packages being left at Beth's, but not much else. "But what about Beth being so against adoption, so against a woman giving up her child?" Carrie said. "I mean, that's what her argument with her mother is all about, isn't it? Robin, I don't understand."

"We've gotten to be friends, and we've talked, a lot. I think she's finally beginning to understand what can happen, why a woman might give up her baby not because she doesn't care, but because she does. I think she's come to realize that letting go is a special kind of love, too. So..."

"Have she and Victoria made up?"

Robin frowned slightly. "Not yet, but I don't think it will be too much longer." She patted her stomach again. "This little guy is going to help."

Carrie watched Robin, seeing the gentle caring movements of the girl's hands as she touched the taut mound that contained her baby. She heard the love in Robin's voice.

"Are you sure—about giving up the baby, I mean? You know I'd be willing to help you in any way if..."

Robin was shaking her head. "I'm sure, Carrie. The time isn't right. I might wish with all my heart that things were different...." She hesitated, and her blue eyes filled with shadows. But she blinked, and the shadows melted away. "But they aren't. I'm not ready to be both mother and father to this baby, but Beth and Stewart definitely are. So it's perfect. And Beth, Stewart and I will stay friends and in touch, so I'll always know how he's doing and that everything's all right. And when the time comes, if he wants to know me, I'll be there for him—not as a mother, but as a special friend.''

"Oh, Robin!" Carrie leaned forward, hugging the girl tightly. "Both Mac and Eddie said you probably knew all along how things would work out."

"I guess I did in a way," she replied. "Even before I met Beth, I knew there was someone out there who needed my baby, who could give him the home I can't."

Carrie smiled through the tears in her eyes. "You always refer to the baby as a 'he.' Are you sure about that, too?"

"Oh, very sure," Robin declared. But as she spoke, she reached up onto the couch, pulling down her bag of crocheting. From the bag she pulled out the baby blanket she'd been working on, the blue blanket. Giggling, she held it up for Carrie to see. "Can't you tell?"

Around the blue rectangle, she'd added a lacy pink border.

They laughed and cried a little together and stayed up late discussing lofty philosophies of life and love and the future, like two girls at a slumber party, until not even cups of hot tea could keep them awake any longer. Then they hugged again, and Carrie thought she would never consider Robin a girl again. She was a woman. No girl could make the difficult choice she had with as much love and caring.

But later, when Carrie was in her bed, staring up at the misty sky framed by the skylight, she was thinking of a different woman, one who had faced the same choices as Robin. Had that woman reasoned as Robin had when she was deciding to give up her child? Had her decision been made with as much love? And was Caroline the woman's name?

Carrie never remembered consciously deciding to open the envelope. One moment she was lying in her bed, Pandora curled against her side and questions spinning round and round in her mind, the next she was in the hammock, the shoe box in her lap. She took out the envelope, stared at her name on the front, then opened it and removed the single sheet of paper. And looked at her birth mother's name.

Violet Durning had been right. It was Caroline. Caroline Warner.

And a name didn't answer any questions at all.

THE NEXT DAY was the first of July, and the afternoon was bringing the first summer storm of the season.

Carrie stood on the deck, looking out across the water. The sky was a strange yellowish gray, and dark clouds were gathering over the distant hills like an army massing for an attack. The air was still and warm, oppressively so, and when a faraway rumble of thunder sounded, the downy hair on her arms rose ticklingly.

Rubbing at her arms, Carrie turned and headed back inside. She'd felt jittery and restless all day, and it would have been easy to blame the feelings on the approaching summer storm. But she knew the weather was only part of it, a small part.

In the kitchen, she put the teakettle on. Her grandmother, Carrie remembered, had been a firm believer in hot tea as the universal panacea, regardless of the weather, a belief Carrie had come to share. But she couldn't help thinking as she stared at the telephone on the wall, that right now a call from Mac would do her a lot more good than anything else.

And the phone did ring, just as the kettle began whistling. But it wasn't Mac, it was Peter, and Carrie's stomach sank to her toes the minute he said his name.

When the investigation had started, she'd never considered the possibility of coming to like the people they would deal with so much that disentangling from the lies would become a very personal problem. But that's exactly what had happened. And to make things worse, at the moment she wasn't even sure whether Mac had told Peter the truth yet or not.

Peter's first question didn't give her a clue. "Are you all right, Carrie," he asked.

Carrie lifted the kettle from the burner. "Yes, fine. Why?"

"Well, a couple of reasons," he replied. "First, I missed you at Monday's meeting. But then Janice told me you'd gotten your birth mother's name and I figured you just needed some time to take it all in—that happens to a lot of searchers."

"Oh." She didn't know what to say. Should she blurt out the truth? But Mac had said he would handle it.

He had. "Then this morning Mac called me, and told me just how you'd gotten the name . . . and why," Peter said.

So it was an apology Carrie blurted out. "Oh, Peter, I'm so sorry about deceiving you. When I first agreed to help Mac, I didn't realize everything would get so . . . involved, but I truly never meant to hurt you or Janice or anyone."

"Hey, don't worry about my feelings," he said gently. "I understand. Janice . . . well, she's upset, but then she wasn't very up front about things, either, was she? Really, it's you I'm worried about."

"Me?"

Carrie could almost hear Peter nodding. "That's the reason I called. You see, I suspected all along that you were troubled about this whole search thing, though I couldn't figure out just why. But then this morning, when Mac told me you didn't care about the details of your past at all, that you never had and you never would..."

"He said that?"

"Right," Peter confirmed. "He was extremely definite about it. And I got to thinking of the times I'd sensed genuine concern in you and I...well, I just wanted to make sure you were okay."

Carrie couldn't believe Peter. She'd lied to him from the start, used him and Triangle, and he was worrying about her feelings.

"Thanks," she said sincerely. "I'm fine, but it means a lot knowing you care. And I am sorry, about the other."

"Don't be. It doesn't matter." He paused, as if he was considering something, then said, "I would like to know, though, if Mac was wrong, if you might want to keep on with your search. If you might want to contact your birth mother."

"No, I...I don't think so." Carrie twisted a length of phone cord round her finger.

"Is that your choice, or is it because Mac is so dead set against searching, if you don't mind my asking?"

Carrie's mouth was suddenly dry. "Did he tell you that? That he's...against searching?"

"In some very emphatic words, Carrie," Peter replied wryly. "So I want you to know that if you do decide to go on, I'd like to help. I've been through it, I know how emotionally draining it can be, especially if you don't have support from those around you. So just let me know, okay?''

Carrie's mind didn't entirely register Peter's offer; it was still whirling with his other comments. Mac had told Peter he was against searching, in some "very emphatic words." What exactly did that mean? And why would he have assured Peter she had no interest in continuing her search, now or ever? He'd never asked her about that, after all. So why had he simply assumed he knew her feelings?

Why? For the same reason he'd never even asked her about the envelope Janice had given her the other night—because he'd just *assumed* it would have no importance for her? Because he *wanted* it to have no importance for her? Just as he wanted her to have no interest in continuing to search?

"Carrie?" Peter's voice interrupted her scrambling thoughts.

"Yes, I'm sorry," she said quickly. "I'll call if I change my mind. And Peter, thanks again."

She hung up the phone and crossed to the stove to pour boiling water into the teapot. She needed the tea now, more than ever. Peter's call had raised some dreadful questions in her mind, questions she didn't even want to consider. But she couldn't avoid them.

Mac had made some broad assumptions about her and her attitude toward searching. But what if he discovered those assumptions were wrong? What would happen then? How would he react? Would he still love her if she didn't fit the mold he'd fashioned for her?

Of course he would, she told herself, stirring sugar and milk into the tea. He loved her. He'd once offered to call off the whole investigation if it was going to bother her, hadn't he?

And she'd assured him that pretending to search didn't bother her, that she'd never been interested in searching, couldn't even imagine being interested in it. And that night he'd made love to her. That night he'd said he loved her.

But what would have happened, a little voice asked, if she hadn't given him that assurance then? And what would happen now if she decided to continue her search?

Suddenly, Carrie was thinking of Doug Bannerman, ripping up her acceptance letter from the publisher. "I did it for us," he'd said. And she was wondering, if Mac had had the envelope containing her birth mother's name, would he have simply destroyed it without telling her. If challenged, would he have said, "I did it for us."

No, Carrie told herself. Mac wasn't like Doug Bannerman. Not at all.

But she took a sip of her tea, then another and another, even though it was so hot it burned her tongue. She wanted the warmth. Because in spite of the stifling heat running before the approaching storm, she was suddenly very cold.

And she wondered how close Mac was to finishing his article, because she needed very much to see it. She had the feeling she'd find the answers to her questions in what he wrote, and she needed them . . . now.

IT TOOK HER twenty-five minutes to get to Mac's house in Stinson Beach. And for every one of those twenty-five minutes, Carrie told herself she was doing a very foolish thing. If Mac had finished his article, he would have phoned her or come over. So, since he was undoubtedly not finished, she would be interrupting. To say what? I have to see your article right away because I'm cold? Because I'm worried? Because you didn't ask about my birth mother's name?

He'd think she had lost her marbles—and he would probably be right, she admitted ruefully. But in spite of increasingly strong misgivings, she kept going until she was pulling into the driveway beside Mac's beach bungalow.

She climbed the four narrow steps to the veranda running around three sides of the house. The door was on the beach side, and as she walked toward it, she was very conscious of the hollow thumps of her shoes against the wooden flooring. As she rounded the corner of the house, she paused, looking out across the beach. The breaking waves were tinted greenish brown by the strange sky, and fell sluggishly against the sand. There was virtually no breeze, and the little air that did move off the water didn't carry its usual salt-sweet smell.

And Mac's house was so quiet. As she stood in front of the door, about to knock, it struck her that there should have been some sound—the typewriter, music on the stereo, something. Unless he wasn't home. Probably he wasn't, she thought, almost hopefully. She knocked, lightly, then slightly harder. Finally, a shuffling, grumbling sound came from the other side of the closed door and a moment later it opened.

Mac was wearing only a pair of rumpled, ragged cutoffs. His hair was mussed, his eyes were red-rimmed like those of a man who'd gone far too long without sleep, and at least one and probably two days growth of dark beard shadowed his lower face. But his smile was still as warm and wonderful as ever when he saw her.

"Carrie Prescott, you must be psychic," he declared, and even his voice was raspy with exhaustion. "I finished..." He lifted his arm, but there wasn't a watch on the wrist. "What time is it?" he asked, rubbing a hand across his face. Carrie told him. "Well, that means I finished the article an hour and thirty-four minutes ago. And I started to call you, you know. I sat down on the couch and reached for the phone...and crashed. Sorry. But you must have gotten the message anyway, huh?"

"I must have," she answered quietly.

He reached out for her hand, drawing her inside. "And am I glad you did, mermaid," he said, a smoldering fire in his eyes as he looked at her. "I missed you like hell, and you look so absolutely gorgeous, I'd like to..." He started to pull her into his arms, but stopped suddenly and rubbed his hand over his face again. "And I must look like something the cat dragged *out*!" he said, wrinkling his nose. "I think I'd better clean up a bit before we continue this conversation, okay?"

Carrie nodded, unwilling to trust her voice.

"Make yourself at home," he called out, heading for the bedroom and bathroom at the back of the house. "And the article's on the desk, if you want to look at it—but no fair criticizing my typing. I know I'm the world's worst."

A few moments later the shower came on, and Carrie moved slowly to the teakwood desk in one corner of the room.

Mac was right about his typing, she discovered immediately as she leaned against the desk, reading. His typewriter keys still needed cleaning, "there" was still one big smudge, and he had more words with typos than without. But it wasn't the typing that made the article so difficult to read—it was the content.

It was worse, far worse, than Carrie had ever imagined it could be. It was an extensive piece. As Mac had it laid out, there would be a main article and several side bars telling individual stories of searchers and people who'd been found. But both the main story and the individual ones were so slanted that Carrie thought they should have slipped right off the paper they were typed on. Slanted and absolutely unfair.

Mac had presented only the negative side of searching, only the most extreme cases, only the most fanatical opinions. There was nothing in his article showing the real problems inherent in a system based on secrecy. There weren't any of the statistics on adoptees' higher rates of emotional and psychological problems. There wasn't even a hint of the real need some of them felt to know the truth.

And worse even than the slant was the article's tone. It was by turns biting, sarcastic and downright cruel. Using selective facts, stories and quotes, Mac had painted a very vivid picture of searchers as self-pitying neurotics, engaging in sneaky illegal enterprises just to further their own selfish ends, and not caring that they were hurting many other people in the process. He'd demolished the whole concept of searching so very deftly, and Carrie couldn't believe the award-winning, unbiased Mac Kincaid—the Mac she loved—could have written anything so horribly unfair.

And he'd taken some of his nastiest swipes at the adoption search and support groups, like Triangle. They served no function, he indicated, but to cater to the irrational whims of searchers, formulate excuses for the immoral actions of their members and promote unethical search methods under the guise of attaining "rights."

Although he hadn't actually used names when describing their experience with the "illegal underground," he had managed to get both Janice's and Peter's names into the text, in very unflattering ways. After describing several heartbreaking results of illegal searches, including a probable suicide, he quoted "two leaders of the local support group, Triangle. When asked their opinions of the morality and ethics of using illegal methods to gain access to sealed government files, both Janice Sedgewick and Peter Millheiser would respond only with 'no comments.' Similarly," he went on, "Irene Orrock, a social worker with one county adoption agency, who does have access to such files, refused to even speak to this reporter when she learned the subject of my investigation."

He hadn't come right out and accused them of anything at all, yet he'd tried and convicted them of immoral and illegal acts with two sentences. And while Carrie couldn't help feeling that Irene Orrock deserved anything she got, she couldn't bear reading what he'd done to Janice . . . and Peter.

Carrie hadn't heard the shower go off, but suddenly Mac was coming out of the bedroom dressed in fresh corduroy shorts and a snug maroon T-shirt. He was shaved, his hair was neatly combed and still damp from the shower, and he was more devastatingly handsome than Carrie had ever seen him look before. And she loved him, with all her heart and soul. But at the moment, with the sheets of his article clenched in her hand and its words ringing in her brain, she didn't like him at all.

Mac, though, seemed totally oblivious to the raging emotions she was sure must show on her face. He crossed the room, flicked a finger at the pages she held and grinned.

"Well, what do you think?"

"I think," she began softly, "that you can't possibly publish this."

He laughed, but it wasn't his usual warm laughter; it was hesitant and forced, and there was suddenly a wariness in his eyes. "Hey, I warned you my typing was lousy...."

"Mac, it's got nothing to do with your typing," she said, cutting him off. "And I think you know it."

He snatched the papers from her hand, his grin hardening into a scowl. "All I know is that this is the best work I've done in a long time," he declared.

"The best...?" Carrie couldn't believe it—he actually sounded proud. "Mac, you couldn't pass a first-year journalism class with that biased piece of muckraking. It's all insinuations, skewered facts and distortions."

"I don't distort facts or make insinuations!"

"You don't? Then what would you call these 'no comments' you attributed to Janice and Peter?"

"That's what I got when I called them, told them about the article, and asked for a quote."

"Yes, I heard about your call to Peter," she said. "He called me this morning to—"

"Oh, he called you, did he?" Mac interrupted, rolling the sheets of paper he held into a tight tube. "How nice of him."

Anger spurted through Carrie. "No, Mac, it wasn't nice at all," she snapped. "It was damned embarrassing to hear you'd been telling him how I felt and what I was and was not going to do.''

Mac's scowl changed to a puzzled frown. "What are you talking about?''

"You told Peter I wasn't interested in searching, that I didn't care about it at all.''

"So? He asked and I told him—what's wrong with that?''

"What's wrong is that you never asked me how I felt.''

"Of course I did. We talked about it in the very beginning.''

"In the beginning, yes. But not lately. And certainly not after Janice handed me the name of my birth mother.''

"Oh, that . . .'' He started to dismiss it, then his eyes narrowed. "Carrie, don't tell me you opened that envelope!''

She smiled, a sad little smile. "You never even considered that I might, did you? You were too wrapped up in your vendetta to notice anything so inconsequential as that.''

Mac whacked the tube of rolled papers down onto the desktop. "Damn it all, Carrie, what are we arguing about here? My article or my insensitivity?''

Carrie looked at the sheaf of papers he'd thrown onto the desk. They were slowly uncurling now, like something alive. "They're pretty much one and the same, aren't they? Your insensitivity is what made the article so wrong.''

"There's nothing wrong with that article!''

"There's plenty wrong with making every person interested in searching look like another Priscilla.''

Mac's eyes flashed angrily. "Who the hell told you about Priscilla?"

"Beth told Robin who told me...so I can understand why you're concerned about the whole concept of search," she said, more gently. "And I agree totally with some of the points you made about the necessity for safeguards and restraint. But, Mac, you ignored the real problems adoptees face, the real need some of them feel and the rational approach a lot of them take to searching. You twisted things to make them all look just as insensitive and selfish as Priscilla...."

"It didn't take any twisting to make them look that way."

"Mac, don't you care that this article will hurt a lot of innocent people?"

"This article will stop innocent people from being hurt by a bunch of fanatics so hung up on the past that they don't care what they do or whose lives they destroy."

"But not every searcher is a fanatic. It isn't right to condemn them all...."

"They're all part of the same thing, and it needs condemning," he stated flatly.

Goose bumps raced up and down Carrie's arms and she moved away from the desk, away from Mac. Turning her back to him, she asked, "Would you still feel that way if I was one of them?"

"Oh, Carrie, I'm too tired to play games," he snorted.

"Answer me, Mac. What if I wanted to search? Would you condemn me, too?"

"How can I answer an absurd question like that? You're not like them. You don't need some story from the past to define yourself. That's why I love you so much."

Carrie stared out the window, at the swampish-colored waves and darkening sky. Mac had said he loved her, but he was almost shouting, and it didn't sound very much like love.

"Maybe that's the only reason you fell in love with me in the first place," she said softly. "Because I seemed like the opposite of the woman who hurt your mother so badly. Because I wasn't interested in searching and so I filled the image you wanted."

Suddenly he was behind her, his breath warm against her neck. "Don't be ridiculous, mermaid. I fell in love with everything about you, not because you fit some anti-Priscilla model." His hands were sliding up and down her arms, tentatively, little questioning touches. And Carrie wanted more than anything to answer by relaxing back against him, by letting herself be enveloped in the strength and security of his caresses. But it wouldn't solve a thing.

"Then it wouldn't make any difference if I decided to continue my search," she said, "if I decided I wanted to use the name Janice got for me to find my birth mother, would it?"

"You wouldn't!" His hands closed tightly around the softness of her upper arms and he turned her around to face him. He stared disbelievingly into her eyes. "Carrie, you wouldn't dare! You couldn't do that to..."

"To you, Mac?" He had cut himself off, but Carrie knew what he'd been about to say. She smiled, a brittle angry smile. "No, I wouldn't do it *to you*," she said, "but I might do it *for me*. If Charles Wieland and Irene Orrock and some blasted clerk in Sacramento can all know the details of my past, then I should be able to know them, too, if I really want to. So I might decide to go on with my search, and if I do, no one is going to tell me I don't dare. And that includes you, Mac Kincaid!''

Slowly, very slowly, Mac opened his hands, taking them from her arms and holding them out from his body as if they might be contaminated. His brown eyes were hard and cold as he looked at her. "Well then," he said, each word distinct and arrow-tipped, "I guess we're even. Because I'm not changing my mind about my article, either. It's staying exactly the way I wrote it—every goddamned word!''

The army of clouds had been advancing across the sky, and all at once the room was plunged into gray darkness. Carrie tried to take a deep breath, but the air felt not just oppressive, but fetid, nearly suffocating, now. She looked at Mac, at the rigidity of his expression, at the coldness in his eyes, then turned and started for the door.

But as she came even with the desk again, she paused. Stretching out her hand, she yanked Mac's ring from her finger and tossed it onto the desk. It landed on the half-curled pages of his article, making a small dead sound.

"We're through pretending, aren't we, Mac?" she murmured, just as the storm broke and big fat ploppy drops began splashing against the roof, the windows, the sand and the sea. Carrie walked out into the rain.

CHAPTER NINETEEN

DAMN HIM!

Carrie twisted the key in the ignition and threw the car into reverse, carefully not looking back at the beach house. She didn't want to know if he had come out onto the veranda, if he was watching her drive away or not.

Damn Mac Kincaid!

The wheels spun on the damp gravel drive, then caught with a squeal and a jerk. Carrie flicked on the windshield wipers, backed up, then shifted into first. Then second, and third. At the corner of Mac's street she couldn't help herself—she glanced into the rearview mirror. But there was nothing to see but rain, the house and a shadow at one window that might or might not have been that of a man.

Damn him, damn his article, damn him for sounding more like Charles Wieland or Doug Bannerman than the man she'd thought she loved. Damn his stubborn blindness, damn his "you wouldn't dares"... damn him for making her love him and then not loving her enough. *Damn!*

The phone booth loomed up out of the silver rain like some netherworld creature she'd conjured with her profanities, and she pulled up in front of it as if in a trance. She dropped a coin into the slot and dialed. A mechanical voice demanded more money, and then Peter Millheiser was saying a pleasant hello.

"Peter," she said quickly, before she could change her mind, "will you help me find Caroline Warner?"

SHE DROVE a few more miles before the hot stinging tears began to well in her eyes. She pulled into a turn-off just as the world became one big blur. Crossing her arms over the steering wheel, she rested her forehead against her wrist, and let the tears come. Because she couldn't stop them. Because it hurt. It hurt more than Doug, more than anything. . . .

And the hot tears spawned huge heaving sobs that seemed to rip from a place somewhere deep inside her that she'd never even known was there, each one chipping a tiny sliver from her heart until it lay in a thousand sharp and tiny pieces. She sobbed, and sobbed, until she started to wonder if she would ever be able to stop.

But eventually there weren't any tears left to shed, there was nothing left but the ache of her splintered heart. Carrie turned her head, pressing one wet cheek against her wrist, and realized the windshield wipers were still going. Shh-shh-ish, shh-shh-ish, back and forth, pulling fat raindrops into streaks across the glass and whispering like a mother comforting her child after a bad dream.

Only this wasn't a dream, she thought weakly, spent from the force of her tears. It wasn't a dream, and she wouldn't wake up tomorrow to apologies and early-morning lovemaking. Mac wouldn't give in this time, and she couldn't. This time there would be no yellow roses.

"LIBBY, YOU CAN'T PRINT Mac's article," Carrie said.

Libby Sandowski leaned back in her chair, studying

the young woman sitting across from her. Normally she did not take at all kindly to anyone trying to tell her what she could and could not print. But this case was a bit out of the norm.

Mac Kincaid had been in late yesterday, tossing his finished piece on her desk with all the defiant bravado of the school-yard bully drawing a line in the dirt with the toe of his tennis shoe and challenging anyone to dare cross it. He hadn't stayed while she read it as he usually did; he'd simply asked how soon she could get it into the paper, looked extremely dissatisfied with her noncommittal answer, and left. A whole teacup full of shiny new paper clips, and he hadn't stayed long enough to maul a single one!

This morning Carrie had called, asking for an appointment. And now she was here, looking like something a vampire had feasted on all night, and telling Libby she couldn't print Mac's article at all.

"Why can't I?" Libby asked curiously.

"Has Mac brought it in yet? Have you read it?"

"Yes, to both."

"Then you must know it's all wrong."

"You mean Mac got his facts wrong?"

"Not the facts, just his interpretation of them. He's taken everything we heard and retold it with a sneer. Libby, you knew about what happened to his mother, didn't you? Surely you suspected he wouldn't be able to do this article fairly?"

"I suspected," she admitted. "Which was one reason I pushed him into contacting you—hoping you could give him the balance he needed." Libby didn't catch her slip until too late, but it didn't matter. Carrie was too preoccupied to notice the "one reason," and wonder what others there might be.

"Well, it didn't work out that way," she said, the words sharp and bitter, filled with anger and agony. "His article is totally unfair. He refused to listen to anything we heard that contradicted his preconceived ideas. You simply can't print what he's written."

Libby sighed, wondering exactly what had happened between Mac and Carrie, and how deep the wounds were. But that couldn't be her concern at the moment.

"I can, Carrie, and I have to," she said firmly. "I don't censor Mac. As long as he has the proof to back up any accusations he makes, as long as he's given anyone unflatteringly named in his article a chance to explain, respond or tell us to go to hell, and as long as he doesn't screw up the facts, his work goes into print just as he writes it."

"But Libby, his reputation for fairness, for seeing all sides of controversial issues, will go right down the drain. His credibility..."

"May be hurt, for a while at least. But Mac will survive. He's too good a reporter not to."

"And what about the adoption groups? His article presents them in a terrible light and it will hurt some very nice people who don't deserve it. Can you just let that happen?"

Libby made a church and steeple of her hands, leaning her chin thoughtfully on the point made by her index fingers. "I hope I don't have to," she said. "What we need is an opposing viewpoint article, one that shows the other side, the side Mac ignored. It would balance Mac's article... and teach him a thing or two as well, I think." She looked pointedly at Carrie.

"Me?" she gasped, her green eyes wide. "You want me to write an article contradicting Mac?"

"Only if you feel some of what he's written is wrong."

"You know I do, but..." Carrie could only think of Mac's reaction if he saw her opinion printed in direct opposition to his, presenting the point of view he couldn't—wouldn't—understand. He would be furious, he would feel betrayed. He would never forgive her.

All of which—furious, betrayed and unforgiving—he felt already, she realized suddenly. So writing the article wouldn't make any difference at all, except to the people in the adoption groups—some very nice people, like Peter.

"All right, Libby," she said softly, more miserable than she'd ever been before in her life. "I'll do it."

CARRIE VICIOUSLY CRUMPLED another piece of paper and tossed it across the sun room. Pandora didn't even bother to watch where it landed.

Each day for the past week, Carrie had worked on the article for Libby. And each day the sun room floor had ended up strewn with paper balls, as if some dreadful snowstorm belonging in a land of giants kept mistakenly hitting her houseboat instead. Pandora had lost interest in the recurring "storm" the second day.

Carrie hadn't expected writing the article to be so difficult. She'd planned to simply take each of the points Mac had made in his article, one by unfair one, and refute them. Simple.

Only it hadn't turned out that way. After asking permission, she wrote the stories and experiences of people like Peter, Allyce and her twin sister, and several others at Triangle, contrasting them with the totally negative stories Mac had presented. She went into great detail trying to explain the need some adoptees felt to know the truth of their pasts, a need Mac had dismissed, a need she believed was often very real. She showed how Triangle, with its attention to the three sides of the adoption triangle, was trying to promote understanding and make improvements in the adoption experience for everyone concerned, not just encourage searching.

She presented contrasting facts, contrasting stories. She had an argument for each of Mac's most unfair points. But her story still wasn't working. It argued, but it didn't say anything of its own. She wasn't getting across all the feelings and emotions and needs involved that made adoption search such a complicated issue. And she couldn't keep Libby waiting much longer; she had to give her something soon.

But worst of all, working on the article this way was like living through her argument with Mac all over again every day. And each time hurt just as much as the first.

The knock on the front door a short while later was a welcome reprieve. Calling to Robin that she would get it, Carrie scrambled out of the hammock and crossed the paper-littered floor, kicking white balls out of her path.

It was Peter, and his grin was a toothy half moon in his chestnut-colored beard as he presented her with a sheet of paper. On the paper was written what looked like an airline flight number, date and time.

"Peter, what is this?" Carrie asked, her brows lifting curiously.

"That, Carrie Ann Prescott, is your flight reservation to San Diego for this coming Friday morning."

"And why would 1...?" she began, then stopped uncertainly.

Peter nodded, handing her a second piece of paper. "Here is Caroline Warner's married name—Caroline Heston—and her current address in San Diego."

Carrie's knees turned to jelly, and she quickly moved to the couch and sank down. "How did you find out?"

"I told you this part would be easy, didn't I, when you called the other day?" He sat beside her.

Had he, she wondered. She didn't remember much of that phone booth call.

"Marriage records are public in California," he went on. "Anyone can go to the State Department of Health, Vital Statistics Section, give them a name and a small fee, and request a copy of the records of any marriages made by that person during a ten-year period. The fee's only slightly higher to cover a twenty-year period."

"Anyone can do that? You mean you don't have to be a relative, or anything?"

Peter nodded, and Carrie thought: how strange. Something as personal as marriage records were open not just to the parties involved, but to anyone, yet her past was supposed to be sealed away from her forever. How very strange.

"So it wasn't difficult to learn that Caroline Warner married in San Diego county three years after your birth. Fortunately, she and her husband stayed in the same area all these years. They're in the San Diego phone directory."

"I can't believe it was so easy," she said, stunned.

"This is the computer age, Carrie. You can find anyone who isn't deliberately hiding, once you have a name. So Friday, if you'd like, we can fly down...."

"We?"

A hint of red stained his cheeks above his beard. "Only if you'd like company, of course, and if you don't mind waiting a couple of days. I can't get away before then. If you'd rather go sooner, or take someone else with you, it's fine, Carrie. But I do suggest you have someone along. That first contact can be emotionally harrowing."

Carrie stared at Peter, not believing it was all happening this way, so quickly, so abruptly, without any real effort on her part.

"Or if you're having second thoughts, it's all right," he continued. "I would understand. Lots of searchers need to back off a bit at certain points, especially if they're getting a lot of...static from people they care about."

Carrie hadn't actually explained her relationship with Mac, or its end, but Peter had obviously been able to put two and two together to get at least three and a half. And his comment had reminded Carrie of Mac telling her she "wouldn't dare" continue her search. Yes, she supposed she had got some "static" from someone she cared about, she thought, the hurt stabbing red hot through her all over again.

She shook her head once more, her tightening fingers making wrinkles in the papers she held. Robin was still four weeks from her due date and feeling fine, so there shouldn't be a problem with Carrie being away for a day. And maybe really finishing her search, once and for all, would give her the perspective she needed to do the article the way it should be done. Maybe this was exactly what she needed.

"No, Peter," she said firmly. "Friday will be just fine."

WEDNESDAY NIGHT Carrie was in her room, tucked in among the pillows in the window seat, struggling again with the article—and far too frequently letting her attention drift to the two small sheets of paper she'd paper-clipped to the front of the folder containing her article notes. She should really put them away somewhere, she thought. Her birth mother's married name and current address and her flight reservation weren't making concentrating on her work any easier.

She didn't do it, though, just as she hadn't phoned Peter any of the several times in the past two days when she'd decided to cancel the trip. She felt so torn inside, partly excited, partly apprehensive, partly just plain uncertain. More than once she'd thought she should cancel the flight, put away the name and address and forget about the whole thing. But each time she had reached for the phone to call Peter and tell him her decision, she would remember Mac's taunting words, and Charles Wieland's and Irene Orrock's. . . .

Carrie was a million miles away—or at least several hundred—and absently running a finger over the paper holding her birth mother's name, as if the contact might tell her something important, when Robin appeared suddenly beside her.

"Carrie?" the girl said softly, and Carrie jumped, her breath tripping on the startled thump of her heart.

"Oh, Robin! I didn't hear you come in." She looked at Robin and smiled.

The girl was wearing a long, full, Victorian-style nightgown of soft white linen edged with blue ribbon and lace. Her fair hair was loose and fell to her hips like golden silk. Her cheeks were rosy, her blue eyes bright, her lips curved in a slight, knowing smile. She looked like something out of a fairy tale, a princess carrying the future heir to the kingdom.

But as Carrie watched, Robin's whole expression changed and she turned so that she was leaning against the edge of the window seat. Her body seemed to loosen and relax, she stared straight ahead, her hands came up, making small slow circles on the mound of her stomach, and she was breathing rhythmically—two slow, deep breaths, then several shorter quicker breaths, then a flurry of very quick, very shallow little breaths.

It was all Carrie could do to remain where she was, waiting quietly so as not to disturb Robin until the contraction was over, until Robin's eyes focused again and she smiled.

"How far apart?" she asked then. "How strong?"

"It's time," Robin said simply. "Call Beth and Stewart, please. And the doctor."

Carrie's hands were clumsy as she flipped through her address book and dialed Beth's number. She knew she shouldn't be nervous. Clearly Robin wasn't, and their Lamaze training was supposed to have assuaged the typical fears and confusion. But the baby was nearly four weeks early and Robin was a lot further along in her labor than Carrie had expected her to be when they left for the hospital. Just because she and Robin had studied every stage of the birthing process from beginning to the actual birth itself didn't mean she felt ready to play obstetrician, she thought.

She listened to the ringing of the phone and whispered, "Hurry up, Beth, Stewart . . . please!"

But it wasn't Beth or Stewart who answered. It was Mac.

"Hello?" His voice was as sweetly rich and sexily husky as Carrie remembered, and it seemed like years, and only minutes, since she'd heard it last.

Though when she'd heard it last, it had been sharp with anger and coldness, and it wasn't now. Now it was warm and filled with the hint of a smile, as if he'd been laughing just before picking up the phone. Carrie's heart started doing wild and crazy somersaults inside her breast, and she couldn't think of a thing to say.

"Hello?" Mac said again, and then muttered something rude that was obviously preparatory to putting down the phone. Carrie forced out words.

"Ma...Mac, it's Carrie. Robin's in labor and ready to go to the hospital. She wanted Beth and Stewart to know, and asked me to call and...."

"They'll meet you there," he abruptly interrupted her babbling, the trace of a smile gone from his voice. And Carrie fully expected to next hear the connection being sharply broken. But after a long silent moment, Mac spoke again.

"Is Robin all right?" he asked gently. Another pause, then, "Are you?"

"We're fine," she replied, her throat constricted. "But tell Beth and Stewart they shouldn't waste any time."

She put the receiver down, gently, too. And licked away a salty tear that had trickled down to catch at one corner of her mouth.

THE BABY WAS BORN, crying lustily, two hours and ten minutes after they arrived at the hospital.

"A bouncing baby boy!" the doctor announced after Robin held her breath and pushed one last time, and the baby's body slipped from hers. "Even if he did decide to rush his birthday a bit."

A collective sigh came from Beth, Stewart and Carrie. Robin turned her flushed, sweat-soaked face to Carrie and said, "I guess I didn't need the pink border after all."

For a few minutes, bits of post-delivery business occupied the doctor, the nurses, Robin and the baby. But then a tiny bundle in a thin blue blanket was being brought over to the bed and placed in Robin's arms.

She carefully took the bundle and eased the blanket back from the tiny wrinkled face, from the downy golden hair. She stared down at him, and stroked his pink cheek with one fingertip. Then she raised her head, looking up at Beth and Stewart. Slowly, she held the baby out toward Beth.

"Here's your child, Beth Abramson," she said, very softly. "I hope you and Stewart wanted a boy."

Beth was crying, tears spilling silently from her hazel eyes. She moved to the bed, slowly, hesitantly, and her hands trembled as she took the blue-wrapped bundle from Robin. Much as Robin had done, she eased back the covering and stared down at the baby, and in spite of her tears, she was smiling joyously. Stewart moved up beside her, putting an arm around her, looking down. And then at Robin.

"He's absolutely gorgeous," he said, after clearing his throat a time or two.

"Gorgeous," Beth echoed, her voice trembling. "But Robin, are you sure about...this? Much as we want him, we don't want you to be unhappy, to ever regret your decision."

Robin shook her head. "In one way I'll always regret that things had to be this way," she admitted honestly. "But I won't ever be unhappy that he's going to be your son. I know you'll love him as much as I do, I know he'll be happy with you and Stewart. I know it's working out just right, for all of us." And she smiled that fey smile of hers.

But when the baby had been taken to the nursery and Beth and Stewart had gone to tell Mac everything was fine and wonderful, Robin turned to Carrie, a plea in her shadowed eyes. Understanding, Carrie sat down beside her on the bed and put her arms around the girl. And Robin fell heavily against Carrie as if her own bones could no longer support her. Her head resting on Carrie's shoulder, she began sobbing.

"It's right...and perfect...and I'm so very...glad it's all working out so well," she murmured between sniffling sobs. "But, oh God, Carrie, it hurts. It hurts so...very...very much."

Carrie stayed with Robin until the girl fell wearily asleep. Then she gathered her things, ready to head home.

Only she didn't feel like going home. She knew she should—it was nearly four in the morning, and being a birth coach, though obviously nothing compared to actually giving birth, had been as draining and exhausting an experience as she'd expected. But it had also been incredibly exciting, watching a new life come into the world, and into the lives of Beth and Stewart. She was so happy for them...and so deeply sad for Robin...and she felt like she'd been bouncing around inside a cyclone for hours—exceedingly tired, but emotionally wired.

She was far too keyed up to sleep, she knew, and just as certainly knew she was also far too jittery to be awake, and alone. What she was undoubtedly facing, she thought, was the very unappealing choice between tossing and turning in bed and restlessly pacing the floor for the next few hours.

Resigning herself to her fate with a sigh, she decided to stop in the waiting room and get a cup of machine coffee. It would taste dreadful, but at least it would be hot.

But she didn't get her coffee right away. Because when she entered the small room, Mac Kincaid was there, slouched down in an upholstered chair, sound asleep.

Carrie stood in the doorway, staring at him, bells going off in her ears like the ringing of an angry alarm clock. She hadn't known Mac had come with Beth and Stewart. She and Robin had already been in the birth room when they had first arrived, and afterward, when they'd said they were going to tell Mac about the baby, she'd assumed they meant by telephone.

But he was there, and she couldn't resist looking at him as he slept. His head was thrown back, resting on the pillowed chair back, exposing the vulnerable line of his throat, the pulse beating slowly at its base. The lashes of his closed eyes brushed against the tops of his cheeks, fluttering just slightly, as if he might be dreaming. Was it a good dream, she wondered.

His mouth was slightly open, just enough to give a hint of the soft, moist pinkness inside, and his lower face was shadowed by an early-morning beard. Carrie bit her lip, suddenly tasting Mac's mouth, feeling its moist heat combined with the tantalizing sandpaper of his jaw rasping across her chin, her breasts, her thighs.

A hot quivering started in the center of her body, and Carrie told herself she should turn around and leave, should end this torture instantly. But she didn't move, couldn't move. She shifted her gaze to his hands, resting in his lap, palms up, the fingers just slightly curled—but that was no better. Images of those hands touching her, arousing her, holding her as their bodies merged together, thundered through her mind, and she moaned softly.

Mac sat up suddenly, rubbed briefly at his eyes like a little boy startled awake, then looked up.

"Hi," he said, smiling easily, warmly, as if truly happy to see her standing there.

And then he remembered. She could see him remembering as the smile faded and the warmth disappeared. He pushed himself to his feet.

And they stood there looking at each other, not saying anything, not knowing what to say, but unable to break the electrified connection. The air between them hummed, and a smoldering heat seemed to roll across the space between them.

"Are...Beth and Stewart still here?" Carrie asked finally, awkwardly.

Mac shook his head. "No, they left. But Beth asked me to stay and thank you for all you've done for her and Robin," he said evenly, as if he was reciting a little speech Beth had taught him. "And to tell you she's on her way to my parents' house—to apologize to my mother for not understanding sooner."

"Oh, Mac, that's marvelous," Carrie cried happily, unconsciously taking a quick little step toward him. A step that would have led to her throwing herself into his arms—if things had been different.

Mac saw the movement, saw her abruptly catch herself, draw back and turn away from him. And it was like she'd just stuck a knife into him, and twisted it.

She moved to the coffee machine, digging in her purse for change—which she didn't seem to be finding. "Did you see the baby?" she asked.

"Yes." Yes, he'd looked at the baby. And pictured a similar night, a similar trip to the hospital, with Carrie in labor and him at her side as she gave birth to their child. The picture had grown too vivid, and he'd had to leave the nursery area. He'd come back here, flopped into the chair and fallen asleep, only to be haunted by the same image in a dream. But he couldn't tell Carrie that.

"Funny how newborns look like miniature little old men, isn't it?" he said. "Cute, but ancient, and so wise...like they know all the secrets of life and love—" He broke off, dropping a coin into the machine for her. She whispered a thank you and pushed a button without looking up.

Mac stood there, breathing in the lovely scent of her. He'd missed that scent. Lord, he'd missed everything about her!

Deliberately, he shifted his thoughts. "Beth told me what a wonderful birth it was. Is Robin all right?"

"She will be," Carrie replied, leaving a lot unsaid. "But the doctor would like her to stay at least twenty-four hours."

The machine had splashed pale brown coffee into a Styrofoam cup. Carrie lifted it from the little cubbyhole and took a sip. Lukewarm.

Mac watched her lips part over the white cup rim. "Won't that keep you awake?" he asked.

"I decided I wouldn't be able to sleep anyway, not after all the...excitement." Her shoulders twitched slightly. "But it is getting late...."

"Right. Guess I'd better find a phone and call a cab...."

"A cab?" She looked at him then. "Didn't you drive over?"

"With Beth and Stewart. But they took the car to go to my parents'."

"Oh, well, there's no need for you to try to get a cab at this hour, Mac," she said quickly. "I can drop you at Beth's."

"No, I wouldn't want to put you out."

"It's nearly on the way."

"Well, if you're sure you don't mind."

She shook her head, but her face was pale. "I don't mind."

CHAPTER TWENTY

CARRIE SHIFTED THE CAR into reverse, and her knuckles brushed against Mac's thigh.

"Sorry," they muttered, in unison. Mac quickly moved his leg.

"MIND SOME MUSIC?" he asked a few minutes later.

"Not at all," she answered. They both reached for the radio knob, Mac's hand came down warmly over hers, they both jerked back. And the radio stayed off.

STOPPED AT A RED LIGHT, with nothing to occupy her attention but the low-voltage electricity that seemed to be emanating in hot waves from Mac, Carrie turned her head, irresistibly drawn. And found him watching her, his eyes glittering with a longing she'd never thought she would see again.

She faced quickly forward again and shifted gears, even though the light was still uncooperatively red.

CARRIE EDGED THE CAR up to the curb in front of Beth's and Stewart's condo and looked at Mac again. He was staring forward this time, not making a move to get out, not saying anything. But he was running one finger along the silver edging strip on the dashboard. She watched him, watched his finger stroke slowly back and forth, back and forth, three times.

"I don't want to be alone tonight, Mac," she said softly.

"Neither do I, Carrie," he said fiercely. "Neither do I."

THEY WERE GREEDY, the first time. The week apart, the last tension-ridden half hour, had sparked an eternity's worth of hunger in them. At the houseboat they didn't turn on a light, didn't speak, couldn't wait even for the bedroom. As Mac kicked the front door shut he was already reaching for Carrie, she was already moving into the circle of his arms.

Their bodies pressed together even before their mouths met hotly, feverishly. There was no hesitation, no slow wooing, only a deep delicious need that had to be quenched. Hands tore impatiently at clothing, grasped eager burning flesh.

Mac's fingers slid urgently over Carrie's body, kneading, caressing. He felt the already bead-hard tips of her breasts tighten yet more at his touch. He felt the ripple of her stomach as his hands moved lower, massaging, calling up a moan from deep inside her. He felt the invitation of her warm moistness as she writhed against the shelf of his palm, against the silken invasion of his fingers.

Carrie's mouth moved on Mac's shoulder, tasting saltiness, tasting him. And her hands moved on his body, paralleling the path his were taking on hers. Down over the hard muscles of his chest, tickling through soft, fine hairs, across flat nipples. Splaying wide, then sliding over hipbones, down along the taut muscles of his legs as far as she could reach, before moving inward and starting upward again, slowly,

slowly, until she was cupping him, stroking him, feeling the undeniable strength of his desire.

Mac groaned, reaching a hand to cover hers, to still her too-intense touch.

"Carrie, I won't be able to wait," he murmured as their mouths came together again.

But Carrie's hand wouldn't be still. And she was stretching up onto her toes, molding her hips against his, urging him to her, into her.

"Don't wait, Mac," she whispered. "Please don't wait."

THE SECOND TIME was different. The desperate hunger was assuaged; a compelling craving remained.

After their first urgent coming together, Mac lifted Carrie into his arms.

"Where to, mermaid?" he asked, his voice a warm blanket wrapping around her.

Smiling into the hollow of his shoulder, Carrie considered the possibilities. "The shower, please," she replied.

Mac pulled the shower curtain across the tub, enclosing them in a cozy cocoon. The clear plastic curtain was printed with a brilliant rainbow and it splashed their bodies with jeweled ribbons, ruby and emerald, sapphire and amethyst. Carrie turned on the water, and its warmth fizzed over them, glazing skin and hair with a silverish sheen. Misty steam began to fill the room, and they weren't in a hurry now.

Mac took the soap that smelled faintly of wildflowers and misty woods, and rubbed it between his palms. "Turn around," he told Carrie. "I'll do your back."

She did, and his soapy hands glided slickly, slowly, down the length of her spine, over the soft, sensitive curves of her bottom, across the tops of her thighs.

"Lovely," she murmured, her head falling forward. He kissed the nape of her neck, his nose nuzzling into damp strands of cinnamon hair, as he soaped his hands again. But this time his arms circled her, pulling her back into the cradle of his thighs, while his hands slid round to her front. Soap-silkened fingertips tickled across her stomach, then skimmed upward in the hollow of her diaphragm. His palms cupped the wet fullness of her breasts, his thumbs dancing erotic little circles around their swollen peaks.

A fine heat spread through Carrie, splashing sparks across her senses. She tried to turn around, to touch Mac's body as he was touching hers, but his arms tightened. Holding her in his embrace, he shifted his weight and eased one leg wetly, warmly, between hers.

A seizure of longing stabbed through her and she moaned with the intensity of it. She could feel Mac's smile against the soft skin of her neck, and she raised her arms, reaching back over her shoulders to thread her fingers through his hair, moist with drops of spray.

"Mac, please..." she said, trying to turn again, filled with the need to run her hands over his body, to kiss him. A sensuous chuckle rippled through him.

He turned her to face him then, but when she would have reached for him, he grasped her hands, twining their fingers together. Holding their paired hands out away from her body, he bent slowly.

Carrie's fingers clenched in the soft net of Mac's hands as his mouth closed possessively first over one breast, then the other, his lips hotly caressing, his tongue recreating the dance his fingertips had done before.

"I can taste your heartbeat," he said against her sleek skin, and violent eddies of pleasure swirled through her.

And then he was sinking all the way down to his knees, his mouth following a rivulet of water down across the taut flatness of her stomach.

"Mac..." she cried, her knees threatening to buckle as even her bones seemed to melt with a need beyond anything she'd ever felt before.

But he caught her, releasing her hands to cup her bottom, to lift and hold her against his ravening mouth. Until she writhed in the seductive flame of his embrace. Until her hands grasping his shoulders tightened, her nails biting into his flesh. Until she cried out again.

"Mac, please, oh please."

And slowly, so slowly, he eased her down, over him, around him. Their mouths met, greedy again, her knees fell naturally to either side of his hips, and their bodies became one, one beautifully pulsing flame, growing brighter, hotter, wilder, as the shower spray splashed over them.

THE WATER was growing decidedly cool when they finally ended their shower. Mac helped Carrie to her feet and pulled back the shower curtain, reaching for a towel.

He shook his head. "Carrie Prescott, there is water all over the floor in here," he announced with a mock scowl. "Whatever would your mother say if she walked in the door right this minute?"

Carrie looked at him, her emerald-green eyes moving slowly from his head to his toes, stopping significantly on the way down.

"If my mother walked in right this minute, Mac Kincaid, I doubt she'd notice the floor at all," she said giggling, and then yawned hugely.

"I think you're ready for bed," he said, and yawned, too. He began gently drying her body with the terry-cloth towel.

Carrie pretended to pout. "Well, I was thinking of the hammock...."

Mac laughed, and pulled her into his arms again. "Later, my insatiable mermaid," he whispered. "Later."

And when they were nestled in her bed, Mac's arms still around her, Carrie hugged the word to her heart. Later, she thought, smiling sleepily to herself. Everything was going to be all right now—and later.

BUT WHEN CARRIE WOKE UP a few hours later, everything was not all right. Because Mac wasn't in the bed with her, pressed naked and warm against her back, his arms holding her tightly. He was dressed and sitting in the window seat. And in one hand he was holding the file folder containing her notes and the draft of her article, the folder with her birth mother's name and address paper-clipped to its front.

Carrie sat up, clutching the sheet to her. The look in his eyes made her nakedness embarrassing.

"Mac, I...."

"No wonder Libby's been putting off publishing my article," he said, his voice white-hot with anger. "She's waiting for this, isn't she? For this fatuous defense of searching and Triangle and Peter Millheiser!"

"I just wanted to present the other side of things, to be fair...Mac, you have to understand...."

"Forget it, Carrie. We've had this argument before, and frankly I'm sick of hearing the same old garbage." He stood and dropped the folder onto the window seat. But not before pulling off the two small pieces of paper. He looked at each one and then at her. "And besides, I see you're going on a trip tomorrow," he sneered. "With dear understanding Peter, no doubt."

She wanted to lie, to tell him no, she wasn't going with Peter, she wasn't going at all. But she couldn't.

She nodded, her neck aching with the small movement, all of her aching as her mind careened this way and that, trying to think of some way, any way, to stop what was happening. To fix it. Before it was too late.

But it was already. Mac crumpled the pieces of paper and tossed them onto the bed. "I'll catch the ferry back to the city," he said, and walked out of the room without looking at her again. A moment later the front door slammed. And his footsteps sounded on the dock, growing fainter and fainter. Until Carrie couldn't hear them at all. Until he was gone.

SAN DIEGO SPRAWLED from seaside to desert, encompassing rolling hills and flat mesas, rocky cliffs and green canyons. It was a bustling city and a lush resort, several distinctive communities linked together by a name, sunshine and sea breezes.

Caroline Warner Heston lived in a northern section of town, in a pleasant housing development riding the crest of a hill. The houses were similar in their California-casual style, distinctive enough to avoid monotony, and old enough to be surrounded by mature, lush landscaping.

The Heston house was white with chocolate-brown trim. It had a wide, well-manicured front lawn and one ancient oak tree bearing a swing on one thick limb. A seashell wind chime hung from a corner of the front porch roof, tinkling gently in the light breeze.

Sitting in the rental car parked across and just down the street from the house, Carrie stared out the front window, trying to feel...something. She really wanted to feel amazement, excitement, a sense of triumph, something. After all, she had come almost to the end of her search, she had done what so many people had told her she couldn't do, she had found her birth mother. So she should be feeling...something.

But she hadn't felt anything, not since yesterday morning, when Mac had walked out of the houseboat. Out of her life. She was beginning to think she would never feel anything again.

"Carrie, are you sure you wouldn't like to call first?" Peter, sitting behind the wheel, put his hand over hers, feeling its chill.

She smiled at him. He'd been so nice, so understanding, even if he had attributed her long silences and her glassy-eyed stares to nerves over her upcoming meeting rather than to their real source. She probably hadn't spoken more than three sentences to him since he'd picked her up this morning to go to the airport—and that included the time spent over their recent lunch at a restaurant on San Diego Bay. But he'd seemed content just to be with her, offering support and friendship. She suspected he would be willing to offer a lot more than friendship, too, if she wanted it. But he was sensitive enough to know she didn't, and wise enough not to press.

When they'd arrived at the San Diego airport, he'd made the same suggestion he was making now—that they call Caroline before going to her home. But despite the logic of the suggestion, for some reason Carrie hadn't understood herself, she'd refused. She'd wanted to come directly here, to Caroline's house.

Peter had obliged, they'd pulled up near the brown-and-white house with its tinkling wind chime, and Carrie had just sat here, looking at it, for the past fifteen minutes. And feeling...nothing.

But suddenly the front door of the house opened and a small boy toddled out, followed closely by a young woman. A man was behind her, walking beside another woman—a middle-aged woman whose hair glinted cinnamon-copper as she stepped into the sun.

The young woman caught up with the little boy. "Say bye-bye to grandma," she said, lifting the child into her arms. Turning back she called, "Bye, Mom. See you tomorrow." The boy waved, and his grandmother waved back.

"Take care, Caroline," the man said, and then hurried to open the car door for the woman and child. They all got in and, waving, drove off.

The other woman stood on the porch, a contented smile on her face, watching the car until it was out of sight. While Carrie, her hands clenched in her lap, watched her, desperately searching for a resemblance, a connection, between Caroline and herself.

There was the similarity in hair coloring, and something in the bone structure perhaps, she thought, but nothing more. And that didn't seem right. Shouldn't she be feeling some instinctive pull, some biological recognition, some intrinsic bond with this woman who had given her birth, she asked herself. Shouldn't she be feeling the urge to dash across the wide green lawn and throw herself into this woman's arms in one of those ecstatic reunions? Shouldn't she?

Alone now, Caroline turned, paused to break a few dried buds from the bleeding heart plant spilling over the edges of a hanging basket near the door, then went inside. The door shut behind her.

And Carrie sighed, her hands unclenching, going limp. Because it didn't matter. A woman had come outside, waved goodbye to her daughter, son-in-law, and grandson, neatened a plant and returned to her house. And it didn't make any real difference to Carrie.

The woman was a stranger. A stranger bearing a slight resemblance to her, but still a stranger. And, Carrie realized, even if she looked exactly like Caroline, her feeling would be the same. She wouldn't have felt anything more than this dispassionate curiosity. Yes, it was interesting to finally put a face to the name, just as it had been interesting to first look at the name. But it didn't mean anything special to her. There was no connection, no intrinsic bond. She was still the daughter of Oliver and Helen Prescott; she still didn't care what blood ran in her veins.

But then why was she here, sitting in a rented automobile, spying on a woman she didn't know—and didn't really want to know? Carrie asked herself. Why?

Because people had told her she shouldn't, she couldn't, she didn't dare—that was why. At first she had felt curious and admittedly bothered at discovering that not everything she'd believed about her adoption was precisely true. The blank spaces on her birth certificate had piqued her interest, and the mixed-up dates and learning she'd been adopted twice had furthered it. But it wasn't until Charles Wieland and then Irene Orrock had accused her of wanting to snoop into a stranger's life that she'd first begun to actually wish she could find out the truth.

And even then, the wish might have died a natural death, fading gradually away, if it hadn't been for Mac's article, and for Mac telling her she wouldn't dare to go on with her search. But he had, and she, afraid he was another Doug Bannerman, had responded like a child, determined to have the one thing she was told she couldn't. She'd tested Mac's love with the threat of continuing her search, and when his love hadn't proved strong enough to survive the test, she'd decided to carry out her threat as what...a kind of revenge...a kind of defiance?

Whatever it was, it wasn't the real need some adoptees felt, the genuine need that drove them sometimes too far. And she had no business being here. No business at all.

"Peter, I want to leave," she said.

He patted her hand. "I understand," he said. "It happens to all of us. You search, never really believing you'll find, and then one day you're there, looking at the house or the person...and you ask yourself what will I find? Good news or bad? Will I be rejected again? And it's terrifying."

"No, it's not that," she told him. "I'm not afraid. But this was a big mistake. I got caught up in the search itself, in wanting answers because I was told I couldn't have them, not because I really cared. I don't need to be here. There's nothing Caroline can tell me that will matter in the least, so why should I invade her life, delving into a past that must have been hard for her?"

"She might be very happy to see you," he said. "Lots of birth parents hope their children will search for them."

Carrie nodded. "She might, and I'll leave my name in with the registries just in case. If she really wants to find me, she'll make the effort, too. But I don't need to find her. There's nothing missing in my life."

That wasn't quite true. Mac was missing. But that didn't apply at the moment.

"I'm a person already," she went on, "with all the pieces in place. There's nothing for me here."

"I understand," he said again. "In a few days, or weeks, you'll be ready to face it, Carrie, and we'll come back. It's okay."

He said it with the same touch of supercilious condescension that Janice had used once when she'd claimed any adoptee who said she or he wasn't interested in searching was just deluding herself or himself out of fear. Peter undoubtedly shared that view. She could almost hear him thinking she was only making excuses because she was afraid to face the truth.

And she knew, too, that nothing she could say would convince him otherwise. That was the kind of issue it was, she decided. One that polarized viewpoints, one in which everyone was too defensive about their own side to bother trying to understand the other's.

But at least she finally understood herself. Even if it was too late for her and Mac.

"I want to go home, Peter," she said firmly. "Now."

CHAPTER TWENTY-ONE

CARRIE TWISTED HER KEY in the lock and pushed open the door of the houseboat. But she didn't immediately go inside. She'd been gone less than twenty-four hours, yet it seemed to her that the houseboat had the musty, deserted atmosphere of a place long empty and abandoned. In fact, the whole dock had seemed deserted as she'd walked from her car. Eugenie Brindle hadn't been in her rocking chair to greet Carrie with some ribald comment. Eddie hadn't been home, either, though he'd left her a peculiar note taped to his door: "Gone hunting, darlin'." Since she knew quite well that Eddie was not a sportsman, all she could do was wonder just what he was hunting, and how.

Robin wasn't there, either. Surprisingly, she'd gone directly from the hospital to Victoria Kincaid's motherly care. Robin had explained that she wanted to know all of little Alexander Stewart Abramson's family, and she thought they should have the chance to know her, too.

But the houseboat wasn't quite as empty as it first appeared. The moment Carrie stepped inside, she heard Pandora's slightly accusing meow. Setting down her suitcase and turning the plastic wand to open the miniblinds at the front window, she looked for the cat. Pandora, she knew, wouldn't be far off—just far enough to let Carrie know her opinion of being left alone all day, even if Eddie had fed her. She was under the redwood-burl table this time, staring at Carrie with unforgiving aloofness.

But the cat was willing to exchange aloofness for a place in Carrie's arms while she went around the house, opening all the blinds and windows to let in the fresh evening breezes. Then she poked into cupboards and the refrigerator in the kitchen, trying to provoke her flagging appetite without success. And the whole time, no matter which room she was in, she couldn't keep from looking at the telephone, or when there wasn't one in the room, thinking of it. Thinking of calling Mac to tell him she had changed her mind about contacting her birth mother, that she hadn't done it, and knew now she didn't need to.

She wanted so much to call him. But deep down, she knew that even if she did, it wouldn't make any difference. There had been more to their argument than this one detail, and it would take more than this one change to end it. But knowing didn't keep her from staring at the phone, wishing she could call. Wishing he would call her.

Eddie's "hunting" expedition turned out to have been a search for the ingredients for something he called a Greek-Hungarian stew, including ground lamb, eggplant, tabbouleh, pine nuts and several spices with unpronounceable names, all of which he'd "bagged." He brought the whole collection to Carrie's and insisted she help him prepare the dish, ignoring her protest that she wasn't hungry and didn't feel like cooking.

"Think of it as therapy, darlin'," he told her. "Dr. Ed thinks you'll feel better after a good dose of KP."

He was right, though it wasn't the cooking that had therapeutic properties. There was a lot of cutting and mixing to do, and the stew needed a lot of simmering. Which left plenty of time for Carrie to talk and Eddie to listen and inject an occasional thoughtful comment. By the time the meal was ready, Carrie found she was hungry—no, starving—after all; when Eddie kissed her later and lightly bumped her chin up with his fist, she realized how much better she felt. She'd stopped thinking of the telephone, and decided what she needed to do.

In the sun room, she took her legal-sized pad of paper and a pen, climbed into the hammock, and started writing. She wrote a very different article from the one she'd begun before, the one Mac had read. This one wasn't so much in opposition to Mac's article as it was a description of her own search. She put down everything, all her questions and confusion, all the secrets and the people, all the good and bad she'd seen of searching, all the experiences and feelings that had led her on her odyssey, an odyssey ultimately leading her back to the knowledge that she didn't need to know all the answers to be complete.

She worked feverishly for the next week, the hours flying by in long, long stretches, the words seeming to pour directly from her soul onto the paper. She ate when Eddie dropped in to insist, and slept when exhaustion overtook her. But mostly she wrote and wrote, for Mac. She knew a wide audience would see the articles—hers and Mac's—in the paper, and didn't care. She also knew Mac would probably never read what she'd written, that he wouldn't want to. And that even if he did, he wouldn't let himself understand what she had said. But that didn't matter, either. She was still writing for just one person. Him.

"IT'S DAMNED GOOD, Carrie," Libby Sandowski said, dropping the papers onto her desk. She looked at the young woman across from her, at the dark circles under her green eyes and at the lifeless expression in those eyes. "The article's perfect. But you look like hell."

"I feel like hell," Carrie admitted, a weak smile touching her pale lips. "I'm going away for a few days, I think, right after Robin leaves for New York."

"New York? What made her decide on the Big Apple?"

"A friend of Stewart's from New York was out here visiting, and had to see the baby, naturally. She also saw the painting of children on a merry-go-round that Robin had given Beth and Stewart. It turns out this woman is a well-known patron of the arts, and one of the things she sponsors is a ballet troupe. So, liking Robin's work, she asked her to come east to paint portraits of all the ballet company members. She's going to put Robin up at her estate on the Hudson while she works, and is paying a hefty fee besides. It doesn't mean instant success, but with this woman as her patron, I think Robin is really on her way."

"Good for her."

Carrie nodded. "She leaves Friday morning, so I thought I'd head up to Mendocino then, and stay for a couple of days. I'm caught up on the column for a while, and my neighbor, Eddie, is willing to cat-sit, so now that the article's done..." She let the thought drift off, as so many thoughts seemed to do lately.

"I can recommend a great place to stay just south of Mendocino in the little town of Elk," Libby said. "It's a guest lodge on a cliff overlooking the most stunning cove and stretch of ocean the north coast has to offer.

It's quiet, beautiful and the perfect spot for getting away from...whatever.''

"It does sound perfect," Carrie agreed, but without enthusiasm. She didn't really care where she went, as long as it was away, away from the phone that didn't ring—at least not with the right person on the other end.

After a spin of her Roladex, Libby wrote out the number of the inn and handed the paper to Carrie. "Have a good time," she said gently, then added, "The articles will be in Sunday's edition."

"Fine," Carrie responded dully, knowing it wasn't. Because putting the two articles into print would be like engraving them in stone, solidifying Mac's and her opposing opinions, making permanent the rift between them. And then all hope—that things might change, might somehow magically turn out differently—would be ended.

But then, she'd lost all hope anyway.

AFTER CARRIE WAS GONE, Libby tilted back in her chair, lacing her fingers behind her head and staring up at the ceiling. She felt guilty. Mac Kincaid and Carrie Prescott were two of her favorite people, and the first time she'd thought of them together, she'd decided they were perfect for each other. So she'd bulldozed Mac into contacting Carrie. True, she'd done so partly for legitimate editorial reasons, wanting to give Mac some perspective on his article. But she was honest enough to admit that if there hadn't been an editorial justification, she probably would have invented one. She'd liked the idea of them together and of matchmaking, so she'd meddled—and now the two of them were walking around like shell-shocked war veterans.

And she had two very different articles to publish.

Tilting forward again, she opened a drawer, taking out Mac's article and putting it beside Carrie's. She read one, then the other, shaking her head. She supposed asking Carrie to write a sort of rebuttal had been another bit of meddling, but she'd truly needed something to balance the definite bias of Mac's piece. What she hadn't suspected was how Carrie's story was going to not only balance the bias of Mac's, but actually point out its faults and weaknesses glaringly. If Carrie had argued each point of Mac's article, one by one, she couldn't have done a better job of showing where he'd gone wrong. She'd demolished him with honesty and understanding.

Carrie's article was terrific. So what was going to happen when Mac saw it? Libby poked a loose bobby pin back into her topknot, thinking. Mac would probably be furious, at first. For a day or two, his personal involvement would stand in the way of his judgment. And then...?

Libby knew Mac Kincaid. She knew how great a reporter he was; she knew how sympathetic and caring a man he was, too. She was sure that when the first fury wore off, he'd be unable to ignore the truth of Carrie's story. The reporter in him would see the mistakes in his own piece, and he would wish he could call it back, change it, correct it. But the printed word couldn't be called back, so for the rest of his life, he'd regret the one story he'd really blown, he'd feel guilty for the hurt he'd unfairly caused.

Of course, Mac the reporter would probably learn to live with his professional guilt. But Mac, the man, would have something worse to live with....

Libby sat there awhile longer, staring into space. Then she reached out and flipped the button on the intercom.

"Yes, Ms Sandowski?"

Ah, that voice. She smiled. "Tim, get Mac Kincaid on the phone and tell him I want him down here as soon as possible after lunch," she said. "Tell him there's a problem with his article—that should guarantee his speedy arrival."

"Will do, Ms Sandowski. Is there anything else?"

Libby glanced at her watch. "Yes, Tim. Speaking of lunch, I know a place where they serve Glenmorangie, a single malt Scotch whiskey that'll knock your socks off. Care to join me?"

"Och, weil, I couldna refuse such a bonnie invitation as that, now, could I?" Tim replied. And only then did Libby think of Tim's last name: MacDonald. She laughed.

THE INN LIBBY HAD RECOMMENDED was as perfect as she'd promised. Built in 1917 by a lumber company as a guest lodge for entertaining company executives and customers, it blended the rugged beauty of redwood with the elegance of another era. Carrie's top floor corner room was huge, with a fireplace and windows looking out through tall cypress trees to an expanse of north coast sea dotted with artistically craggy rock formations.

But it was the atmosphere more than the scenery that appealed to Carrie. She'd been doubtful about the inn on Friday evening when she'd pulled off Highway 1 and directly into its small parking area. From the highway side the rather old and worn building, nestled beneath the trees, was interesting but unimpressive. And she couldn't imagine feeling "away from it all" in a place sitting almost on the road with its steady flow of gawking tourist cars and roaring lumber trucks.

Like Alice through the looking glass, though, stepping through the front door of the lodge was like entering another world. A quiet, serene world, unhurried and untroubled. Carrie wasn't sure just what made it that way. Whether it was the isolation of the lodge, perched on the bluff overlooking the private cove, or the graciousness of the innkeepers. Perhaps it was the garden in back, blooming with jewel-toned flowers and fresh vegetables, or the delicious meals served in the dining room facing the sea.... Or it might have been that there was no phone in her room to mock her with its silence, or that she'd never made love with Mac Kincaid in the huge beds here, and never sat in front of this fireplace sipping wine with him.

Whatever the reason, Carrie began to feel, if not wonderful, then at least better. She began to unwind. After eating all of her Chicken Paprika Friday night, then sitting out on the patio drinking tea and watching the sun's final glow fade from the sky, she went to bed early. For the first time in weeks, she slept soundly, without bothersome dreams. Saturday, she roamed the New England-style community of Mendocino, poking through antique shops and art galleries, browsing bookstores, admiring the picturesque architecture of the cluster of historic frame houses and restored Victorians gathered on the headlands above the midnight-blue Pacific. By Saturday night, when she lay in her bed, watching shadows cast by the dying fire dance across the ceiling and listening to the soothing sound of the waves crashing on the rocks beyond the cove, she realized she was going to survive.

She might always love Mac Kincaid. She might never be able to forget him. She might never love anyone as she did him. But she was going to make it. She was even, she thought, smiling up at the ceiling, looking forward to the next day.

She'd forgotten the next day was Sunday.

PART OF THE INN'S old-world graciousness included supplying a Sunday paper with Sunday's breakfast. So that when Carrie came down to the dining room bright with sunlight reflecting off the water and took her place at one of the tables, she was greeted by the front page teaser: "'Adoption Search—an Odyssey to Find One-self'—see today's Life-style section!"

It all flooded back over her. She reached out a hand toward the paper, but the hand shook and she drew it back. And just sat there looking at the glaring lines of type. And wondering.

Where was Mac this morning, she asked herself. At Beth's where, she recalled with a faint smile, there weren't many people to fight over the Sunday edition? At his parents' house, where Tessa used to lay in wait for the paperboy just to get 'Dear Carrie' before anyone else? Did she still do that, Carrie wondered wryly. Or was the column, like everything else about Carrie, out of bounds? Did the Kincaids all despise her for being like Priscilla? How would they feel when... if...they read her article? Would any of them understand at all?

Or was Mac at his own house in Stinson Beach? Was he alone, staring at the teaser on the morning paper as she was, and trying to decide whether or not to open it and see what Libby had done with their articles. Carrie reached out again.

"Coffee or tea this morning, miss?" a pleasant voice said, and Carrie jerked her hand back guiltily. She looked up at the young girl who was serving and tried to smile.

"Coffee," she answered, her lips stiff, barely able to form the words. The girl didn't seem to notice.

"We have ham and cheese omelets, banana nut bread and cantaloupe this morning," she said, turning Carrie's china cup upright on its saucer and pouring dark-roasted coffee from a glass pot. "I hope you're hungry."

But Carrie wasn't hungry, most definitely not for omelets, which reminded her of another, happier, morning. Her stomach flip-flopped agonizingly, and she shook her head.

"I think I'll just have the coffee," she said, and pushed back her chair. "In my room." She snatched up the cup and saucer and started to leave the table.

"Are you sure, miss? The omelets are made with eggs from our own chickens...."

"No, thank you," Carrie cut in. "Really."

And she turned away, leaving the newspaper on the table.

But she'd been in her room only a few minutes when there was a knock at the door. The girl was there, holding out a small bundle of letters addressed to "Dear Carrie." The bundle, tied with a red ribbon and marked "Urgent," had been delivered just moments ago, the girl explained.

Carrie thanked her and carried the bundle over to the white wicker chaise lounge in front of the fireplace, a puzzled frown wrinkling her brow. Libby must have sent them, but Libby knew Carrie would be back home in just a few days. And besides, she'd just turned in the next several weeks of columns. So what could be so urgent that Libby had sent these letters specially on? And why hadn't she included a note of explanation?

After lighting a fire in the fireplace, she sat down with her coffee and the letters in hand. Untying the red ribbon, she opened the first one curiously.

"Dear Carrie: Help! I've been a complete fool and lost my girl. I was stupid, arrogant, impossible and pigheaded. How can I win her back?.... Broken-hearted."

Carrie smiled, an answer popping instantly into her mind. "Dear Broken-hearted," she would reply, "Send her a copy of your letter to Carrie. Good luck!" Easy to answer as it was, though, there certainly wasn't anything urgent about the letter.

She hadn't intended to work today, but doing so was keeping her mind off the newspapers on the tables in the dining room downstairs. She opened a second letter, and was still more puzzled. It seemed to be from the same writer. And the next two were the same. Which made Libby's sending them to her even more puzzling.

In each one, the poor writer lamented the mistakes he'd made that had cost him the woman he loved. In each one, he wanted to know how to win her back. And all the letters were typed, by a not very talented typist, and on a machine with very dirty keys. A machine with indecipherable "e"s and "o"s, that turned the word "there" into one big smudge....

Carrie gasped, and began ripping open the rest of the letters, barely stopping to read them, only checking to make sure they were all the same. And then she reached the last envelope, a larger, bulging manila one. Her hands were shaking so badly she couldn't work the silver clasp. Finally, she simply ripped off the top end of the envelope.

There wasn't a letter inside. Instead, the envelope was filled with bits of shredded paper.

Disbelievingly, she dumped the contents out onto her lap and picked up one piece, then another and another—and recognized words and phrases of Mac's article, even a handwritten alteration or two she remembered being in the original copy. But what could it mean? Could it . . . could it possibly mean . . . ?

She jumped up, scattering the pieces of paper over the floor like snowflakes. She headed for the door and a copy of the *Times*—where she suddenly knew she wouldn't find Mac's article.

And if she didn't, how long would it take her to reach Stinson Beach, she wondered frantically. What if he wasn't there? What if he was out of town? What if . . . ?

Almost running, she reached the door to the hall and yanked it open. And he was there, lounging back against the opposite wall, looking almost relaxed. Except for the key ring he was twisting round and round on one finger.

"Carrie Prescott, you must be the slowest reader in the world!" he accused. "I thought I was going to die of nerves out here before you ever opened that door."

"Mac! Oh, Mac!" It was a good thing he had the wall backing him up, because she flew into his arms then with enough force to have bowled them both over. She clung to him, needing to feel him, touch him, smell him, needing to convince herself he was really there, really smiling down at her.

"Mac, you're here!" she whispered against his neck. "You're really here."

"Can you ever forgive me for being the most stubborn jackass in the whole wide world? For refusing to see or listen or understand?"

Carrie pulled back, just enough to look up at him, to gaze into his warm brown eyes. "And do you understand now, about everything?"

"Well, it took some of Libby's best steamrolling tactics to get me to sit still long enough to read your article...and then another couple of days for me to cool off enough to take it all in...but then, yes, Carrie, I did understand. That's why I pulled my article. And that's why I realized what I should have seen from the start—that you would never do anything to deliberately hurt another person, no matter what. But I know that now, so even if you do decide you need answers to your past someday, it will be okay."

"Even...?" Carrie stared at him wonderingly. "Mac, are you saying it wasn't just my changing my mind about contacting Caroline that made the difference, that even if I did decide someday to do it, you'd still be able to understand, you'd still—"

"I would still love you as much as I do now, unless—" he smiled and kissed her lightly "—unless I love you more by then, which seems a distinct possibility to me."

But one light kiss wasn't enough for Carrie. Taking Mac's hand, she drew him into her room.

"You will if I have anything to say about it, Mac Kincaid," she said. Her fingers began working on the buttons of his shirt.

Mac grinned. "You may be a slow reader, Dear Carrie," he murmured as his arms went around her, as his hands slid down her back to the roundness of her hips.

"But you sure do give the right answers. I think I'll write more often."

"Promise?" she asked, reaching his belt buckle.

Mac's voice was a husky growl. "I promise, mermaid. I promise."

IT WAS A GOOD WHILE LATER before Mac thought of anything but the wonder and magic of Carrie in his arms, and when he did, he had to search the area of the room between the door and the bed to find his shirt where it had been carelessly dropped behind a chair. He was digging into one pocket as he returned to the bed.

Sitting beside Carrie, he lifted her onto his lap, loving the way her green eyes widened in surprise, and then widened yet more as he took her hand and slipped the Kincaid diamond onto her finger.

"Marry me, Carrie," he said softly. "I love you, and that's no pretense. It's for real, for always."

And Carrie smiled. The way newly engaged women are supposed to.

THE WEDDING WAS BEAUTIFUL, and filled with joy from beginning to end.

Libby Sandowski unabashedly announced the marriage of her top reporter and her most popular columnist on the front page of the paper, so presents and letters of congratulations poured in from readers as well as friends and relatives. Carrie and Mac loved them all, sharing the opening of every single one like two excited children. But there were a few that had very special meaning.

One was a card of congratulations from "Spinster," also thanking Carrie for her letter about finding Mr. Right. Carrie had blushed wildly, explaining to Mac about Spinster's first letter, and how she'd finally been able to answer the girl's questions—after Mendocino.

Another was a tiny redwood carving of a mermaid, with a short China-doll haircut, from Eddie.

Robin gave them a painting of a man sitting out on the deck of a houseboat, in the rain, yellow rose petals strewn around his feet.

And another was a letter from a woman named Caroline, which began, ''I read the article you wrote and contacted Charlie Wieland to see if by any chance it was me you'd been searching for...''

The day of their wedding dawned clear and bright. Carrie wore her mother's wedding dress, her grandmother's pearl lavalier, and the Kincaid family diamond—plenty of old. She ''borrowed'' Victoria's floor-length baby-net veil with its pearl headpiece; she had a fancy blue silk garter on one thigh. And for new, she wore the sexiest white lace teddy she'd ever seen—one Mac had picked out for her and presented along with his whispered list of the things he was going to be doing to her tonight as he removed it.

And for love, she carried a bouquet of yellow roses.

Harlequin Superromance

COMING NEXT MONTH

What readers say about SUPERROMANCE

Harlequin Intrigue

Because romance can be quite an adventure.

Available wherever paperbacks are sold or throug

Harlequin Reader Service

In the U.S.	In Canada
901 Fuhrmann Blvd.	P.O. Box 2800, Station "A"
P.O. Box 1325	5170 Yonge Street
Buffalo, N.Y. 14269	Willowdale, Ontario M2N 6J3

INT-6R

Harlequin Intrigue

WHAT READERS SAY ABOUT HARLEQUIN INTRIGUE . . .

Fantastic! I am looking forward to reading other Intrigue books.

> *P.W.O., Anderson, SC

This is the first Harlequin Intrigue I have read . . . I'm hooked.

> *C.M., Toledo, OH

I really like the suspense . . . the twists and turns of the plot.

> *L.E.L., Minneapolis, MN

I'm really enjoying your Harlequin Intrigue line . . . mystery and suspense mixed with a good love story.

> *B.M., Denton, TX

WORLDWIDE LIBRARY IS YOUR TICKET TO ROMANCE, ADVENTURE AND EXCITEMENT

Experience it all in these big, bold Bestsellers— Yours exclusively from WORLDWIDE LIBRARY WHILE QUANTITIES LAST

To receive these Bestsellers, complete the order form, detach and send together with your check or money order (include 75¢ postage and handling), payable to WORLDWIDE LIBRARY, to:

In the U.S.
WORLDWIDE LIBRARY
901 Fuhrman Blvd.
Buffalo, N.Y.
14269

In Canada
WORLDWIDE LIBRARY
P.O. Box 2800, 5170 Yonge Street
Postal Station A, Willowdale, Ontario
M2N 6J3

Quant.	Title	Price
_____	**WILD CONCERTO**, Anne Mather	$2.95
_____	**A VIOLATION**, Charlotte Lamb	$3.50
_____	**SECRETS**, Sheila Holland	$3.50
_____	**SWEET MEMORIES**, LaVyrle Spencer	$3.50
_____	**FLORA**, Anne Weale	$3.50
_____	**SUMMER'S AWAKENING**, Anne Weale	$3.50
_____	**FINGER PRINTS**, Barbara Delinsky	$3.50
_____	**DREAMWEAVER**, Felicia Gallant/Rebecca Flanders	$3.50
_____	**EYE OF THE STORM**, Maura Seger	$3.50
_____	**HIDDEN IN THE FLAME**, Anne Mather	$3.50
_____	**ECHO OF THUNDER**, Maura Seger	$3.95
_____	**DREAM OF DARKNESS**, Jocelyn Haley	$3.95

YOUR ORDER TOTAL	$_____
New York residents add appropriate sales tax	$_____
Postage and Handling	$____.75
I enclose	$_____

NAME _____

ADDRESS _____ APT.# _____

CITY _____

STATE/PROV. _____ ZIP/POSTAL CODE _____

WW-1-3